Mammoth Boy

John Hart

Matador
9 Priory Business Park,
Wistow Road, Kibworth Beauchamp,
Leicestershire. LE8 0RX
Tel: (+44) 116 279 2299
Fax: (+44) 116 279 2277
Email: books@troubador.co.uk
Web: www.troubador.co.uk/matador

ISBN 978 1780881 744

British Library Cataloguing in Publication Data.
A catalogue record for this book is available from the British Library.

Typeset in 11pt Aldine401 BT Roman by Troubador Publishing Ltd, Leicester, UK

Matador is an imprint of Troubador Publishing Ltd

Printed and bound in the UK by TJ International, Padstow, Cornwall

Mammoth Boy

To the memory of Don Marcelino Sanz de Sautuola who discovered the cave of Altamira in 1879, thereby opening the magical world of prehistoric cave art to modern eyes.

CHAPTER 1

S mell drifts in the air, brushes on to the boy from those plants that grow only here as he crawls through them, trying not to touch their acrid leaves. To a hunter's eyes no two plants stir alike in a breeze. This the boy knows.

Plants that thrive only here, in the shade of the overhang. Bits of white stone from the scarp overhead fleck the dark slope of soil where the plants root. He creeps onwards till he sees the cave-like hole just beneath the scarp. A scrape of bare earth shows where something climbs to its lair, then skids back down through the plants.

He watches till the sun moves behind the scarp, chilling the air, and he shivers, not only from the chill. On knees and elbows he worms backwards through the plants, faster and faster until he is able to get up and run down the combe, legs working with a will of their own, through the bracken down to the tree-line and the sun-lit meadows beyond, where women are moving slowly from bush to bush, one holding an infant, another suckling her child under her short summer cape.

They espy the boy – not one of theirs – and go on with their berry-picking. One gestures at the bushes; for the stray boy, a sign that says 'eat'.

The mothers. They know nothing of the smell, the rank weeds below the cave, his secret place.

More smells drift, home smells, soot and charred bones. These the boy often dreams of, stirs in his sleep when he does.

Good times of burning fat, suet, marrow, plenty.

The boy trots ahead of the women into another combe, wider, well-treed, with a brook running down its centre forming pools and cascades. Far up the combe looms the distant bluff that seals it off from all beyond. The boy trots on, to turn towards wisps of smoke filtering through brushy growth on a rock face.

He hoists himself to peer over the cave ledge. Only the old woman is there, by the fire. She rocks on her hunkers, mumbling, grimy and shrivelled. At his appearance she shrinks back: fear of beasts, of males, of violence on old women. But it is only the boy. She cackles, prods the fire till blue flames lick up the smoke.

Fire-crone, guardian of warmth.

"Food?"

Again she cackles, tooth stubs worn to the gums.

Old Mother, feeder of young. Her long-gone young. This boy. A young male.

She holds out a thigh-bone, broken off at one end. Meat hangs on it.

As he gnaws, sinews running through his teeth, flesh filling his mouth, she crinkles with pleasure.

"You like?"

"Uh-huh."

"I keep for you. One day you strong hunter." He is used to her broken speech. Unlike most of the women, she has never learnt the clan language well. She was traded from far away, from beyond the mountains – when she tells the boy, her hand flaps over and over for the many days travel to a high land where the great ice lies, even in the warm times – and from a language she has never unlearnt. *Land of herds, of plenty, of her young time.*

Often she rambles back into the tongue of her girlhood. He listens, staring with wonder at the strange sounds. His mother had lulled him in her tongue too, sweeter, less rasping than fire-crone's.

2

His mother, her woman-smell under the furs, unlike any other woman's. That he remembers.

Maggots slither out of the broken end of the bone on to the rubbish-strewn floor of the cave-shelter, squirming into the debris, droplets of life for the boy to squat and catch. They taste of unripe, milky kernels. He taps the bone on a flat stone to knock more out, a whole handful.

The old woman watches, her leathery face creasing with pleasure to see him eat, the motherless boy, a no-one's child.

She draws beasts in the dirt for him, scratching outlines with a bone pick.

"Bull?"

"Not bull."

It is bigger even than the aurochs, glimpsed deep in woods on the low lands.

She scratches in huge ears, hints of shaggy hairs on the flanks, adds tusks, croaks the name in her own tongue. The boy repeats it, with mounting excitement.

On the flank now she draws the shape of a heart, colours it with pinches of reddish ash from her fire, makes spear-casting gestures for the boy to mimic. An urge grips him to dance round the sketch, stabbing at the heart, in the high-stepping dance of men before a hunt. She chants him on, a hoarse rhythm, clapping in time.

They had been alone in the shelter, under the escarpment, that day. A good day. Old Mother, succour of waifs, her cackle of pleasure. Her old-woman reek. *Mammurak,* she had said, *mammurak.*

"Boy, what are you doing?"

He fled, down the slope, stones pelting past as he ducked and wove.

3

Blows. An old woman's wails. Men, the beaters, punishers, strong hunters, stealthily back by the fireside in their strength, thighs gory, arms and arm-hairs clammy from the gralloch and the huntside feast of kidney fat and offal. They exulted. Together they had overcome the bull, the solitary of the deep woods. Their kill made them one being, limbs moving in unison, a single tireless file, as tireless as the bull hunted down, hewn into cuts and borne to the shelter for the feasting.

Beyond the firelight, round the shelter walls, huddled the women, children clutching tresses, holding on to fur tatters, groping to suckle. Tonight there would be meat for all, bones to gnaw, whole collops even from the hissing and sizzling in fire-crone's hearth. Delicious smells filled the air, well-being lulled the hunters sprawled round the fire, the seven sires, their clouts cast aside in the warmth.

When he judges the hunters have gorged themselves into a drowse, or disappeared beyond the firelight with a woman, the boy creeps back, stomach twitching at the roast smells.

"Boy."

He flattens himself, the small threatened animal.

"Boy. Here!" It is Blueface, so called from a birthmark across his jowls. He is not the worst. The boy senses this summons means no harm.

"Boy, what were you doing?

"Dancing."

"Dancing what?"

"Dancing *mammurak.*"

"What, dancing a what?"

"A *mammurak.*" The boy sees the old woman looking up at him from her grovel amid the ashes at the word, her word.

"Bah."

4

Her girlhood, the land over the hills, land of herds and plenty. No maid had fetched more spear-points, antlers engraved with tiny deer entwined, the does of the women-spirits, than she at the great meet of the tribes that year.

This the boy would remember. *Remember the mammoths. Her. She who had known his mother before her death, who knew his mother had called him Urrell.*

He waited till it was safe to crawl in and sidle past the hunters sprawling glutted with meat from their kill. Scraps abounded. Gnawn bones, crackling, half-eaten lumps of meat lay in the rubbish of the shelter floor, food galore for a waif. No-one bothered him. The women had ceased bickering over their share of the feast and nursed infants, groomed one another, nipped lice, rubbed berry juices on their faces and breasts. Newest among them, barely older than himself, a girl was streaking dye in bars across her cheeks; berries threaded her hair, a foreign custom. Under her loose cape the boy glimpsed young breasts, rounder, paler than other women's.

This would be fire-crone's last year. The men had spoken. When the time to trek came, as the cold began, she would stay by her hearth. Another would carry the fire-log. Food would be left for her. By next spring, the shelter floor would have been picked clean. Only the black patch of charcoal and ashes would be there, ready. Thus it had always been.

The boy knew. She knew.

That summer the boy wandered further, stayed away longer, unheeded. He knapped his own flints, fire-hardened his own spears, and practised with a cast-off spear-thrower as he had seen hunters do. His strength was not enough yet to hurl a full-sized javelin. The old woman watched him whenever they were alone, pleasure creasing her wizened face. When sinews parted she helped

5

him twine new ones. One day she reached under her rags and pulled a kind of necklace, black with age, over her head. It was threaded in a sort of string, something unknown to the boy who knew only plaited thongs. Perhaps it was a keepsake from her girlhood, or a trade swap. The cord was unbreakable, a true material for binding. The boy's surprise over its strength gratified the old woman.

"Where from?"

"From plant." She uttered a name that meant nothing to him.

As she had drawn the mammoth for him, he said, "Draw for me."

On a shoulder-blade bone she outlined in charcoal a small plant he recognised immediately.

"You gather. Put in water." With effort she described to the boy how to ret fibres from the plants by steeping them in water, then twine them into cord, skills recollected from her girlhood, skills for which no words existed in the boy's language.

With interest, almost a passionate desire to learn, the boy carried out her instructions, delighting the old woman. He waited till the hunters and the women were out foraging to bring his ill-twisted yarn to her. She showed him how to ravel it on a wimble she made for him with sticks bound together, then how to tighten the strands into an unbreakable cord. Her fingers followed movements taught them many years ago when she had learnt to braid fibres and mammoth hairs into cords and bindings for the hunters of her tribe. The boy saw her face grow young as her fingers took her back in distance and in time, tears smearing the grime of her cheeks, although she was not being beaten.

She told the boy tales of her folk, how great beasts roamed her land, some with stripes and fangs, strange horns, woolly flanks, and of huge bears that did not flee from hunters as did those of these valleys.

He knew this must be so when he found an engraving on a rockface high up the valley where birds nested. He was stealing eggs. It was the outline of a bear, faint under the lichens. He scraped it clean, excitement mounting as he revealed the top of the head, the little ears, a humped back graven to show the bear lumbering away into the past. His shoulders trembled. A quivering inside him. He placed berries in a crevice as offerings, with a perfect spearhead in red flint he had found and kept as a charm. This for the bear.

Father bear. Old bear. His secret bear.

In his search for nests – eggs and nestlings, delicious morsels – he sometimes found wild hives in clefts and looted them in a frenzy of honey-lust, an orgy for the sweetness found in nothing else, a lust which led hunters to scale cliffs and risk swirling swarms of bees that sent them to their deaths below. Bees that women clapped to their limbs to cure aches, and to their bellies to quicken with child.

Untaught, the boy learnt to follow a single bee till it led him to its hive. Often his patience ended at a cranny or hole too deep to pillage, thus he learnt the wisdom of this best of flies.

He roamed ever farther afield, nothing and no-one holding him back. He lived off the food of summer – berries, grubs, nests, nuts, fungus. He stalked does in the hope of tracing their fawns. Once he found one, lying still in the bracken, a few hours old. It fed him for several days, raw, the surplus flesh wrapped in the pelt. The kill made him feel manly, a hunter, although larger game ignored him, busy grazing, browsing, fattening ahead of the rut and winter survival. Herds might look up, shift uneasily, then settle back to eating, sensing this lone manling was no threat.

He was several days easy travel from the bear engraving when he reached the head of the valley. Here the escarpments closed in from both sides. Where they met, a long thin waterfall spattered down, little more than a snail's trail as seen from a distance. This was the source of the brook he knew so well as it tumbled down his valley, past the cave shelter and wound down to the lowlands and the far-off sea. When he reached the foot of the fall he lay and drank, startling small fishes in the deep green water. He savoured the cool, damp air under the ferns and hanging plants of the wet rock-face.

The boy looked up at the fall. It led on and up. On impulse, he started to climb. A jumble of boulders brought down by centuries of spates blocked his way. Among and between them he squirmed, spears in one hand, bag over his shoulder, lithe as the lizards he startled but did not stop to snatch. Beyond the rockfall his way rose clearer, less impenetrable than it appeared from below, beckoning him on. The waterfall itself helped: ice and snowmelt had cut steps where the rocks were softer, forming pools from which the water spilled cascading to the next level.

Water-fowl, unused to men, scarcely heeded him; smaller birds called warnings at this intruder crossing from one side to the other in search of the easiest way up. They darted from overhanging banks where eroded roots hung, ideal places, as the boy knew, for streamside birds to sling their nests among the rootlets, beyond the reach of egg-thieves. Against his instinct he ignored them, impelled by desire to reach the top.

His climb lasted till early afternoon. He surfaced, at the hottest hour, on a scene new to him: an undulating moor. It stretched as far as he could see. Beyond, so remote as to dissolve in a haze, ran a range of mountains, from one side of the world to the other.

Fire-crone's mountains, land of mammoths.

He set off at a trot towards them, his feet springing on the moorgrass and the ling.

As he went, the boy stunned lizards sunning themselves on stones; or spied on the flight of moorland fowl to guess where their nests lay cupped in the tussocks and heather. This way he found clutches of good-sized eggs that he ate on the spot, fresh or half-hatched, crunching them as he crunched the lizards, scarcely pausing in his onward trot.

By nightfall, the long sundown of summer, he was far into the moor, drawn towards those mountains that lured him on, ever-receding into their haze. That night he curled up in a hollow, snuggling into a patch of bracken, and slept with the immediacy of an animal, safe in this open land of wheeling hawks, moor fowl, hares and silence.

Three days he travelled, in a relentless line towards the mountains, never coming nearer, till late in the third afternoon the light changed as though after rain and the air grew transparent. His eager eyes could see snow on the summits and shoulders of the vast range, but what excited him most were the streaks of ice, huge glaciers, reaching down the valleys. *Land of ice even in the summer time. Old Mother's girlhood homeland. She who had drawn him a mammoth.*

He pressed on now. The hot weather continued. Trying to reach water in a peat pool he sank into a moss-hag and only by dint of crossing his spears on firmer tussocks and spreading his slight weight was he able to wriggle to safety over the quaking slime. Thenceforth the boy sought water in stony outcrops where sometimes small pools formed in hollows of rocks, tiny inland seas for water-boatmen to navigate and dive in fright as his face appeared above them.

On one such outcrop he chanced on a hawk's nest and stole the nestling's meal, a half-eaten hare, and was pursued and bombed by an enraged parent bird as he scurried away gnawing his prize.

Perhaps the fifth, perhaps the sixth day the moorland ended

abruptly so that the boy found himself, soon after sunrise, high on the rim of an escarpment, higher than his home one and no longer overlooking a valley and familiar brook but unbroken forest in every direction. These trees were darker than his home ones, his mixed woodlands, for these were conifers. To right and left, as far as he could see, the scarp ran unbroken.

He sat on his hunkers in the buzz of summer insects, the sunlight slanting from his left side as he waited to know which way to go. No wish to turn back welled up. That much he knew.

Far beyond the vast forest, no nearer now than when he had set out, rose the mountains. He waited for an impulse to guide him onwards, as a grazing herd drifts one way or the other, or a beast of prey slinks this way or that, following no plan, yet ready to bolt or spring when the need arises.

The boy waited. He knew he would go on, but which way? He knew too that the summer warmth was short and the buzz of insects would be cut almost overnight as the long iceland winter covered the land. To be caught in that cold meant death. Strong hunters seldom survived a winter alone. All this the boy knew but it was not on his mind at present as his eyes focussed, alert to the slightest signs of movement, his hearing quickened to catch the least untoward sound, each helping his flared nostrils to sense what might be alive and stirring in the forest below. Out on the open moors he had felt safe; down there he would not.

He gathered his spears, his satchel holding spare flints, scraps of food, the trinkets a boy collects and keeps through his boyhood, and set off to his right.

He had gone a day and a half along the rim with no way down, and no sign of anything to tempt him down, when he saw what seemed like wisps of smoke rising from among trees below. There he settled for the night, comforted that perhaps humans existed down in the woods. He ate berries and bivouacked under briars and bracken above the spot, to be ready to spy further as soon as light broke.

When he awoke all signs of smoke had vanished like morning mist. The conifer canopy stretched away below him. He resumed his way along the cliff top, eating berries as he went, but moving cautiously, the carefree days on the open moors behind him. There was no knowing what the forest might conceal. Any tracker could be tracked. His boy's spears would be as much defence against hunters as a fawn's kicks against him.

Yet he felt drawn to find those people, danger or not, after so many days alone. Perhaps they knew the land of ice and mammoths.

It was a while before he found a place that led down to the forest.

The overflow from a tarn had cut a ghyll or chine down which a small beck ran. He scrambled down the incline and followed the stream till it ended at tree-top level before it tumbled over the edge into a pool below. The boy crouched, scrutinising the forest for signs of life, before daring to scale down the remaining part of the cliff. He threw his spears and satchel ahead and climbed down after them, grasping the small trees and tangle of roots that the fall of water had encouraged to grow along its margin.

Once down, his spears and pouch retrieved, he lay under the boughs of a conifer to gather his breath and to listen. There was nothing to hear. Not even the twitter of birds. He drank from the brook and backtracked in the direction of the smoke, the cliff-face now to his left. He was feeling a need for human proximity.

It was cool in the gloom of this forest, the densest he had ever seen. He travelled by instinct, trotting along the pine-needle floor, among these endless trees. There would be little to eat here, few clearings for raspberries, bilberries, little by way of recognisable fungus, and no game that he could sense.

CHAPTER 2

Whenever he saw a hollow or overhang at the foot of the rockface he approached it cautiously, half-hoping to find a hearth, half-fearing he might. But no sign of human habitation appeared in any. Once he disturbed bats and several times old droppings showed that game animals huddled in these natural pens for shelter.

Spoor and signs of bigger beasts along the foot of the cliff made him redouble his alertness. Any breaks in the forest canopy, where sunlight encouraged drifts of raspberry canes and other food plants to thrive, made him especially wary. So when he came to a small clearing where he would need to cross open ground and was approaching with especial stealth, stooping under the sweeping boughs of firs, he saw something that stopped him dead: in the open, its huge head bowed till its shaggy underlip brushed the ground, stood a full-grown bison bull.

It was motionless. Urrell remained still too, under a downswept bough. A rogue bull bison was more than a grown hunter would face single-handedly, let alone a boy. He was about to draw back to make a detour through the forest when a slight movement in the thickets opposite caught his eye. For a while he saw nothing more. Then, as the brushwood stirred again he knew it was being moved by a living creature, and that the creature was a hunter stalking the bison.

With his attention now intent on the far side, Urrell saw not one but several hunters slowly closing in on their prey from behind brushwood screens. The men were invisible. Only their camouflage, as they inched forward, revealed their presence to Urrell, if not to the bison.

Urrell's excitement rose as he watched. The bison must be wounded or exhausted, having been harried, perhaps, for days.

When they judged they were within range of their quarry, five hunters rose as one man from behind their screens and hurled their javelins at the bison. Urrell glimpsed the points of the weapons, their tips longer and sharper than those his clansmen fashioned. The movement alerted the bison, but too late to avoid the missiles which struck its flank. It bucked and snorted, shrugging its body as it strove to dislodge the spears, its small eyes alight with anger as it turned to confront its tormentors. Three javelins remained embedded. Faced by the bison the hunters withdrew with their brushwood shields, shorter stabbing javelins held ready. Urrell guessed they were enticing the beast to charge, ready to jump aside and drive their javelins deep between its ribs.

The bison appeared to guess this also, feinted a charge, then turned and galloped off down the clearing into the forest. Only then did Urrell notice that its left rear hoof was entangled in a sort of wickerwork box-trap which, for all its bucking and kicking as it fled, the beast could not shake off.

In his excitement Urrell jumped up in sympathy with the hunters – but as quickly quailed back. Too often had he seen the killer lust of hunters injuring hapless creatures that got in their way.

The men picked up their javelins and examined the points. One showed the others the broken tip of his, no doubt embedded in the bison's side, a good hit after all.

They were clad in leather breechclouts made from pelts of smaller animals, and skin jerkins, much like Urrell's clansmen. All wore belts hung with pouches and pokes while one, perhaps the leader, wore a baldrick, whereas Urrell's clansmen out hunting seldom bothered with more than a pouch slung over one shoulder into which they stuffed spare scrapers, cutters and scraps of meat. These men, moreover, were streaked in ochre and white on any bare brown skin, with white zags across their faces. Urrell shivered a little at the sight.

They appeared to be in no hurry to take up the chase. Instead they squatted, emptied food from a satchel and set to. As Urrell watched his stomach gurgled with hunger until he feared they might hear him.

There was nothing to do but wait. Not far beyond the clearing there must be an encampment where Urrell knew he might cadge scraps from the women and any camp-bound old men, as well as rummage for food amid the rubbish strewn around in the abundance of summer's good hunting. No-one would bother about a scavenging lad while food was so plentiful.

When the hunters had eaten they conferred. The one in the crossbelt scratched a plan or design on a bare patch of ground, which all looked at intently for a while and discussed. Then, as one man, they leapt to their feet, brandished their javelins, jigged round the patch of ground, uttered a single howling whoop that startled Urrell almost into giving away his hideout, and trotted off in single file in pursuit of the bison.

It was some time before Urrell felt safe enough to steal out to the gnawn bones marking the spot of the hunters' repast. He regnawed every one clean of the least shred of gristle, fat and sinew, his belly quaking for such nourishment after days of raw fungus, handfuls of berries and grubs prised from rotten logs. Then each bone was cracked with stones for marrow and juices to suck dry.

Only after the last splinter had been dealt with did Urrell think to look at the drawing on the ground. It was the outline of a bison, the bison he had witnessed, with spears in its sides and a rear hoof caught in that trap-like box.

He was absorbed in this when his heart tripped as he heard a tread and realised that he, in turn, was being intently observed.

CHAPTER 3

U rrell crouched stock-still, eyes locked with the watcher, who appeared to be alone. He too kept still, offering no threat of violence.

They had time to examine each other. The stranger was little above the lad's height, with shaggy hair and a remarkably intense gaze from yellowish, goat-like eyes. He seemed to understand how hungry the boy was. From a pouch he drew out a sizable chunk of cooked flesh, still on the bone, and held it out invitingly. As the boy did not budge, he beckoned with the other hand. Still the boy dared not shift.

The rank weeds, the fetid smell.

Holding out his offering, the watcher slowly advanced towards Urrell, pausing to instill trust before moving forward again. Urrell saw he was unarmed and limped. It was clear he meant no harm, even meant good. When he was a few paces away he tossed the meat to the lad and squatted to see how it was received, never taking his light eyes off Urrell's face. He uttered a few words in a strange language, underscored by gestures urging the boy to pick up the food and to eat. It was enough to allay some of Urrell's wariness, enough for him to pick up the joint and sniff it: venison, cooked right through. He bit. It was delicious. He chewed and tore at it, his hunger overcoming fear. An expression of pleasure and approval on his provider's features was accompanied by more words, ones conveying a tone of friendly interest. Urrell nodded and grunted.

"It is very good," he said. "I am very hungry."

"Good. Then you eat, eat," said his benefactor in the boy's own language. He spoke it haltingly, as if recollected from a far past.

So Urrell did as bidden, ravenously, on his hunkers opposite this strange short man who had appeared out of nowhere bearing sustenance and was now squatting a few paces away watching him eat his fill.

That the watcher spoke his language did not surprise the boy much.

He was used to hearing different languages among the women in the camp when they conversed among themselves, or crooned to their infants. They came from distant places, exchanged and traded at moots, or stolen, bringing with them strange ways and words, so that boys like Urrell hanging round the camp picked up smatterings of words, mainly names of things, leaf movements, animal moods, ghostly occurrences, and objects brought from faraway places, passed from hand to hand and held to be valuable or potent due to their very rarity. His red spearhead, now the bear's, had been one.

"Where you come?"

The boy answered by pointing up and over the cliff he had been following.

"How many days?"

Shy to risk speech with this unusual being and loth to look straight into that yellowish, enquiring gaze, Urrell kept his eyes fastened on his venison haunch-bone and held up one hand, fingers outspread, clenched and outspread twice, to signal how long he had been travelling.

The answer seemed to satisfy his questioner who left him to get on with his meal.

Then: "How you called?"

"Urrell."

"Ah, Urrell, Urrell," repeated the stranger, savouring the name, fluting the sound.

16

As the boy said nothing, the man volunteered: "I, Agaratz."

By now the bone was picked clean. No excuse remained for staying crouched, so Urrell stood up slowly, unsure of himself, avoiding sudden movements that might look hostile. His spears he left on the ground.

Agaratz also rose. Although he was scarcely taller than Urrell he had a grown man's breadth of shoulder and a powerful chest, as well as adult hairiness. Indeed he was hairier than any man Urrell had ever known. His head hair grew coarsely down the back of his neck, sprouting from the nape, its rusty colour matching the yellow eyes. Agaratz noticed the boy's hesitant look. A gleam of playfulness lit the strange eyes, as in a feline's when chasing and tumbling in play with other kits outside their den. Was it a prelude to a half-playful, half-hurtful gambol? Urrell tensed, ready to retreat or dodge.

Instead, Agaratz turned to show his back in profile, to show the boy that he was crookbacked.

Urrell's surprise must have shown – he knew that malformed babies were not kept, even if their mothers tried to save them. He had heard their screams as the men of the clan wrested the cripple from its mother, threw it into the air and skewered its falling body on a spear to avert evil befalling the encampment. Again that half-playful gleam played across the yellow eyes as they noticed Urrell's discomfiture and appeared to prelude a pounce, making the boy feel like the smallest cub confronting the biggest of a litter.

But no pounce came. Instead, Agaratz spoke, forgetting the boy did not understand his native tongue. It was some kind of explanation, perhaps to do with his back, in no way threatening, so Urrell relaxed a little and stared.

"Ah," went Agaratz, brought up by the boy's blank look. "Ah-ha, I say that I *konkoraz*." Then, to show what he meant, he pointed at his hump.

17

Urrell nodded, more to show friendliness than comprehension.

It was then that Agaratz did an astonishing thing. Placing his hands on the ground and kicking his legs in the air, he walked about on his palms. Instantly Urrell understood why. One of Agaratz's legs ended in a club foot, hence his limp. Instead of toes, the foot split into two horny extensions from the callused heel. The lame leg was hairier than the other, thinner, more sinewy. Urrell had never seen anything like it and his face showed his astonishment when Agaratz sprang upright from his handstand.

Impulsively he stepped forward to look closer, then as quickly drew back, alive to danger. Agaratz's arms could have broken every bone in his body with ease. But there was no menace in Agaratz's stance, not a hint of danger in the gleaming eyes that seemed to say, 'Look at my skill and singularity', with a look that changed to wistfulness no sooner had Urrell shrunk back. It was that look which told Urrell, as no words could, that Agaratz meant no harm. This time he stepped forward and did not step back, but placed his hand on Agaratz's forearm, a gesture as natural as when he had set off up the course of the waterfall and across the moors.

In his turn Agaratz placed his hand on Urrell's and they remained motionless for a while in this gesture of friendship.

CHAPTER 4

Agaratz stirred first, to pick up Urrell's spears. He examined them attentively a few moments before handing them over. The fibre bindings, tested with a thumbnail, seemed to meet his silent approval. Old Mother's fibres that she had shown Urrell how to ret.

Without a word, Agaratz leading, they set off across the glade into the forest. Under the downswept boughs of the first fir Agaratz stooped and recovered a pouch, several javelins and smaller objects bound in a bundle with thongs. Urrell realised Agaratz had cached these things before coming out to meet him, perhaps to avoid frightening him. It roused in him feelings he could not name, this rare kindness. He felt safe, glad to be trotting behind this being with the rolling gait from the odd foot, the roll of powerful shoulders humped under the russet hair.

Urrell now had time to notice his new companion's garb. Never had he seen the like for stitching: the man's trews fitted to below the knees, sewn down each side, the leather supple. Over his back and chest Agaratz wore a seamless jerkin that reached mid-thigh. Small ornaments like quills were stitched to the front. Over this was slung a pouch, also ornamented with quills, coloured to make patterns in white, reddle and black.

He could also see that Agaratz's javelins were beautifully crafted, finer than anything he had ever seen, the shafts incised with tiny heads of deer, bison and other creatures. The tips, long and wrought in a reddish stone new to Urrell, delighted him. His were poor, boyish things in comparison.

Their route ran parallel with the cliffs in the same direction as Urrell had intended to go in the hope of finding a settlement. Neither spoke, nor did Urrell think to ask where they were going. Despite his club foot Agaratz travelled with the tireless trot of hunters, barefoot on the springy pine-needle floor of the forest, broken now and again by clearings where a beck ran down the cliff face and created a little glade with light enough for deciduous trees and bushes to grow. At these Agaratz was careful to pause, look and listen before crossing over. What he was wary of he did not say.

They had come to one of these when Agaratz said: "We stop. You hungry?"

"Yes." He was tired too.

"Good. Look." So saying, Agaratz pointed with his javelins up the clearing to the cliffs at an overhang at ground level. It looked unexceptional to Urrell. Agaratz made for it and he followed.

Charred wood and ashes in a small hearth near the back wall betokened a hunters' shelter. It had none of the usual rubbish, bones, broken flints, cast-off shreds of pelts that littered camps, nor their stench, to which Urrell was used.

"Your camp?"

"One my camp."

"Where is your main camp, your tribe?"

For all response Agaratz waved a hand in the general distance towards which they were travelling. It seemed an inconclusive answer but Urrell dared not question more. Instead he squatted by the dead hearth awaiting what Agaratz might do or offer. His own pouch was bare. Since the venison hours earlier he had eaten only a few bilberries and raspberries grabbed as he trotted behind Agaratz. Food would be welcome in this forest seemingly bereft of game, apart from a few fowl that whirred aloft before they were within range of even a weighted throwing-stick.

"You look, Urrell."

Agaratz dragged a pine log from the weeds outside and leant it against the inner cave wall. Snags stuck out of it like rungs. Using these, Agaratz climbed to a ledge under the ceiling of the shelter where, invisible from below, were cached provisions: a bundle and a joint of meat. These he tossed to Urrell and followed down his scaling pole.

"I kindle fire. You find wood."

Keen though he was to see how Agaratz made fire, Urrell did as bidden and was soon back with an armful of dry twigs and cones from beneath the nearest firs. Agaratz was twirling a fire-stick in a hollow log and already blowing on tinder till it flared. Several times Urrell was sent to fetch more fuel, Agaratz intent on building up substantial heat. Urrell expected him to thrust the joint into the flames or dangle it over; instead he built up a bed of embers.

"Now cook."

He parted the embers with two stones till the glowing mass lay open before Urrell's inquisitive eyes. Agaratz placed a flat, much-blackened stone in the bottom of the hearth, placed the joint on top, drew the embers over and squatted to wait. Urrell had never seen this done, nor had his surprise gone unnoticed. When he glanced at Agaratz he saw in the crookback's eyes that playful gleam, like the one when he had astonished Urrell with his handstand, a look which said, 'See, another trick you did not know'.

It was a trick worth knowing; Urrell's nose twitched and his stomach rumbled at the savoury smells rising from the roast. When he judged it done, Agaratz scraped away the embers and with two pointed sticks speared the meat and placed it on a flat stone, as Urrell followed every move. First he brushed off ashes and coals then, from a belt pouch, produced a flint knife, longer than a man's handspan, exquisitely knapped to a fine edge from the same reddish stone as his javelin points, and with it sawed the joint in two, half for Urrell, half for himself, handing the lad his share skewered on one of the roasting sticks.

In companionable silence they set to, Urrell savouring a feast he would long remember.

But it was not yet over. Agaratz surprised Urrell again by producing from his pouch a bark bundle which, unfolded, revealed most of a honeycomb. He halved the delicacy with the same flint knife and gave Urrell one piece and kept the other – something no man in his own tribe would have done. Urrell wavered before the offer, expecting a cuff if he reached out for it.

"Take, Urrell. For you. I bring for you." Then, perhaps to coax him the better, he said, "*Etzi*" in his own tongue.

"Honeycomb."

"Ah, honeycomb," repeated Agaratz, savouring the new word.

"Etzi," said Urrell, in the same spirit. Their eyes met in a look of complicity and Urrell saw an expression new to him on a human face: a sly grin, part fun, part knowingness, part mockery, which gave him a curious sense of pleasure and comfort, so that he laughed as he never had before and clapped his hands. This incited Agaratz to do another handstand round the fire, then drop on all fours and begin mimicking the gait and movements of different animals, delighting the boy who called out the names of the creatures being imitated, identifying them from the performances before him: "horse – foal – mare in foal – boar – sow with young – bear – buck – doe – stork…"

Plainly his pleasure redoubled the performer's, encouraging Agaratz to move from mimicry to imitating the calls, grunts, sounds made by each animal with such accuracy as to make Urrell think, eyes closed, that the beast was in the shelter. His repertoire seemed to include all creation. At least all creation that the boy knew – until Agaratz rose on his toes and knuckles, rounded his back even more than his hump made it, and circled Urrell on toes and knuckles with a rolling, massive gait, rocking from side to side, burbling and rumbling, till without warning he emitted a blaring trumpeting that echoed out of the shelter into the woods, startling Urrell from his happy state.

Urrell was lost. His puzzlement pleased Agaratz.

"You not know what is that?"

"No."

"Is *ummook*. Look, I draw."

With a twig, in one swift, continuous line Agaratz drew a mammoth, raising the twig only to sketch in the tusks of a big bull and to hatch in a hint of his hairy flank.

Urrell hopped about with excitement. "*Mammurak, mammurak,*" he almost shouted, the word from Old Mother's language, the only name he knew for the great beast. Her word. It reminded the boy of her, the old woman who had befriended a small boy when no-one cared whether he lived or died. Her cackle of laughter when they were alone. Sometimes the men laughed, but it was the laughter of bullies, of males guffawing at others' falls, laughing at a woman nursing a wrist broken in a beating, at a small creature wounded to use as target practice. If the women laughed it was in scorn of one another, spiteful.

Old Mother. Her last season before the cold.

"Where are the *ummook*? Where?"

The boy's eagerness about this beast seemed to amuse Agaratz. The sly, elfish grin Urrell would grow to recognise flitted across the long face framed by reddish sideburns over the ears.

"*Ummook, ummook,*" he echoed, "*ummook* long long way." One hand made an up-and-over movement, as though unrolling immense distances, pointing towards the remote snow-capped mountain range.

"Agaratz, please, have you seen them, have you seen *ummook*?"

23

"Once I see." The souvenir did not appear to be a happy one. "When cold times and I small."

Then, changing expression, he said with a tone of finality, "Now we go."

The preparations were soon done. Watched by Urrell, the mammoth-mimic shinned up his improvised ladder to stow the fire-stick, fire-log, spare tinder and odds and ends of the bundle in the gap under the shelter roof, and came back down the climbing pole, which he hid in the undergrowth outside. He then trod the ashes, some still glowing, the heat not seeming to affect his feet, the club foot or the other, scattered the hearthstones and swept away the mammoth sketch and their footprints with a fir branch till the shelter floor looked as though no-one had been there for months.

Urrell wondered why but did not ask. His own clan hunters never troubled to hide their passage.

When all was as he wanted, after a last glance round, Agaratz led the way onwards in the same direction as before, broadly parallel with the cliffs which were gradually becoming lower. The forest scene was changing too, the fir trees giving way to ash, beech, oak and their accompanying understorey, more like the woodlands Urrell was accustomed to.

CHAPTER 5

As they went on, Agaratz grew warier, pausing occasionally to listen; the boy obediently stopping too. Apart from a few bird sounds there seemed to be nothing to hear. Although they saw deer, always at a distance, game was less plentiful than in Urrell's home valley. In any case, Agaratz was evidently not bent on hunting but on arriving at his destination. Whatever it was that kept Agaratz alert remained invisible.

In this unquestioning way Urrell kept behind his guide, hunter fashion. By nightfall the cliff-face, which had been declining in height, was little more a than a long bluff, broken by scrub-filled gullies. Streams became more frequent and the wooded landscape through which they had been travelling opened into grassland interspersed with clumps of trees.

Agaratz paused, crouched and pointed towards a bluff. "Cave: you come."

At this, Urrell scanned the bluff for signs of life, expecting the tell-tale smoke of cooking fires, a hint of movement. But there was nothing. This was so much against his boyish experience that he exclaimed in surprise, "Where are your people?"He remembered those bison hunters. "Were the bison hunters from your people?

"No. From far."

Agaratz being obviously disinclined to expand on the matter, the boy kept his questions to himself.

They now moved forward again, Agaratz no longer wary. He turned towards the bluff, leading the way through the scrub at its foot till a cleft appeared, scarcely noticeable a spear's cast away, and entered it. Urrell followed. There were none of the signs of life that indicated a home camp – no rubbish, no trampled plants, no smoke. It must be another of Agaratz's camps, like the one they had eaten at earlier that day.

The cleft angled sharp left and opened out into a sort of small gulch, a self-contained and hidden patch of grass and scrub surrounded by rock walls. In the left-hand rock-face the opening to a small cave could be seen, well beyond reach, at twice the height of the tallest man.

"You stay, Urrell."

Agaratz searched among the bushes at the foot of the rock-face to lift out a climbing-pole, as he had done at the earlier shelter, and propped it beneath the cave entrance. It was over twice the height of that first one. Was Agaratz about to toss down another roast, more fire-making material?

"You follow, Urrell." Agaratz swarmed up the pole, his club foot no hindrance. With his pouch and spears, the boy followed, feeling less nimble.

When they were both up Agaratz hauled in the climbing pole and laid it along one side of the cave, a cave which Urrell saw was the entrance to a gallery that disappeared into the bluff. Its floor was clear of all litter. Ranged round the walls were bundles and piles of objects, shadowy in the gloom. He squatted, not knowing what to expect. His trust in Agaratz was complete, but was this just another resting place on the way to the tribal camp of his people? It looked more permanent than the camp they had stopped at earlier yet he could not fathom why there were no hints of anyone else using the place. Why there were no signs of hunting parties coming and going? He would wait to ask.

"You want eat, Urrell?"

Agaratz was ferreting among things in a recess as he spoke.

Urrell recognised another fire-log, tinder and a hardened fire-stick. The stick twirled with a deftness that entranced the boy, the tinder soon smouldered, was blown alight and twigs added to start a fire in a hearth Urrell now discerned against a wall. He glimpsed the sly grin on the long face lit by the first flames.

"You make fire next time, Urrell."

In his home clan, an old woman kept the fire alight, her role to carry the fire-log with its embers on the long trek to the upland hunting grounds in spring and back down in the autumn when the snows drove the clan to the lowlands and the sea shore. Woe betide the fire-keeper who let the embers die. Re-kindling was not easy. Urrell knew it was done, but never had any of his tribe conjured up fire so magically, so effortlessly, as Agaratz had before his dazzled eyes.

He was to be shown how. His breast swelled with pride. "Tomorrow I make fire, Agaratz?"

"Yes, now I cook." Agaratz pulled out bundles of bone-dry twigs from a pile and built up an almost smokeless fire against the wall. Urrell's people used a hearth away from the wall, always the same.

In the firelight Urrell made out side entrances and recesses, as well as piles and bundles around their sides. Yet more bundles hung from pegs and from frames made of boughs. There was a permanence about the arrangements. Agaratz must live here much of the time. But where were his kin?

Urrell saw too, from the blackened wall, that this was the regular hearth – though not in the propitious mid-rear of the shelter. Another puzzle. Old Mother would have known the answer, keeper of the flame in the true spot the spirits knew.

Tomorrow he would learn to make fire; Urrell the fire-maker-to-be.

Agaratz was fanning the blaze with a leafy branch, dispersing the little smoke the fire made. He was crouched in profile, lit by the flames, the club foot, almost cloven, was turned towards Urrell, with its hairy shin.

"You eat *perretxiko?*"

"*Perretxiko?*"

"Like… like mushroom."

Urrell knew some funguses could be eaten, some not. At certain times, the women gathered them when they went berrying, if game was scarce or the men's hunting had failed. It was not men's fare; hunters spurned funguses unless driven by extreme hunger. He had learnt from the women which kinds to nibble by following them when he was small and ousted from the camp with stones and cuffs, the lot of orphaned boys everywhere.

"You eat fungus?" Urrell's voice must have conveyed boyish disbelief.

"I eat. They *mamu* food."

"*Mamu?*"

"Give strength. Give…" he sought a word in Urrell's language… "give power."

Urrell knew hunters sought hunting powers, held secret rituals that women and boys must not witness, on pain of spearing. Some foods, some signs, weakened power, deflected weapons from their mark. No hunter touched fish, from the water world, because of this. Some foods women might eat, but not men; some men alone might eat. That lore he knew.

"If it is power food, am I allowed to eat it?"

"You eat. I let you."

The finality of this empowering statement comforted Urrell.

An idea occurred to the boy. "Agaratz, may you eat fishes?"

"Fishes, yes."

"For my people fish is… like spirit food. Hunters never eat fishes."

Somehow he felt he had impressed his protector. The golden eyes rested on him, with a stare devoid of the sly grin, empty of malice or of friendliness, looking beyond him. Urrell crouched still, caught in the stare, a small creature paralysed by a greater. Had he crossed an unseen line, transgressed, as a boy chancing upon hunters' rites might transgress, unwittingly? He had once seen a boy speared through the legs for this.

The rank smell, the hidden den. A secret place.

Then, with the same finality as earlier, Agaratz stated: "I *accalarrak*. Eat spirit food, fish food, fungus food. One day you be *accalarrak*. Eat spirit foods."

Agaratz raked the embers from the glowing hearth stones and arranged several big white mushrooms, of a kind unknown to Urrell, on them, having first smeared them with grease. When one side was done and the aroma began to tease Urrell's nostrils, Agaratz turned the mushrooms over with two sticks to sizzle thoroughly. Not till he deemed them done did he spear one for himself and another for Urrell.

The flavour was something quite new to the boy.

"You like, Urrell?"

"Oh, yes."

"You eat before?"

"Not this kind, not cooked."

"You eat not cook?" That impish grin again which told Urrell he had said something odd, boyish. Perhaps eating funguses raw was taboo among Agaratz's people, like fish among his.

"Where is your camp?" he asked.

"This my camp."

"But where are your kinfolk?"

"I no kinfolk. Alone."

He said this matter-of-factly.

"But I saw smoke, before the bison hunters, before you. Who were they?"

Agaratz looked up from the second toadstool he was spearing

for them both. The yellowish eyes fixed on Urrell's again, making him feel important, he, a boy, the bearer of important information. "I saw it from the clifftop, like mist, but it was smoke."

Agaratz pondered the information, nodded to himself but made no comment. Perhaps it explained his wariness in the woods.

"Now we sleep," he said.

Before he could do so, Urrell knew he needed to relieve himself. In his home camp it was no problem. Men stepped out a little; women a little further the other way. Here there was no stepping out, not even to climb down the pole as Agaratz had hauled it up. He wondered what Agaratz would do. He had not long to wait. Agaratz drew aside a curtain of pelts to reveal a recess piled with pine branches and bracken, on top of which were spread several hides including a bison's. Urrell had never seen the like. "Here sleep," said his host. "First follow."

Taking a brand from the fire as a torch he led Urrell into the gallery till it forked then took the lesser opening, which led to a side chamber. Its use was obvious to Urrell, its earthen floor absorbing the result. A heap of moss and grasses lay nearby, their use evident. Agaratz stuck the torch in a crevice for a sconce, a familiar place, and left Urrell to his needs.

When Urrell made his way back by the light of the dying brand he found Agaratz hunched by the fire waiting his turn. Urrell wondered at such behaviour, why the crookback should wish to be alone for that.

"Now we sleep," said Agaratz on his return. He banked the fire and they both crawled into the recess, Urrell to the back, snuggling into the bracken and pine branches and drawing a pelt over himself. He was asleep in seconds.

When he awoke, Urrell knew with animal immediacy where he was.

Agaratz was gone. Raising the curtain of skins, he crept out but his host was not in the cave either. He saw that the climbing-pole had been lowered: Agaratz must be outside. Finding Agaratz seemed the first thing to do so he scaled down the pole and set about exploring the little gulch. He soon found a freshet rising from the foot of the cliff, forming a natural basin that overflowed and meandered into the vegetation. Signs showed that the basin was someone's drinking place, Agaratz's no doubt, as well as other smaller creatures. He lay on his face and drank from the surface, seeing his face, brown with dirt and sunburn, reflected in the still pool. A fuzz was beginning to darken his upper lip. He ran his finger along the down, pinched it, made faces into the water.

Thus engaged in self-exploration, he had not heard anyone approaching. A "ho" from Agaratz announced that he had come up silently and was warning him of his presence. "Ho," answered Urrell, caught unawares.

Agaratz had been foraging, as a skin held by the four corners to make a carrier revealed when he laid it down for Urrell to inspect. It held several kinds of funguses, several rodents and some raspberries wrapped in big leaves. He watched Urrell's reactions, with a communicative gleam in those yellow eyes that Urrell had never known in anyone, not even in Fire-crone's when she took pleasure in explaining things to him, or talked of her girlhood land.

"Good, now eat," said Agaratz.

They went back up the pole and Agaratz revived the fire. As before, he made a rude oven of hot stones to bake the rodents while others served to braise the heads of funguses. Urrell watched all this, between acting as fuel-fetcher from the woodmow, noting every move which, once seen would be recalled perfectly, like spoor. From Agaratz's manner he knew there would be more to learn: he squatted happily, as happy as those rare times when he and Fire-crone had been alone in camp and she had rambled on about her youth, shown him binding skills, described strange beasts and told him stories of olden times in that mixture of her girlhood tongue and his camp's which he had grown to understand better than anyone else.

The marmoset-like creatures proved good eating, creatures that his clan eschewed, nobody knew why. If Agaratz ate them, Urrell felt safe to do so too. His camp's taboos held no power here. He memorised each fungus Agaratz gathered and ate, and learnt their names, known only in Agaratz's language.

When they had finished eating, he saw how Agaratz gathered the bones and leftovers to burn in the fire, something no-one would have bothered to do in his home group, where leavings lay where they fell, to be trampled into the shelter floor.

CHAPTER 6

He had no notion of what to expect next. Only that it would be good, new knowing, like Old Mother's knowing when they were alone in camp, by her fire.

"You know how to make… spear-caster?"

"For throwing spears? I have seen some, in my tribe."

"Come."

Agaratz went to one of the recesses at the back of the gallery, lighting his way with a burning stick from the fire. Inside, laid out on a skin, were spear-thrower heads. Some looked yellow with age. Each was carved in the shape of an animal – bison, deer, horse – so as to wed purpose and shape in one thrust of the shaft straight to its mark. Urrell's eyes widened.

"Oh."

"You like?"

"Oh, I like them, yes. Did you make them, Agaratz?"

"No. These olds." His eyes lost their lustre for a moment. "These, keep. I make you one."

They went back by the fire. Nothing stirred outside in the sunlit gulch. From the bundle that he had been carrying when Urrell first met him, Agaratz drew out a collection of flint and bone tools – scrapers, chisels, burins, drills, blades – which he laid out in rows on a bit of leather before Urrell's intent gaze. Then he went to one of the piles of objects ranged round the sides of the cave and selected a piece of hard, dark wood, of the kind that Urrell knew was found in bogs. It was crooked, like an elbow.

"You watch, Urrell."

Gripping the wood upright between his good and his cloven foot, Agaratz began to shave and pare the wood with a two-handed scraper. Urrell squatted to watch. When the scraper bluntened Agaratz stopped to sharpen it, not as the boy thought he would, by tapping the blade edge with a flint. Instead Agaratz chose a burin from his array and, with small, rapid pressures on the flint edge, prised slivers of stone off. His speed and deftness dazzled Urrell. Soon the scraper was keen again and Agaratz resumed work for a while.

"Now stop."

He stowed his tools back in their bundle, tied the thongs that Urrell had noticed on that first meeting, when the bison hunters had sped off after their prey, and replaced the bundle with the wood on a natural shelf. Agaratz then swept up the flakes and shavings with a handful of twigs and, to Urrell's surprise, instead of throwing them out of the cave, dropped them in the fire, muttering something.

"Now go find food. Hunt. Come."

From a sort of rack Agaratz took down a spear-thrower from among several others, complete with grip dowelled into the throwing piece whose cup to hold the javelin butt Urrell saw was shaped from two stags confronting each other, forelegs and antlers locked in battle.

"Did you carve these, Agaratz?"

"No. Father." It was Agaratz's first reference to any kin.

Urrell durst ask no more. Instead his eyes fastened on the stags. That Agaratz had had a father who could create such a thing roused in him even greater awe of his mentor. The men of his own tribe made plain throwers, wooden or bone dog-legs, sometimes adorning them with sketchy shapes of game animals to 'bring good luck' during the hunt. Boys made their own in imitation of their elders to chase small game and birds. But nothing like Agaratz's stags.

As Agaratz chose two javelins with long blade-like points to use with the thrower, Urrell could not resist asking: "Agaratz, where are your people?"

Immediately he knew he had overstepped some invisible mark. Agaratz shrugged, his eyes clouded as Urrell had seen them do before, but the impression was gone no sooner than expressed while Agaratz went on choosing hunting gear.

He selected a second weapon, a throwing-stick unlike anything Urrell had seen before, a short shaft ending in a cup or dub the breadth of a man's hand. Agaratz saw Urrell's interest. Pointing to the cup, he said, "Mammook" – the sly grin – "see, is carved mammook." Urrell looked closely at the grain, yellow with age, knew it was not bone but ivory, ivory like the beads Old Mother wore in the dirt round her neck, keepsakes of her youth. The boy's excitement overflowed: faintly but distinctly engraved round the edge of the cup ran a series of miniature representations of mammoths, in profile, follow-my-leader. The artist had hinted at each beast, etching in the bulbous head, the ears, the outline of the back, its long curving tushes overlapping the animal ahead so that they went round the rim in a never-ending line, each no larger than a child's thumbnail. Urrell could scarcely contain his urge to skip about at the sight.

Old Mother of the Mammoths. Fire-crone.

"Agaratz, take me to the mammoths."

His mind, fired by the miniatures round the cup rim, overflowed into a state of excitement that he had never experienced before. While part of him remained aloof, another part seemed able to leap distances with the power of dreams and conjure up the old woman crouched in her usual position by her fire, only now it was by Agaratz's hearth. Her face turned up towards him, but her old hag's cackling humour was no more; her stare as remote as stone. "Old Mother, Old Mother," but the vision vanished, and the part of him which had remained aloof told the part of him that dreamt that Old Mother was dead.

Old Mother…

He was back in Agaratz's cave, a lad developing in strength, alone with a hunchback. Those yellow eyes intent on his face told Urrell that they had seen what he had seen, had been present in his vision, shared his woe.

"One day, Urrell, when you strong, we go find mammoths."

Urrell knew then, with the knowing that is true knowing, that he would never return to his tribe, beyond the cliffs and across the moors. Henceforth his life lay wherever Agaratz led. Through him he would find the mammoths.

CHAPTER 7

Instead of mammoths, that day's hunting was to take on homelier quarry. The climbing pole once lowered and stowed among bushes, they left the gulch, Urrell following his leader through the cleft and out into open country, but not before Agaratz had scanned the outlook as far as they could see. Summer's high grasses rose to the lad's knees, so that both humans seemed to wade through a vast inland sea of grass, broken in places by islands of trees. Ahead, in the distance, ran a long reef of more trees, a continuous line, and it was towards this that Agaratz travelled, moving at a steady trot with the rolling gait peculiar to himself, as though the grassland heaved underfoot. The sun shone. At each step they disturbed tiny blue butterflies, insects of all kinds and grasshoppers, these last the boy snatched without pausing and crunched as he went.

After half the day of travel the line of trees was growing closer. Far off a herd of horses grazed at walking pace. Sighting the two humans, they paused as one animal, heads turned to watch them; then, caught in heedless panic, galloped off across the grassland, gliding over the green surface on hooves and fetlocks hidden from sight in the deep grass. Urrell watched them until they were a frieze skimming along the horizon.

The nearer they came to the tree-line, the more evidence of herds showed in the grass – droppings and trampling of horses, deer, even bison. These Agaratz ignored, eyes on the trees.

"River soon."

Once into the woodland they saw more evidence of herds

37

sheltering. Several times remains of kills attested to the presence of predators. "That lion, those wolf, and here one by…" Agaratz was lost for the name "… like big cat." As he seemed unconcerned by these signs, Urrell felt unconcerned too.

The river was a considerable one, flowing strongly and smoothly between banks thick with rushes which grew some way out into the current. As they emerged from the tree cover Agaratz signalled to Urrell that they were to start stalking but he was not in time to avoid disturbing a flock of ducks which rose from the rushes and flew off upstream.

"We hunt," and Agaratz pointed at the disappearing ducks. Wildfowl were seldom pursued by Urrell's tribesmen, being hard to bring down with javelins and beyond the range of stones and throwing-sticks, however accurately flung. Sometimes where roosts were known, fowl were caught by stealth at night: this was hunting that boys could and did do. How Agaratz intended to capture ducks, Urrell could not guess.

"You watch, Urrell. Not move."

Javelins and spear-throwers were set aside in favour of the cup-shaped device with the mammoth carving that had so excited Urrell. With this, and three egg-sized pebbles from his pouch, Agaratz crept off through the undergrowth to reeds along a spit of land which gave him a better view of the rush-beds. Urrell watched, wondering.

Soon the calls of a duck attracting drakes rose from the reeds where Agaratz was hidden. For a few moments even Urrell was fooled: Agaratz was mimicking a female; several drakes, equally fooled, settled among the rushes in search of the caller.

The calls intensified, luring the birds closer inshore. When he judged they were close enough, Agaratz changed calls to a sort of whistle that disturbed the drakes, causing them to fly up and circle the reeds were he was hidden, bringing them within range. With astonishing speed Agaratz loosed a pebble with all the extended power of his arm and the shaft of his cupped thrower, hitting a fowl in mid-flight, recharging his thrower with his free hand and sending the second missile at another drake with such smoothness of action that it struck its target as the first duck landed in the rushes. His third shot at another drake, by then at tree height, missed by a finger's breadth.

"Come," he shouted and plunged into the waist deep rushes to retrieve the downed birds. Urrell leapt in and made for the spot where the second one had fallen, finding the dead bird easily whereas the first one made efforts to escape and kept Agaratz engaged longer in its capture.

The excitement of the hunt showed on the boy's face.

"You like? asked Agaratz, pointing at the stone-thrower.

"I have never seen one before."

"My people use."

Fleeting sadness passed across the light eyes, but Urrell thought better than to enquire further. A shrug would have been his answer. "Now we hunt more, Urrell."

By late afternoon, when they turned back towards home gulch, the two bore between them seven game birds brought down by Agaratz's marksmanship plus pouchfuls of freshwater mussels and crabs that Urrell had been detailed to gather. The boy felt that it had been the happiest day in his life. There was much to be learnt with Agaratz. He vowed that he too would become skilful with a stone-thrower, this new hunting device.

"Agaratz, will you show me how to use a stone-thrower like yours?"

"I make one you. For boy."

What made Urrell sense that his request had struck a chord in the breast of his strange, hairy protector?

A grin, the sly smile. "But now eat duck."

There was little to do by way of preparation when they got back in the dark. Agaratz revived the fire, Urrell fetched wood, Agaratz plucked and burnt off the feathers of two ducks, filling the cave with the smell of singed plumage. When the fire had been well built up, Agaratz made an oven with stones, placed the ducks inside to roast and scooped embers all round and over.

While waiting they ate the mussels and crabs, raw, by the fire, as the short summer night drew into the dawn. Never had Urrell feasted as he did then, with a whole duck to himself, gnawing and crunching his way through it, entrails and all, till only the charred bill and cracked bones remained. Happy, glutted, he reeked of singed feathers and burnt fat from his ragged hair to the tatters of fur round his breechclout and jerkin, whereas Agaratz had picked his duck clean without smearing himself in grease and juices. The crookback grinned at Urrell. "You like?" Urrell could only nod.

"Come."

Agaratz lowered the pole in the dark and Urrell followed him down, wondering why, bloated from his feast. They went to the spring. Here Agaratz wet a handful of grass and rubbed his arms and face vigorously, signalling for Urrell to do likewise. He explained: "Smell bad." Urrell knew that hunters sometimes rubbed themselves with strong-smelling plants to mask their own scent. Children splashed in brooks for fun and he knew women washed off their berry-juice designs to paint on new ones, but this was different. He scrubbed with a will to please his teacher, stood in the pool and rubbed his legs for good measure, enjoying the tingling freshness.

Then Agaratz indicated, by gesturing, that he was going one way to fulfil private needs and that Urrell should go in the other, before they returned up-ladder to sleep.

This day set the pattern for the next ones, Urrell swiftly learning from Agaratz by example. Agaratz seldom explained. True to his word, he made a stone-thrower for Urrell and set him to practise in the gulch till his aim became passable. He refashioned the lad's javelins to sit well in the spear-thrower that he finished carving and paring from the bog-wood elbow. He showed Urrell how to improve spear points and glue them with resin on to the shaft. Agaratz himself used points with tangs that fitted into a slot at the tip of the shaft, an improvement new to Urrell.

They went fishing along the river using harpoons to spear a fish unknown to Urrell.

Izokin, Agaratz called it.

Agaratz's technique for harpooning salmon was to lie along the trunk of a tree overhanging a pool in a bend of the river and wait till a salmon swam into range. His bone harpoon-tip had barbs and was attached to a line of finely plaited thongs. Urrell watched as at the second or third throw from his perch Agaratz hit a fish, the harpoon tip detached and remained in the salmon's back while Agaratz paid out line, playing the fish until it weakened enough to draw it inshore for a final spear thrust – Urrell's task from the bank.

They ate part of it raw, stowing the rest in a pouch to bake later.

Urrell wondered why Agaratz never cooked anything away from the home cave, however far afield they roamed. One day he asked: "Why not cook meat here?"

Agaratz was silent. The pause was so long it seemed he would not answer. Then he said, quietly, "Bad. Hunters see smoke."

Since the bison hunters on the day he had met Agaratz, Urrell had seen no sign of humans in all their hunting trips across the savannah, or to the river. Only herds of horses and bison, far off, fattening for the migration south as winter would arrive, the time when Urrell knew his home group would migrate in parallel with the herds to the plains by the salt water to seek shellfish, crabs and

41

flightless birds that drifted on the sea currents in vast flocks and sometimes came too near inshore in pursuit of shoals of fry, becoming stranded when the sea withdrew. Those were cold and often hungry times. Even the sea froze in places. Hunters died in the snowy wastes as they pursued game into the frozen woods where bison and horses sheltered, browsing on brushwood and bark, made alert by packs of wolves and all the members of the cat family, that preyed upon them. Some years when the cold became very great, the deer with the wide antlers were driven to the coast in search of grasses and lichens under the snow. His group lived out these months in caves beside the sea, as generations before them had, the mounds of cast-off shells from the food the women gathered at low tide proof of how long they had been coming. When hunting had been good and the fire blazed hot, old men told of monsters and huge beasts from those far-off times, creatures long since vanished. Yet deep in caves Urrell knew there were paintings of great power where these monsters lived on, secrets only a few initiates might visit.

When and whither would Agaratz migrate – along the river, perhaps?

"Agaratz, when the cold comes, where do you go?"

"Stay."

"Stay – in the cold?"

"Yes, stay in cold."

Urrell had heard tales of hunters dying on their own, unable to hunt enough to stay alive. Surviving the cold by the sea was hard, when the wolves, lions and panthers from the forest were famished and ate anything they caught.

"How… how can you live – in the cold, Agaratz?"

"I live. You see."

"I see?"

"You see. You see with me."

Urrell, so far as he had thought at all, knew his future lay with Agaratz, but had not thought of it like this. It was a reversal of all his experience to date.

"But, Agaratz, how can you hunt alone in the great cold?" His voice must have trembled at the prospect of starvation, of freezing to death, for Agaratz was firm yet consoling when he answered:

"You see. I hunt. You hunt." There was no hint of the bullying or bragging of one of his home group's hunters: Agaratz stated what he had done. Experience spoke; Urrell's qualms subsided.

CHAPTER 8

"You like to see wolves, Urrell?"

Wolves. They heard wolves most nights howling afar, responding to one another, or 'singing' as Agaratz called it. Nothing in Urrell's life had led him to want to meet them. Wolves, he knew, unless ravenous, seldom attacked humans so long as one did not encroach on their territory. They warned, and one turned away.

"We go see."

That evening Agaratz roasted two wildfowl and placed them on a shelf, out of reach of rats.

"Tomorrow we go see wolves," he said, "take food." Urrell wondered what he meant. Some sort of bait? Agaratz explained: "Long way. Need food."

That night Urrell, sleeping in his burrow of branches, leaves and ferns, dreamt of wolves, of Agaratz as a wolf, of himself in a wolf's lair eating roast duck. When he awoke, the dreams had been so real he tried to describe them to Agaratz.

All he got was a nod and a grin.

"Take stone-thrower, pouch, spear-thrower, three spears," said Agaratz, selecting three weapons from his store of antiquities, or 'father' as he called them.

These Agaratz laid on the cave floor. As Urrell watched, wondering, Agaratz took a flint flake and drew the outline of a wolf in a single easy line round the weapons, muttering over the drawing in a language unknown to Urrell and sprinkling ashes from the hearth over the three spears. The hunchback was entirely absorbed in his ceremony.

"Now wolf no harm," he said.

It was scarcely light as they set out, not towards the river as Urrell had half expected but straight from the gulch towards the distant range of mountains that the boy fancied as 'the land of mammoths'.

Agaratz moved at a faster clip than usual, as though a great distance lay ahead, Urrell trotting along behind, his excitement slowly subsiding as the rhythm of the journey took over. Agaratz was more alert than usual, so Urrell kept a lookout too. By mid-morning their cliffs had sunk below the grass line. Huge herds of bison, seas of shaggy shapes, grazed slowly southwards. Ponies scattered at the sight of the two humans, galloping off only to stop and turn as if to see whether they were being pursued by such a puny pair. Deer loped away. Overhead vultures wheeled in ever-smaller circles as they descended on a distant carcass.

By the time the sun had passed its zenith the grasslands were beginning to break up into gullies and ravines. "Wolves soon," said Agaratz. He pulled one of the cold fowls from the pouch and tore it into two rough halves, one for Urrell, one for himself, which they squatted to eat, their weapons on the ground by them, their eyes watchful.

Nothing disturbed their meal except marmosets popping up to stare at such unexpected visitors to their domain. When they had eaten, Agaratz descended into the ravine ahead, along a way he seemed to know, Urrell following. Across the bottom and up the other side to the top, where Agaratz beckoned Urrell to move with stealth. Over the rim of the next ravine Agaratz pointed at a burrow in the opposite bank, the earth worn at the entrance.

The secret place, the smell of weeds.

"Wolfs," said Agaratz. He touched Urrell on the arm, sensing his fear.

The burrow remained blank. Agaratz began to make

45

whimpering sounds. Soon a snout and pricked ears appeared at the burrow entrance and a she-wolf emerged, sniffing the air and locating the direction of the sounds. Urrell saw her dugs in milk. Her cubs would be in the den, her mate and the pack not far, ready to defend. Agaratz's whimpering changed to a low call and the she-wolf, ears pricked, loped down the bank, across the bottom and up to where Agaratz and Urrell were crouched. Urrell moved to flee but Agaratz's grip held him back.

"Stay. You see."

The she-wolf came right up to Agaratz, licked his hand and rolled on her back. She showed every sign of pleasure at seeing him and answered his snuffling sounds with snuffles of her own. She turned and went back down the incline towards her burrow. Agaratz slithered down after her. At the bottom he looked and saw Urrell still on the ridge.

"Come, Urrell. Come, safe."

Against all instinct, he did so, his trust in Agaratz overcoming all he had ever heard about not approaching female wolves, bears, lions and other animals with young. The trust was borne out when the she-wolf, at the entrance to the burrow, with whimpering sounds of her own, coaxed out her litter. They appeared, one after the other, biggest first, shy of the visitors, cowering near the entrance.

"Wolfs, eh?" said Agaratz.

"How do you do this, Agaratz, you speak to a she-wolf with cubs?"

"This wolf, my wolf."

"Your wolf?"

"Yes. I keep when small."

She approached Agaratz and when close dropped to a creeping stance, crawling towards him, submissive and friendly in answer to his cajoling sounds.

Shyer, drawn between following their mother and fear of the unknown, the cubs lagged behind, the smallest hanging back farthest. Their mother was three paces from Agaratz when she flattened her ears and looked away up the ravine. Their eyes followed hers. Standing, tail upright, was a big male wolf, slightly ahead of his pack. Urrell knew straightaway he was the pack leader and the father of the cubs. His hand tightened on his spear. If the wolves attacked to defend their pack's cubs, he and Agaratz would be overwhelmed. He glanced up the ravine side: it would be too steep to scramble up with wolves in pursuit. He looked to see what Agaratz meant to do and saw only unconcern. What he was about to witness would raise both his boyish respect of and his devotion to Agaratz higher than ever.

Agaratz fixed his eyes on those of the lead wolf and began to call it in a low, coaxing bark, at the same time crouching wolf-like, bending forward and mimicking the stiff, prancing manner of a dog-wolf approaching a rival. The big wolf responded in kind, prancing forward aslant on the balls of his feet, tail erect, till man and wolf were level, flank to flank. They circled. Urrell stood still, breath held: any sudden movement and they would both be torn apart. The pack, too, held back. Meanwhile, the she-wolf, crouching where she had been near Agaratz, kept up a snuffling sound directed at the two. Her cubs had scampered back into their burrow.

Weaponless, Agaratz circled the dog-wolf as the dog-wolf circled him and such was his mimickry of wolf behaviour that beneath the jerkin and breeches Urrell momentarily saw a wolf in human skin. He blinked his eyes. It was Agaratz again. He had a strange feeling that Agaratz was performing for his benefit, the stray boy, his sole witness.

Suddenly, the tension broke, the big dog trotted over to his bitch, ignoring both Agaratz and Urrell, nuzzling her in greeting. At this signal the pack followed and milled around. Soon the cubs came out again, the smallest last, and began cavorting with elder siblings in the pack. Urrell stood there, unbelieving, his eyes going from wolf to wolf as they moved about ignoring this human in their midst.

When the dog-wolf had broken off the confrontation, Agaratz had straightened up, his attention elsewhere. Urrell noticed the pallor, the vacant look in the eyes, usually agleam with malice, fun and meaning. He shook, or was it a tremor that ran through his body – either as far as Urrell could tell – then he moved towards the she-wolf which was rolling in submission before her mate. The pallor vanished and Agaratz became himself again before the boy's troubled gaze.

"You want wolf, Urrell?"

CHAPTER 9

The question was so unexpected that Urrell, still afraid to move, could find no answer. When he tried, he yammered uncontrollably, unable to use his throat, and instead of words broke into paroxysms of tears that surprised him almost as much as they seemed to surprise Agaratz. He stood there, a little boy again, in an alien place, wolves all around. Dimly he knew that what he had witnessed lay beyond any experience he, his band or even Old Mother had ever known.

Just as dimly he sensed that to enter into such experience needed the companionship of a wolf.

"Yes, I would like a wolf."

Agaratz nodded. "Come."

He led Urrell – pulled him – from the spot where he was rooted and drew him, without the least concern, through the wolves to the cubs and squatted with them. He made the comfort sounds of a she-wolf to her young. They sat on their behinds and looked at Agaratz expectantly. Here he took from his pouch the second roast wildfowl, which he began to tear apart and feed in tidbits to the cubs. Delicately each in turn accepted the treat, taking the shreds of meat from his fingers and gulping them. Last to receive her share was the smallest, the shyest cub, a she, woollier than the rest, the litter's runt. Agaratz picked her up and as she squirmed he rubbed noses with her till she quietened.

"You take, Urrell."

Urrell did, awkwardly, an eye askance at the parents. But they went on with their bonding behaviour, the female on her back wriggling on the ground, her mate standing astride her. None of the other wolves showed any concern.

"Now we go." Agaratz seemed keen to leave. On his way he picked up his own and Urrell's weapons, and followed by Urrell encumbered with his cub, now contentedly cuddled in his arms, they scrambled up the ravine side. Once at the top, they turned to look at the wolves a last time, and Agaratz again surprised Urrell: he threw his head back and howled as a wolf howls in a long ululation, beautiful to hear, and was answered by other wolves and far-off packs along the horizon.

The dog-wolf looked up and replied in song, chorussed by his pack, heads raised and their eyes on the two humans outlined on the rim of the ravine. When the call sank away, Agaratz turned and led off at a brisk clip to the grasslands, towards their distant cliff home, Urrell trotting behind him bearing his furry burden asleep in his arms.

Twice during their journey Agaratz stopped to call the wolves and each time they answered from the direction of the ravine. The third time, within view of the cliffs, as dusk fell, his call went unanswered. They were beyond earshot of the pack.

Urrell's contentment with his newfound companion knew no end. He had once kept an injured squirrel as a pet; sometimes girls nursed and played with fledglings till they flew. But to own a wolfling! His gratitude and wonder at Agaratz's ability to go and fetch one so simply grew greater yet.

Once in the cave, the fire lit and meat roasting, his new charge's playfulness was revealed in full. It chased twigs, played with pinecones, soon learnt not to fear the fire, and adopted Urrell as its leader. That first night and thereafter it cuddled up with him as they snuggled into the leaves and dry grass of the bedding in the recess. He wondered what to call it. Agaratz would know.

Those late weeks of summer were the boy's happiest yet. His wolf cub followed him everywhere, grew fast, losing its puppyish down and taking on the sleek lines of her kind. She mimicked Urrell's behaviour when out hunting and foraging, learning to obey commands and signs.

Agaratz watched the relationship with his amused look, those fleeting grins, as fast to flit across his face as the wistfulness that Urrell had learnt not to question

"Soon, big cold come," Agaratz said one morning when the autumn air felt chill.

"Why not go, like others, like bison and horses, to the lowlands, Agaratz?"

"Stay. My people here."

"Your people, Agaratz? Where?"

"In cave."

"Cave?"

"Special cave. Special for my peoples."

Urrell had heard such caves existed. Old Mother had told him of those of her youth, the land of mammoths. Deep in them sacred pictures from legendary times recorded animals and rites.

"Where is the cave, where?"

"Near."

"Can I see it?"

A cloud of such sadness passed over the long expressive face that Urrell knew he had overstepped a bar. Agaratz noticed the boy's look.

"Other time, Urrell, other time we go. When you older."

Boys had to wait to learn the ways of men.

"Now collect foods, much foods, for cold time, Urrell."

All Urrell's experience was of hunting and gathering and living from day to day. A big kill meant feasting, plenty; no kill meant berries, lizards, carrion. Nothing was hoarded.

"We collect foods," said Agaratz to his doubting charge, "you see."
It was the start of a systematic campaign of gathering. Agaratz
planned each day's activity in a way unknown to Urrell. They set
off with pouches, grubbing sticks, lanyards tressed from thongs,
each day to places Agaratz knew, as he seemed to know all places
within several days' march, in search of storable foods. Urrell,
unsure of the purpose of these expeditions, followed wherever
Agaratz led, the wolf cub happy to gambol from side to side, mock-
hunting insects and anything else in the grass that their footfalls
startled.

Their first expeditions took them to wetlands and water
meadows by the river, the Nani, as Agaratz called it, where a
variety of grasses and sedges throve in the damp, rich silts. The
grasses were familiar enough to Urrell. Like Agaratz he chewed a
few seed heads as they hunted wildfowl along the river, without a
second thought. Now he was to be surprised yet again. Agaratz
went to an old tree with a large hollow and wriggled in to reach up
into the gap, from which he pulled down a hide, bound tightly
with thongs. These he untied and the complete fusty hide of a
bison opened on the ground. Urrell stared.

"Now Urrell collect grasses and bring." He showed Urrell
what he meant by wrenching off handfuls of grasses with ears of
seeds and piling them on the hide spread bare side up. They toiled
at this for a while, Urrell not inclined to ask why. When the pile
was as big as Agaratz wanted, he handed Urrell a cudgel, took one
himself, and said, "Now beat."

As they flailed the heap seeds fell from the ears. They ended up
with handfuls of grain, which Agaratz winnowed by shaking the hide
with Urrell and blowing away as much chaff and awns as he could.

"Good to eat, Urrell, when big colds, no hunt. Eat." He gave
Urrell a big pinch. The grain formed a chewy gobbet in Urrell's
mouth, hard to swallow.

"You like?"

"Yes, I like it."

They spent several days like this, camping and reaping. When their pouches were all full Agaratz replaced the hide in its hollow and they trudged back to the cave, where Urrell watched as Agaratz spread the grain on hides to dry. In a side gallery he had rigged a framework of poles lashed with withes and bast, from which he hung the dried grain in pouches. Round each he sprinkled a circle of grain, muttering as he went. Seeing the lad's incomprehension, he explained: "For rats. Not touch pouches."

Having gathered as much grain, in several such trips, as he seemed to think they might need, Agaratz said, "Now go for *xaurak*." Urrell waited to see what these might be.

For this trip they hugged the cliffs to where they petered out into a gap letting the Nani cut through on its journey to the sea. A long day's march along its bank and they came to groves of nut-bearing bushes Urrell knew well. They grew in his valley, where he and other boys cracked them when in season – cob nuts. *Xaurak*, Agaratz called them.

Agaratz climbed into the low dense trees, swinging from one bough to another, shaking down showers of nuts for Urrell to gather while the cub frisked about to catch hers, cracking the shells and eating the kernels as if wolves ate little else.

By nightfall they had a good heap. Agaratz showed Urrell how to bend hazel wands into a wickey-up for the night. Around them animals foraged, none of them making sounds to alarm them. Only once were they roused when some small forager emptied a pouch of nuts and Agaratz shooed and hissed till it scampered off, pursued by a yelping cub.

"Call her Rakrak," said Agaratz, "make rakrak noise."

In three days their harvest became sizable. How Agaratz intended to transport it he showed Urrell on the third day. He cut two hazel poles, getting the boy to pull them down so that his axe sliced better into the tensed wood. He stripped and laid the poles flat and showed Urrell how to weave wands between them to form a travois, something new to Urrell. He helped the lad to make a lighter one for himself and when both were complete they loaded their bags, pouches and skins full of nuts on to them, bound them with strips of green bark, lifted the butt ends on their shoulders and set off home.

It was hard work. They repeated the trip to the nut groves till Agaratz had enough to see them through the hardest weather, then he announced another crop. "Now we fetch *intauraka.*"

This foray took another direction. They went up the cliff using a chine not far from their cave, across upland and into a hidden valley, a long rift in the plateau created where the surface, in another age, had fallen in. Trees abounded in the shelter provided. Acorns littered the ground and beechmast lay everywhere. Urrell found crab apples starting to fall, a few medlars and in thickets the blue masses of sloes, uneatable till blackened by frosts.

Agaratz was unusually cautious, spear-thrower at the ready. Urrell was soon to see why. A herd of wild boar trotted past as both stood still in the undergrowth, Urrell holding Rakrak's muzzle tight lest she yelped and attracted a charge. Deer abounded. Birds sang. "Here bear live," warned Agaratz.

This was no longer the grasslands, with their open vistas and distant herds of bison, horses and deer that moved on at the sight of humans. Here the humans were the intruders, in a hidden garden, whose denizens might not depart so easily. Urrell was alert, but as if the peacefulness of their mission was clear to the animals of the woods, nothing had befallen the threesome by the time they reached the trees which bore *intauraka.* "Ah, Agaratz, these are walnuts."

"Walnuts, walnuts," Agaratz repeated this new word from

Urrell's language. Urrell, in his turn, repeated *intauraka* to himself. Although both learnt scraps of the other's tongue this way, Agaratz plainly knew Urrell's from some other time or distant source, outdoing the boy's attempts to understand the elusive, shifting language of his mentor.

Some nuts had already fallen, their cases splitting to reveal shells within. They cracked some to eat on the spot, feeding bits to the wolf, which ate anything Urrell gave her. It was an idyllic scene in the sun and shade of the slope, beneath the trees.

Urrell noticed it first. He looked up and saw the bear not a spear's cast away, a massive male, sniffing their scent, drawn perhaps by the sound of cracking nuts.

"Agaratz, bear!"

His companion remained unconcerned. He said it again: "Bear."

All hunters knew how irascible, how unpredictable a male bear's behaviour could be, how irresistible its strength. Even the bravest, ablest hunters shunned them. Any boy knew that. Urrell knew it. He cowered, clutching Rakrak.

"Not move," said Agaratz as he slowly stood up.

The bear responded by standing also. It looked immense. Should it drop on all fours and charge, neither flight nor shinning up a tree would save them. Agaratz was puny by comparison. All he held was a spear in one hand.

Bear and man eyed each other, neither yielding. When at last the bear dropped to all fours, Urrell hoped it would disappear into the woods, satisfied with its stand. Instead it charged, full pelt, at Agaratz. Instinctively Urrell curled up with Rakrak into the tightest ball he could, leaving Agaratz to dodge the bear, even draw it away. When he dared peep up Agaratz was still there: the huge animal, disconcerted, had reared up, fifteen paces from them, and was pawing the air as though inviting the man into a vast embrace. Agaratz grunted bear-like, spread his arms wide, pulled himself up to his full height and seemed to grow as he mimicked the bear's pawing. His bear growls, his fixed stare, had their effect. The bear dropped to the ground, shrugged, grunted a reply, and turned off into the trees.

"Better we go now," said Agaratz. "Bear come back."

CHAPTER 10

Once out of range of the bear they filled their pouches with beechmast, for lack of walnuts, so that their foraging had not quite been in vain.

"Agaratz, are there big cave-bears?"

"Now few. Long ago many."

Urrell recalled his engraving, the bear lumbering away, its head turned as though towards pursuers.

"But ice-bears, Agaratz, bears that live with mammoths?" They were the huge bears of legend, those Old Mother spoke of, like the big tiger cats and the beasts with one horn.

"Only in pictures, in caves, Urrell. Now gone."

"I saw a picture of one, Agaratz."

At this Agaratz stopped and looked intently at Urrell, making the boy feel he had hit on something important.

"Where?"

"In my valley."

"How far?"

"Five, six days."

"When cold time over, you show me."

"Oh yes."

Old Mother of the Mammoths, you would be watching, you who knew the bear.

In the last long weeks of fine weather, as the bison drifted across the grassland, herds of horses with them, fattening as they went, harried by wolves and the furry lions of the forest, Urrell watched

Agaratz's preparations for winter and helped, learning. His muscles were developing and the down over his mouth and by his ears was darkening into hair. He was now slightly taller than Agaratz.

"Soon be man," said Agaratz as Urrell washed by the spring.

"Good."

The wolf, too, was now nearly full grown.

"I take that wolf because smallest. If stay with pack, soon die in cold. Now strong."

They had been scraping hides for several days, following deer hunts where Agaratz's skill and accuracy with the spear-thrower had roused Urrell's admiration, when the lad thought to ask the question uppermost in his mind.

"When deer, bison, horses all go to lowlands what can we hunt in great cold?"

"Boar stay. Snow-deer come. Snow-oxen come. Aurochs in forest. Some big deer in woods. Perhaps… *mammurak*." Agaratz grinned at Urrell. "No, not *mammurak*."

"How can you hunt alone?"

"I hunt. Now you help. But much foods here." He waved a hand at their stores of seeds, nuts, roots, bulbs and pouches packed with fat and suet mixed with herbs.

"But auroch, bison are too strong for a lone hunter, Agaratz."

"You see. Now we go for mushroom."

However, this search was not for the edible fungus that Urrell liked.

Instead Agaratz ferreted under logs, in crannies, for kinds either Urrell did not know or knew were poisonous. In addition Agaratz sought berries no-one touched. In clefts where limestone whitened the cliff-face Agaratz gathered a creeper with a milky sap, as well as its seed pods. Urrell followed, observing.

Back in the cave he watched Agaratz mix and mash these into a sticky paste to be stored in hollowed stems of elderberry wood, using acorns as stoppers. He muttered something rhythmic and unintelligible as he laid the filled stems delicately on a little ledge.

When Urrell asked their purpose he was told, "Soon you see."

On their next hunt Agartatz took a stem with him. Game was scarcer with the approach of winter but deer were still about, if in small wary groups keeping out of range. Without explanation Agaratz had armed himself with light javelins, little more than reeds, tipped in bone, that to Urrell looked inadequate.

After a morning spent stalking they managed to close on a small herd. Agaratz paused to dab paste from his elderberry vial on to the tips of two javelins. The movement alerted the deer. As they raised their heads in alarm he sprang forward and cast both javelins almost together, one from either hand, hitting the buck and a doe. At such range neither animal was much harmed and fled with the rest, the buck's javelin even falling out. Urrell expected disappointment on Agaratz's face. Instead he set off in pursuit, waving over his shoulder for Urrell to follow, picking up his javelin on the way.

On the open floor of the woods the deer spoor was not hard to follow. After a few hundred paces Urrell saw the doe, unsteady, lagging behind her group. Agaratz ran up and speared her dead.

"Urrell, you catch buck." He knew it was an honour, a test maybe.

The male, stronger, less affected by the paste on the javelin, had gone much further before Urrell caught up with it and managed to pierce its tough hide with his stabbing spear, proud to win a four-point stag. Dragging it back to where Agaratz had already gralloched the doe and was flaying and quartering it into manageable cuts was another matter.

They did the same between them with the buck, its flesh rancid from the rut.

"See," said Agaratz, "in winter can hunt."

Half the meat they cached in a tree fork; the remainder they bundled up in the animals' own skins and hoisted on their backs for the return trip. "Tomorrow fetch other, Urrell."

"How do you know which plants and mushrooms to use?" Urrell felt there was more to it than the ingredients, which he had seen and memorised.

"Secret from my peoples."

"Your father?"

"Yes, father. Others."

"Why not use the bane all year?"

"Not ready then. Not time."

Agaratz would, Urrell knew, not expand. He would have to learn the rhythmic chant that went with the paste, to make it work.

In the mornings frost had begun to whiten the grass and sharpen the air. Urrell's breath hung before him. In his home valley his clan would be gathering to leave for the caves by the sea, there to huddle behind piles of seashells discarded by earlier folk, perhaps those who had painted and engraved those very cave walls beyond which only the dead dared venture.

Urrell was wondering why no people trekked along their own grasslands in the wake of the bison, as the snows approached from the mountains of the mammoths across the void land, when his thoughts were interrupted by Agaratz.

"Soon you see people, Urrell."

"Oh, people! Your people?"

"No my people."

"Who?"

"Hunters. They go to Nani, to big salt water."

"My people go. They are going now."

"Yes. I know. I see."

"See?"

"See. See like…" and he turned to Urrell and placed his forefingers on each temple and fixed his stare ahead "…see like that." He said it as he might have said, "That is a stone, yon is a tree."

"Agaratz, when I came, did you see me, see the bison and the hunters?"

"I see," then he added, "I see your folk – seven mans, twelve womens, fourteen childs. One man, blue mark on face."

"Blueface!"

Some people could see ahead in time, this Urrell knew, some could see beyond distance, some even spoke to the dead. It was whispered that some could halt weapons in mid-flight, others cast curses that slew.

Urrell's fear of the approaching great cold lifted: he would be safe with someone of Agaratz's powers.

Agaratz bent over a bone needle, sewing moccassins. Agaratz able to soothe wolves, outface bears, see afar.

CHAPTER 11

Agaratz was also right about groups passing.

The two were returning with bags filled with garlic and onion bulbs for storage when Agaratz pointed at a far-off line of humans advancing across the grasslands, men ahead, women behind with chattels and infants. They too had been seen, so flight being futile, Agaratz squatted to wait, Urrell beside him while Rakrak flung herself on the grass and panted.

Agaratz watched the group keenly. "These different," he said.

They were tall, lithe men, swarthier than Urrell's folk. Black hair hung down their shoulders and each carried six long spears, bone-tipped. All wore necklaces of teeth and coloured stones. When they were half a stone's throw away they stopped and the tallest stepped a few paces in front. Agaratz stood. The man declaimed in a language unknown to Urrell.

His words roused jeering laughs among the man's followers. He twirled a spear over his head in mock-threat at Agaratz, whom he overstood by more than head and shoulders. Agaratz, unperturbed, spoke in what sounded to Urrell like the man's own language, with a hint of warning. Unimpressed, the man strutted nearer, then noticed Rakrak sitting up in the long grass beside Urrell. He pointed at her and said something to his followers, who relayed it to the women who had caught up and were shuffling about in the rear. Whatever he had said, his intention became clear when he raised his spear arm, not at Agaratz nor at Urrell but at the wolf. The lad's panic – he grabbed Rakrak by the neck and pulled her down to shield her –

amused the man. He glanced back at his followers for approval.

As he did so Agaratz, with the speed of the lame, limped forward and caught the man's eye as he turned. Urrell saw the spear-arm freeze in mid-throw. Reaching up on tiptoe Agaratz took the spear from his grip and in a feat of strength that none could have emulated snapped the shaft like a reed. A little 'uh' rose from the crowd. The hunters fell back. Agaratz roused the man with a tap on the shoulder and he resumed his journey, all intentions forgotten, followed by the column of his cowed and silenced clan. As they filed past, Rakrak, interested in the scene, ears cocked, uttered a little 'woof' that sent small children scuttling to their mothers' skirts.

Awe mixed with gratitude in Urrell's heart, gratitude winning.

As on that first day when they had first met, Urrell expressed his feelings by touching the crookback's forearm, his reward the sly grin of acknowledgement of a feat that had impressed.

However, all he said was, "Now time go for *eztik.*"

"*Eztik?*

"From bees"

"Honey."

"Ah, honey." He did not say where or how it was to be found.

Urrell was to discover where and how the next day. Not since that first meeting when Agaratz had given Urrell a piece of honeycomb had honey featured in their searches and garnerings. Now Agaratz chose several quaiches and pouches from his stores, and implements hitherto unknown to Urrell.

"Now go for honey."

Urrell's experience of honey-gathering was to find a hive and raid it. His folk, when they chanced on such a treat, left nothing behind, glutting themselves on combs, honey, grubs, wax, everything, in an orgy of sweetness that no fruit, no berry, however ripe, could rival. He wondered what Agaratz would do with the hives. Would he in his careful way, as with fruit, bulbs, plants, birds' eggs and so on, spare some, muttering low incantations that he never explained?

They set off along the cliff line towards the river, much as they had done to gather cobnuts, but soon stopped at a place where the cliff-face changed to a yellowish, friable stone with a number of holes and cavities.

"Bees," said Agaratz. Indeed, high up bees swarmed in and out of holes far beyond reach. "Follow."

He continued a little further and turned into a cleft that split the cliff from top to bottom. The sides were smooth. On them Urrell saw engravings, the first since his bear.

"Look bees, Agaratz."

A little further was the outlined head and fore quarters of a bear, looking up.

Agaratz said: "Old time." He took a burin from his belt pouch and ran it along the outline of the bear. "You do." Urrell took the burin with a feeling new to him, yet as old as always, and ran the flake along the outline as he had seen Agaratz do. A sense of elation, of strength, of the ability to perform beyond the normal suffused him, like the dream he sometimes dreamt of flying, soaring with outstretched arms above everything else caught in earthbound normality. Waking was always a disappointment. This time when he ended the scrape the elation remained.

"Now bees not sting," said Agaratz.

They followed the cleft, in single file, sometimes sidling to squeeze through, till at a turn a tunnel led off at waist height, round and smooth-bored, large enough for a man to wriggle up lying on his belly or back.

"Rakrak stay." Agaratz made the sounds of a female warning her cubs to lie still and Rakrak crouched, looking up at Agaratz then at Urrell, who repeated the command. She would wait.

"You follow, Urrell." He entered the tunnel head first, on his back, his bowls, bags, and tools strapped to his midriff, freeing his arms to draw himself along the tunnel. When his feet, the normal and the cloven, disappeared into the hole, Urrell lay in the same way and followed up into the darkness.

Soon he was in total gloom, wriggling behind Agaratz whom he could hear ahead. The walls, smoothened by ancient waters, offered little purchase. He heard Agaratz say, "Now narrow," and he came to a gullet which seemed impossible to get through. "Pass things." He did as bidden, his arms half trapped by the narrow tunnel, and felt his things taken one at a time. Then Agaratz said, "Arms first." To get his arms well above his head Urrell wriggled back to a wider part of the tunnel then squirmed his way up to the gullet. Hands took his to ease him through the gap till he squeezed out, like a child thrust from the womb, into what must have been a chamber. Agaratz held his hand to guide him in the total blackness. They felt their way round a rock-face into another low tunnel, stooping, till the total gloom lightened and as his eyes attuned Urrell saw they had squeezed into a huge, high chamber with stalactites at the far end reaching the floor in a forest of stone. Light filtered from on high through chinks and holes – those the bees used. They must have been close behind the cliff-face.

Agaratz ignored all this, his attention fixed on the gaps and chinks near the roof of the chamber. "Up there, *etzi*," he said. "Now fetch pole."

They left their paraphernalia and Agaratz went to a full-size pine log, notched with footholds, lying along the cave wall, unnoticed by Urrell. It was very old yet still serviceable. Who had dragged it there, and how, Urrell was left to wonder. They pulled and rolled it into position and while Urrell steadied the butt Agaratz 'walked' the bole up hand over hand till it was leaning high against the wall.

"Hold, Urrell, I climb."

He brought down two big honeycombs and blew off the bees still clinging to their possession, muttering something as they flew back up to the light. They rolled the log along the wall and Agaratz repeated the operation, never taking more than two combs or a quaich of liquid honey each time. The liquid honey they savoured, miracle of sweetness, in the dark, the combs Agaratz stowed in the pouches they had brought.

"You try, Urrell." The lad went up and found himself peering at an immense hive, the work of years, teeming with bees. As he clung to the pole, undecided what to do next, Agaratz called from below, "Take two *eztic*, with hand. Not sting."

Bees crawled all over his arm, his face, his hair as he reached in, steadying himself on his shaking perch. Very carefully he detached two combs, one at a time, dropping them into the pouch round his waist, and edged down in a cloud of bees. None stung him.

"Only two *eztic*, Agaratz?"

"Two. I tell bees. So not sting."

It was too dark to see Agaratz's expression but Urrell sensed the grin at his puzzlement. Around them the air smelt sharply of honey.

If their trip in had been hard, the return journey was one Urrell would never forget. They worked in stages, pushing their bulging pouches ahead, repeating the wriggling, squirming operation three times to ferry their booty to the entrance for Rakrak to guard. Once all was out, Urrell watched Agaratz dance to the bear, offer it honey, dab the bees with a dot of honey apiece, before they rested and ate a comb between them and gave a piece to Rakrak to gnaw.

Once back in home cave Agaratz stowed quaiches and pouches on ledges beyond any creature's reach.

"Agaratz, you did this before, alone?"

"With father. Now my people gone."

Whether he meant departed, leaving the cripple behind to die, or wiped out by some catastrophe, Urrell was left wondering. It would be unwelcome to ask, though he ached to know more about Agaratz's folk. Agaratz's hints of their powers, of skills he revealed unbidden, as to an apprentice, whet the lad's appetite to know more, to observe everything, to forget nothing. But how to get beyond the sly smile, to enter the mage's mind? Ah.

CHAPTER 12

Summer was beginning to break. Clouds drove across the skies, the air cooled, skeins of geese flew overhead, southerly. Agaratz redoubled activity and Urrell fell in with the new urgency; even Rakrak behaved less playfully.

"Today go for gooses." Rain drifted across the grasslands, shortening sight-lines.

They set off through the wet grass at a hunter's lope, armed with stone-throwers, spears and long lines that Agaratz tressed from thongs. Urrell waited to see what their use would be.

A new stretch of the River Nani was Agaratz's target this time and took them half a day to reach. Late mushrooms dotted the meadows. In brakes, raspberries, bilberries and whortle-berries clustered. Urrell saw where bears had raked pawfuls of fruit into their mouths in an orgy of feasting ahead of their winter sleep.

"Bears," he said. Agaratz nodded. They saw deer aplenty, bison in the distance while herds of small brown horses showed their pale bellies as they galloped away at the approach of two humans and a wolf, gliding over the deep grass on invisible hooves. Hares abounded. Agaratz had other things in mind.

Through a fringe of trees they came to their destination: a loop in the Nani where the current had cut across an oxbow bend, creating a backwater. Floating on the still water were flocks of migrant geese, gathered for their long flight south, sorting themselves out by kind before flying off. So engaged were they in their own affairs that they ignored the two humans standing on the bank. Rakrak sat on her hunkers, looking on with interest.

Urrell was now to see the purpose of the long lines.

"You stay behind bushes and hold." Agaratz handed Urrell one end of the thongs. Then he tied a bundle of reeds into a small raft, divested himself of jerkin and leggings, and entered the water, the thick hair on his neck and shoulders much the same rusty sedge colour as his raft. The end of the lines he held in one hand. Head barely above water behind the raft, he drifted towards the honking, bustling geese. Urrell watched as first one goose, then another vanished underwater with barely a ripple. Agaratz might have gone on all day without the flocks noticing but when he had enough he signalled to Urrell to haul him in.

He waded ashore with nine fat geese, necks broken, tied by a leg to a line. Rakrak bounced about with excitement. The flocks went on as before, oblivious to their trifling loss.

"Now return," said Agaratz, draping five geese round his neck and the remainder round Urrell's.

On their way back they collected mushrooms. Agaratz uprooted clumps of wild, pink-flowering garlic, plucked thyme and marjoram for his pouches, pointing out herbs to Urrell and naming them in his own language while Urrell, where he could, gave names he had learnt from foraging women in his clan who gathered ingredients for their potions and old wives' cures. Each had uses and virtues according to Agaratz, his lore far outdoing anything Urrell had learnt.

Once back and up the climbing pole, which Rakrak had managed, if clumsily, to scale, they set about plucking the geese as the fire was building up for a roast. Agaratz signalled Urrell to pack the down and breast plumage in pouches; the quills and feathers they discarded.

When the fire was hot enough to roast a goose Agaratz gutted one, something Urrell had not seen done before, and gave the giblets to Rakrak, saving only the delicacy of the liver, which he halved with Urrell and they ate raw. Into the cavity Urrell watched Agaratz stuff heads of garlic, mushrooms, handfuls of thyme and clumps of marjoram, the reason why he would soon learn as the goose roasted under its heaped embers while they plucked the remainder: odours such as Urrell had never known increased as the cooking went on. His belly gurgled.

CHAPTER 13

Never had he smelt anything so appetising. By the time the goose was cooked, its companions plucked and hanging from one of Agaratz's frames, Urrell's belly, empty all day but for handfuls of berries plucked on the way to the Nani and back, was quaking for food. Beside him, Rakrak whimpered and pawed the floor.

That goose was a triumph, to man, to lad, to wolf, as they set to in companionable gluttony, hands, faces, paws soon fragrant with goosefat, Urrell's tastebuds lingering on the garlic-flavoured meat and grease, an aroma of thyme, marjoram and other herbs mingling in sensations new to him and memorable for life.

As the last bones and scraps disappeared into Rakrak, the wind rose outside the cave, warning of weather changes coming fast. The flames blew from side to side in the gusts.

"Now make cold-time furs," said Agaratz, more to himself than to Urrell.

"Cold-time furs?" The strangeness of the term intrigued the youth.

"Furs for cold time. I show next day."

They slept that night huddled in the recess, in a torpor of overeating, as the weather outside worsened.

What Agaratz meant by 'coldtime furs' Urrell was to learn over the next few days as the weather grew colder, rain lashed down into the gulch and they retreated deeper into the cave to avoid the worst of the wind.

Agaratz brought out pelts that he had collected over the year, some from hunts with Urrell. From a bundle, he rolled out bone needles, flint knives and burins and set to, cutting the skins into large pieces and piercing holes round the edges with burins or redhot sticks. Urrell was handed tools to do the same.

Over several days and into the nights they worked away till the pile of squares was enough in Agaratz's eyes. Urrell watched to see what came next. This was to sew the squares with thongs and sinews into pokes that Urrell was detailed to stuff with goose down. Thus quilted, the stuffed squares were sewn into jerkins, overgarments, leggings and breechclouts. Agaratz even made double-soled, padded moccassins for their usually bare feet. Such industry was new to Urrell, more accustomed to the free and easy life of his hunting group where the only sustained effort was the pursuit of quarry, not scraping, cutting, sewing. At most, that was women's work.

By the time their garments were ready, the weather relented, though remaining cold as they issued into the sharp sunshine in their new outfits, glutted on gooseflesh and nuts. Rakrak dashed about, letting off pent-up energy.

"Now collect grasses," said Agaratz.

"Grass?"

"For sleep, for warm."

Ah bedding, Urrell thought, to snuggle into when down by the sea his clan would be wintering, men, women and children huddled round fires in caves, not daring to go out into the white wilderness for food. Gales would drive floes ashore, blizzards would blind hunters seeking flotsam, carrion and shellfish, even wrack, along the strand. The weak would starve: he had seen the dead in caves when the thaw came too late for them. How Agaratz meant to survive, inland, nearer the iceland of the mammoths, Urrell knew not: he entrusted himself to his mentor, whose doings and behaviour he shadowed and copied. Agaratz, who seldom explained, this time said:

"When great cold, stay in grass in cave – like bear."

Grass-gathering he found wearisome work. Tuft by tuft they piled it on a hide for Agaratz to gather by the four corners and hump up the climbing pole into the cave. Rakrak entered into the spirit of the task, happy to run about tossing mouthfuls of tore, or dry grass, in the air, pouncing on the summer-fat morsels of mice and voles she disturbed. Most of a week they spent thus, between foraging, benefiting from the cold dry spell, till Agaratz said: "Now woods."

They dragged logs and boughs, bundles and faggots, skinloads of pine cones, to the cave foot. Agaratz let down lines to which Urrell tied loads to be hauled up and stowed deep in the cave.

By the time Agaratz was satisfied that their fuel store would last the winter, Urrell felt his muscles hardening like a man's as he hauled and dragged timber through the early snowflakes with Agaratz. Their flint axes were no match for the trunks of trees, so all their wood was windfall dead wood, to be gathered before snow hid it till spring.

"Soon cold come, Urrell. Then we hunt bison and horse."

Hitherto their biggest quarry had been deer, and that sparingly – Agaratz hunted almost reluctantly. Urrell must have shown doubt.

The grin warned him to expect something untoward.

"Get ready, Urrell. First go to *mammurak* cave, in morning."

Urrell could not believe what he heard. Another of Agaratz's asides? He preferred not to ask.

By way of preparation, Agaratz took a flat stone hollowed in the centre to form a shallow dish. In this he placed some goose fat, then collected embers in a fire-box much like ones Urrell knew from his own clan, plaited wisps of grass and greased them. All this he stowed in a pouch as they set off, Urrell agog at that mention of mammoths.

Three or four spear-casts along the cliff line, the snow now falling thickly, Agaratz pointed at an unremarkable recess in the cliff. "*Mammurak* cave. We go in." He thought a moment, then added, "*Otsoemek* come." The wolf, aware she was welcome, pranced with pleasure.

It was not much of a cave, more a hole into a small chamber. Urrell could sense its size in the dark, Rakrak pressing against his legs.

"Make light." Agaratz opened the fire-box and blew on the embers, his long face faintly lit by the glow, till the grass wick flamed and he stuck it in the lump of goose fat; Urrell's first lamp.

In the still air the lamp burnt clear, lighting the walls of the chamber, smooth and unremarkable. Another tunnel led from it. To this Agaratz moved and beckoned him to follow.

The secret place. The rank weeds. His boyhood fear.

More than fear, elation seized him, the elation he had felt when the bees crawled over his arm, as here, lit by the lamp, he saw four tiny engravings of horses and a bison, none bigger than a hand, etched to perfection at eye level. All four beasts were heading into the tunnel at full tilt. As Agaratz moved on with the light they faded from Urrell's lingering sight. Even Rakrak was loth to move and had to be coaxed.

This tunnel to the next chamber was as short as the first one. But as the light spread inside Urrell stood in fascinated silence, in a trance of attentiveness: on one flat expanse of rock were the concentrated outlines in red and black, superimposed one upon the other, of a fauna of shifting beasts of all sizes — bison and horses, with deer running hither and thither among them – while a frieze of feathery-antlered reindeer topped the display's upper edge where light met dark. To one side, on a separate slab, a vast boar, its bristling mane roughly chalked in, eternally charged towards the centre of the earth.

As the flame steadied – Agaratz had set the lamp down before the mural – more detail smote the boy's ravished gaze. The light, from floor level, revealed a welter of engravings, a criss-crossing of scratchings, each the outline of an animal inter-mixed by overdrawing into a puzzle for his eyes. He saw that the flanks of horses and bisons were shaded in ochre, the white of their bellies carefully picked out, regardless of how they might mask earlier outlines and engravings, as though each artist consumed with a frenzy of creation had possessed eyes only for his own work and had sought a place in this one expanse of rock because he fed on the work of his numberless forerunners, was adding to them, not obliterating. Urrell felt an urge to jig before them, in unison with the gait of bison, horse and deer.

As his gaze travelled to the rim of the gooselamp's range, his widening eyes caught sight of three shapes that nearly stopped his heart – three bulbous forms marched in the shadow on an errand of their own.

Old Mother, Old Mother of the Mammoths.

"Mammoths!" he shouted, his voice echoing and sounding into hollows and caverns beyond sight, as though caught up by giants and passed one to another, roused from immemorial slumber by this over-excited youth. The lamp-flame flickered in sympathy. Rakrak shifted uneasily in Urrell's grasp on her neck.

Only Agaratz was unmoved. *"Mammuraka,"* he said. Then he added, "olds, olds," and to show how old he rolled his hand over and over, as though reeling the mammoths back to the beginning of the world.

Some sign of the purpose of the visit to the chamber now began to make itself evident to Urrell. Agaratz's behaviour changed. He started a chant in his own tongue, directing the song at the mural, oblivious to everything, eyes deadened, his spirit absent. Urrell noticed how Agaratz aimed his chant at a spot in the rock-face where it echoed best. His lowest notes carried into the darkened galleries where Urrell's shout had hardly ceased to bounce and rebound. Agaratz's notes rippled into the distance, in pursuit. Before him the crouching shape chanted on and on in the now failing light of the lamp. One false move – touching the hunchback perhaps – might snap the thread that held Agaratz of the gleaming eyes and sly grin to this misshapen crooning creature. At this point the lamp died. Urrell gripped the thick, warm fur of Rakrak's neck lest she flee and leave him alone, trapped in the blackness of a light suddenly dowsed, a blackness deepened by the aftermath of gleams and flashes under his frightened eyelids.

Urrell stood helpless. He heard Agaratz speak but in another voice, a high thin one, repeating words that sounded like *"Mamu, Mamu, Mammurra."*

Then without transition Agaratz spoke again in his natural voice: "Urrell, wait," followed almost without a pause, as though Agaratz could see in the pitch black, with a touch on Urrell's arm and the word "follow," he led lad and wolf back out into the falling snow.

"Now ready for hunt."

They returned the short distance to home cave. Rakrak, subdued, trotted at Urrell's heels. Snow was falling thickly, in the first true snowfall of the winter, and all three knew, in their own ways, that this was the onset of the great cold. The only sound was the crunch of their feet on the stiff grass now disappearing under a palm's depth of fresh snow.

CHAPTER 14

In the cave, Agaratz returned the fire-box and the lamp to their ledges in his methodical way, then selected spears, a spear-thrower as well as a shorter, thicker javelin tipped with a long point, almost the length of a man's forearm, of a stone Urrell had never seen. It was dark green, its finely-flaked edges twinkled in the firelight where they had been delicately chipped to the keenness of a blade. It was beautiful in the young man's eyes. Agaratz noticed his interest.

"My father, his father, his father make it."

As it was too short and point-heavy to cast, Urrell could not divine its purpose but knew better by now than to ask. Agaratz would reveal by example, his usual way.

"Wolfs help hunt," he said.

"How, wolves?"

"Wolfs. You see. They come."

Besides the spears, Agaratz selected his best flint knives, an axe, bundles of thongs and his biggest pouches. These he gave Urrell to carry, taking the weapons himself. In his belt he inserted an elderwood phial of his hunting bane. Thus accoutred they sallied forth from their home and into the snowing grasslands, Urrell following with his usual unquestioning faith in Agaratz's decisions though wondering how a hunting party as small as theirs might overcome big game, alone, in the snow, the more so since most large herds had already migrated to lands beyond his, or his clan's, ken – to the lands whither the geese flew for all anyone knew.

But the experience in the cave that morning portended something exceptional. Agaratz had given enough proof of his powers – when he outfaced the bear or stopped the hunter in mid-throw to save dear Rakrak's life – for Urrell to have any qualms. Whispered stories overheard when women told tales, or hunters wondered at strokes of freakish luck, hinted darkly at strange forces. Women made magic signs, wore amulets, to avert ill fortune; men marked their spears with totemic designs to help them fly true. Yet none had ever done what he had seen Agaratz do. To Urrell nothing lay beyond the crookback's powers, even the control of wolves.

They had progressed some way when Agaratz paused, hunched a little and became a wolf. He raised his face and howled with such accuracy that Rakrak joined in. Urrell felt again that fear of wolves which had rooted him to the ground the day they had taken Rakrak. No chorus replied, Agaratz unwolfed, and they went on. Not till they had travelled far into the whiteness did a pack sing back.

"Rakrak know these," he said.

The sounds drew closer as they veered in the pack's direction. Urrell's apprehension – fear of wolves in winter when hunger sometimes drove them to eat humans – was not entirely stilled by Agaratz's unconcern.

Another sound now intervened, immediately recognisable: hooves pounding the prairie as bison cantered towards them, driven by wolves.

"Now ready."

Agaratz fitted a javelin to his spear-thrower, smeared the point with the bane from from his elderwood phial, and all three crouched and peered through the driving snow for sight of an approaching herd, a small group to judge by the drumming hooves, a bull or two and perhaps three or four cows, laggards from the major herds.

Agaratz's readiness was not misplaced, the bison were on them in seconds, looming out of the snow, coming straight at them. Urrell darted aside and glanced back expecting Agaratz to follow, but no, the hunched form held its ground until almost within touching distance of the lead beast, a bull. He stepped away at the last moment, making no attempt to lance it. His aim he saved for a young cow just behind, little more than a heifer, prime quarry, which his javelin struck in the flank and held fast. Hardly had the bison appeared than they vanished into the snowstorm, their tracks filling no sooner made.

"Follow," called Agaratz and set off behind the bison.

Only then was Urrell aware that they were not alone – a half-moon of silvery-grey forms trotted silently with them. They ran together, men and wolves, Urrell finding it hard to keep up, encumbered with so much equipment and stiff in his new quilted winter outfit. He called to Rakrak to stay with him but she was drawn by the excitement of her kin and the chase. Soon he was panting along alone, outrun by hunters and hunted. His was not fear of being lost but of failing Agaratz who would need his equipment to butcher and save a kill. There was no way of telling which way a wounded beast might swerve, wolves or no wolves.

He had been in this plight a while, his pace down to a weary trot as exhaustion and cold began to affect his movements, when he thought he saw a shape close by, startling him back to alertness. Another appeared on his other side. He could almost have touched them. His first jolt of fear at the apparitions subsided when he realised they were escorting him. Together the wolves swung half right, and he swung too, letting himself be herded, too tired to care where he went. Much farther on, through driving snow, a dark bulk showed up in the whiteness. He saw shapes around it as he drew nearer: the fallen bison. Agaratz was holding the short spear with the long beautiful blade, bloodied halfway up the shank where he must have finished off the cow where she fell, brought down by the bane or by the wolves. Round the kill silvery-white wolves milled.

Tears of exhaustion, mixed with snowflakes, blurred his vision.

79

He felt inadequate, a weakling, deserving the clouts and shouts that Blueface and the others would have given him had they been there. But instead Agaratz said, "Good, Urrell, you good," and then, "now share with wolfs."

He relieved Urrell of his load of knives, axe, pouches and thongs to proceed with carving and parcelling the carcass, ready to transport the best cuts home.

Exhaustion overtook Urrell and he sank to the snow, warm from the sweat inside his quilts. He was shaken awake:

"No sleep, Urrell, no sleep, or die." Agaratz spoke with unaccustomed urgency. "You look," he said, and gripping Urrell's shoulders fixed his eyes on his. A surge of energy ran through Urrell; his fatigue vanished. "Now help," said Agaratz in his everyday matter-of-fact voice.

Urrell did. He pulled at a flap of the bison's hide while Agaratz cut under it to detach skin from flesh, a long and strenuous task for two. But for Agaratz's phenomenal shoulder strength, and seemingly depthless energy, Urrell knew the work of flaying a bison and butchering it into transportable joints was far beyond any two men, let alone a crookback and a youth. He knew this from hunts in his own clan where its seven-strong group of hunters had work enough with a big kill, when they managed one. Yet he did not doubt Agaratz, someone who bade wolves fetch him and whose gaze delivered strength.

A man who could call up wolves to help him hunt could do anything, so Urrell helped with a will.

Around them, in the stained snow, their allies were feasting on the gralloch, Agaratz having only kept back the suet and some liver for them to gnaw as they toiled. Urrell saw Rakrak happy to chew gut with her own kind. When he called her name she raised her head, acknowledged him, and went on eating.

There was much to learn from watching Agaratz carve with a skill none of his clan could match. He cut round muscle and sinew with speed and precision, sharpening flint blades with a few taps, only using the axe on major joints. Urrell watched and memorised. The haunch came away in one piece.

The beast's shoulder was removed with equal skill followed by the best rib meat. That done they struggled to turn the carcass over in the failing light. Only with Agaratz's strength did they manage. Their problem was to skin this side so as to pull the hide away in one piece. Agaratz sawed though the skin of the massive neck and round each leg, resharpening his blades constantly, showing Urrell how as he did so. The wolves sat watching.

"What are the wolves waiting for?"

"*Oetsemeken* wait we finish, then eat."

"How do you know?"

"They know. I tell."

A last huge effort and the hide came free, dragged from under the carcass. They sat down to recover and chew suet.

"Now cut last leg and go." In the gloom, by touch, Agaratz cut out the second shoulder. The second haunch he left 'for wolfs'.

They packed the three joints with several rolls of flank meat in the pelt, rolled the whole into a parcel, and bound it with the thongs that Urrell had lugged all day and whose purpose he now saw. They made two tump lines and when ready to go Agaratz uttered a low sound to the wolves, one unfamiliar to Urrell, which released them from whatever thrall Agaratz held them in. They leapt forward to finish the bison they had helped to bring down.

"What about Rakrak?"

"Rakrak come later."

Urrell took up his line and Agaratz the other. With their gear piled on the parcel, they set off to haul home enough meat to last them weeks, cached in the snow.

CHAPTER 15

Midnight or later they reached home ground, through the ceaseless falling snow, now mid-shin deep, soft and hampering, piling in front of their burden as they dragged it along, so they had to stop every few dozen steps to clear it away. With unerring accuracy Agaratz headed straight across the featureless expanse, in the whitish obscurity of the arctic night, and brought them safely to their gulch. Whether by design on Agaratz's part or by chance, the kill had been fairly near their home ground. Urrell was too tired to wonder about that, too weary to talk. The haulage took so long because of the parcel's bulk and weight, plus the impediment of soft snow. When the snow froze Urrell knew movement would be easier, despite the greater cold.

They left the meat in its wrapping at the foot of the cave, Agaratz only slicing off two fat collops of rib meat to take up. The climbing pole he left in place 'for Rakrak'.

"Now eat. Need foods. You work well, Urrell. Learn much and be strong. Good."

Never before had Agaratz commented on his efforts or uttered such overt words of praise. That day Urrell knew he had pushed his stamina to the utmost, to exhaustion. He had felt failure, loss. Then to be praised by this being of mysterious talents and powers, not reprimanded, suffused him with gratitude. The visit to the mammoth cave, the hunt with wolves, these had been acceptance tests and after Agaratz's words he felt that he had come through with credit.

The fire seemed to blaze more brightly that night as they

waited for enough heat to build up for their steaks. Meantime Agaratz showed Urrell how to toast handfuls of grains they had spent so long collecting in the river meadows: he parched them on hot stones, releasing a nutty flavour that delighted the boy's palate.

Scuffling sounds heralded Rakrak's return up the pole. Urrell jumped up to greet her as though they had been parted weeks rather than hours, Rakrak placing her forepaws on Urrell's shoulders to sniff and lick his face.

That night lad and wolf slept huddled together for warmth and companionship more closely than ever before.

The trio would now see the wisdom of Agaratz's campaign to lay in winter supplies. Snow fell endlessly for days, monotonously, adding silence on silence. Urrell had seen nothing like this in all his winters spent farther south, at the end of the clan trek to the same stretch of coastline that his group had used as wintering quarters for as far back as oral accounts went. Other groups, with speech much like theirs, camped not far off. The sea-shore was rich enough in shellfish and carrion flotsam to sustain larger populations than the summer hunting grounds.

During lulls in bad weather groups met and mingled, a time Urrell liked. Among these strangers he felt less of an orphan. They accepted him as another boy from a neighbouring camp who showed more keenness to learn than usual. Old men were pleased to have an audience, even of one. By being a good listener, Urrell learnt from an old hunter of the great bears that had once lived in those caves. A forebear of the old hunter had been a boy when the last of them had been slain. There were stories that they still roamed in the mountains to the north, towards the land of Old Mother's childhood mammoths.

"Agaratz, have you ever seen the great bears of the caves?"

"None now. They gone, like my peoples."

"Gone where?"

"Gone."

Urrell knew Agaratz would not elaborate about his kin, so he carried on about the bears: had they gone to the mountains, to the mammoth mountains?

"Not mammoths now. Not cave bears. Not my people."

"But there are bears in the mountains. The old hunters said so, and Old Mother spoke of the mammoths."

"They not know. I know."

"But how can you be sure, Agaratz?" Urrell felt emboldened by the cosiness of the recess, half buried in hay, hugging Rakrak. He noticed how Agaratz's aloofness when questioned was slowly mellowing the longer they abode together, while Urrell increasingly performed his share of tasks and become better company. He could now flake flints, kindle fires, cure hides and cook with almost the deftness of the master himself, coached by him with sly approval, something none of his home hunters would have done for a half-grown youth.

Agaratz did not answer. He remained silent so long Urrell was no longer expecting a reply when Agaratz suddenly spoke out in a high-pitched voice. First hesitantly, as if translating from his own or another language events remembered from the long ago, he gathered fluency in the rhythmic manner of reciters that Urrell had heard from old men down by the sea.

"I tell," began Agaratz. "I tell you. Long time past, long, long time, big bears, *mammurak*, long-tooth cat, and big animal with one horn live in these lands." He paused to search for words in Urrell's language to convey the subtle, more complex original language of the recital.

"Great ice come, all down mountain and never melt."

He went on, speaking to himself in a low voice from his couch in the hay, in words Urrell did not understand, till, satisfied he had recollected the story aright, he resumed, "Winters colder, colder. Very long. Summer short. My people live here then. Living in caves, make snow houses, hunt bison, snow-ox, reindeers. Plenty eat for all. Share with big cat, big bear, and that time they learn to speak bear, long-tooth tiger, wolfs. They hunt together."

"Then ice melt and go back up mountain. Not good for big cat, not for bear. New people come and hunt. Hunt much, so big cats go and bears go. *Mammurak* go. My people stay to keep caves, but they few, then fewer. Now all gone down caves. I last. When go, close cave. No-one find way."

Urrell had listened in utter silence. It was the longest sustained statement he had heard Agaratz make. He, Urrell, the waif, was being introduced into another reality, one in which Agaratz moved with ease, examples of which Urrell had glimpsed. Was Agaratz, its last guardian, testing him, this youth from another people, so that he, the waif Urrell, might become the tradition bearer of such knowledge?

Urrell asked: "Agaratz, can you teach me how to speak to bears?"

"I try."

"Can we go to the land of mammoths, to find them?"

"None now."

Old Mother had spoken of them. She had been in no doubt at all.

"Agaratz, the Old Mother came from that land. She knew the mammoths."

"When summer come, Urrell, we go find *mammuraka.*"

Urrell snuggled down happily with Rakrak, to dream of mammoths.

With winter closing in there was little to do but cure hides, sew garments and keep warm. Urrell grew to asking Agaratz about his people and seeking to be taught anything Agaratz was willing to reveal. Often it meant returning time and again to the same theme.

"Agaratz, why did your people not move when the cold came?"

"They…" he wavered, deciding which word to use "…look after caves." Urrell noticed the explanation did not satisfy Agaratz's sense of what he sought to convey.

"Did they look after paintings?"

"After paintings, yes."

"Who did the paintings?"

"Olds, olds, from old times."

Urrell watched him roll hand over hand to show time long past.

"Were they your people, Agaratz?"

"Before, olds, other kin, all gone."

"Gone where?"

"To *mamu.*"

"Is that where the dead go?"

"Land of *mamu*…"

More he would not say, nor where this land lay, except to wave vaguely into the earth beyond the depths of their cave. At this time Urrell noticed how little Agaratz ate – a few nuts, a handful of seeds. He grew lethargic, he who was so active, slept bouts of many hours in the hay-filled recess whereas his own and Rakrak's appetites remained undiminished. Urrell ensured the fire was kept up.

For many days and nights blizzards drove snow across the open lands, filling their gulch until they could step out of the cave entrance straight on to the drifts. No need for the climbing pole, left poking up through the snow. Before the drifts grew too deep Agaratz had hauled up their cache of bison meat in its hide, and the store of fish, to the lip of the entrance. The emptied bison hide they had dragged into the cave, thawed, scraped, and hung across its mouth. This lessened the worst gusts. Then Agaratz had surprised Urrell by getting him to help to scrape up snow against the hide, tamping each handful till they had built a snow wall, leaving only a small, blockable entry hatch.

"Now less cold."

It left the cave in gloom, but livable, lit and warmed by the fire. As their fuel had dried well, little smoke was produced. Even so, Urrell's hands became black with ingrained grime, his face sooty from the fire.

It did not bother him till his fingers began to itch and the tips split, then he showed them to Agaratz.

"*Ishll.* Bad. Eat plants."

He gave Urrell dried herbs to chew, roots and garlic to eat and the chilblains vanished within days. Such winter afflictions Urrell had known among his own people. He recalled children and women weeping helplessly at their kibed fingers and foot sores.

CHAPTER 16

As the spell of great cold deepened Agaratz grew torpid. He did not waken for two days, his breathing slowing, till Urrell grew fearful and with difficulty shook him awake. Agaratz woke, unconcerned, merely saying, "I sleep bear."

"Sleep bear?"

"Sleep like bear, when cold. You sleep bear, Urrell."

"I can't sleep like a bear."

"Yes. I show."

"But Rakrak can't. She is a wolf. Wolves don't sleep in winter."

"She sleep. I show."

Agaratz made Urrell lie curled up and still, breathing slowly, emptying his lungs and mind. At the same time he held the lad's shoulders and looked intently at him till he dozed off.

It must have worked, thought Urrell, when he came to from a dreamless blank. Rakrak slept quietly beside him in the hay and leaves, her snout nuzzling his side, scarcely breathing. He spent several worried minutes rousing her. Agaratz was nowhere to be seen. Boy and wolf unstiffened their limbs and eased themselves out of their hay-filled den, both compelled by an urgent need to urinate before anything else. They hurried down the gallery, accustomed to the route in the dark. Urrell guessed he must have slept for a number of days and nights, such was the pressure on his bladder and the painfulness of its contents' discharge.

This over, Urrell returned to see where Agaratz might be. Finally, he lifted the hatch flap and looked out on a world frozen into stillness, icier than ever, with all signs of blizzards vanished.

On this perfect snow surface Agaratz's tracks led off, out of the gulch, as though inviting him to follow. He scrambled into his outdoor furs.

The tracks followed the base of the cliff towards the painted cave. Rakrak, in her winter livery, blended with the snowy lower branches of firs, now at surface level. Progress was easy over the frost-crisp surface. It was so cold that Urrell felt his cheeks burn. Even Rakrak seemed subdued, not gambolling as usual but trotting beside him, adding her paw marks beside his footprints, like a fancy stitch along the double seam his made with Agaratz's tracks.

When they were not more than two spear-casts from the spot in the cliff-face where Urrell remembered the entrance into the painted cave ought to be, the tracks stopped dead in a patch of snow between two vast firs. Urrell stopped too, even looking up to see if Agaratz had taken flight and settled on a bough overhead. So bemused was he in the intense cold that even this might have seemed natural. He could see no explanation for the abrupt end in the tracks. No other prints showed anywhere, human or animal. He circled the area and found nothing. Instead of following him Rakrak sat whimpering, her behaviour adding to his unease. With a growing sense of fear, Urrell set off to return as fast as his double moccassins allowed, his face raw from the cold, the icy air rasping his throat, yet sweat running under his quilted pelts, Rakrak pacing alongside.

The secret place, the acrid weeds

But this was no headlong flight of a small boy down a summery combe to meadows below. Youth and wolf arrived back at the cave as to the safety of a lair.

By the fire crouched Agaratz. He raised his eyes as Urrell and Rakrak tumbled through the flap, but seemed not to notice them both, his look elsewhere as though neither was standing before him, still panting. Then the eyes lit up, focussed, and Agaratz looked intently at Urrell's face. He touched the lad's nose and muttered in his own tongue, went to the entrance and came back with a handful of snow. To Urrell's surprise he rubbed his nose and cheeks with it. Urrell felt nothing.

"Bad," said Agaratz. "Sit not near fire. Nose get well, but hurt."

When it warmed it did indeed. His nose and cheeks smarted so much that he did not think to ask why the tracks had suddenly ended nowhere. His nostrils cracked and the chapping of his cheeks made life miserable for days till they healed under the goose-fat plasters Agaratz employed to soothe the frostbite.

Urrell's confinement brought out kinder aspects of Agaratz's character. He lit lamps in a small recess, hung hides across it and they spent hours carving wood, horn and stone with animal designs. Urrell's skills developed under Agaratz's tuition. During those days he became aware that he had passed another unspoken stage of acceptance in Agaratz's esteem.

With each design, each beast, Agaratz recited stories. They were new to Urrell, familiar only with the simple folktales of his own people. In Agaratz's recitals, often made in the high tone of story-tellers, Urrell learnt of an age long past when great beasts jostled and conferred. Men were puny by comparison, tolerated by the beasts as jesters. In those tales humans often played tricks on the animals. None minded. Sometimes the animals had the upper hand. No one hunted for food as it abounded in yon times before the great cold. The lad's imagination was nourished and enchanted by these legends summarised by Agaratz as best he could in Urrell's language.

Indeed, Agaratz's grasp of Urrell's speech improved that winter. A word or turn of phrase new to him and he seized upon it, repeated it once or twice for Urrell to correct, and consigned it to his faultless memory. Sometimes Urrell half wondered if Agaratz made play to learn his language to please the growing lad, able as he seemed to follow wordlessly much that Urrell thought but did not say. Urrell, too, improved his store of words in Agaratz's tongue but could not fluently master its structure, so different was it from anything he knew. It seemed to him of unbelievable complexity, designed to express much he could only dimly perceive, or not at all, let alone understand. He preferred to turn his attention to carving, to making hunting gear, working leather garments, to a background of stories about insects, birds, plants, beasts and their lore. He discovered inner skills of which he had been unaware. Agaratz smiled at his delight in carving mammoths and told him of the wisdom of that greatest of beasts.

During this time Agaratz dipped into their stores to vary their daily fare, devising meals with the skill and invention he displayed in all he did.

A favourite of Urrell's were collops of bison meat, rolled round nuts and garlic before being baked in embers. "Rakrak like too," said Agaratz.

As a treat Agaratz took combs from their honey pouches. Some honey he placed in wooden beakers with water and herbs, where it lay for days till the water bubbled and they sipped it by the fire, rolling the scented liquor round their mouths and feeling it warm their veins.

Urrell's face healed, the cracks closed, his skin grew smooth again. He felt well; down hung a finger's width on his upper lip and cheeks; his body muscles and hair were becoming a man's.

"Soon you grown," said Agaratz.

"Good, then I can hunt better with you, Agaratz, and help you more."

Agaratz remained silent. Then he said, as if coming back from a distance: "Soon you need woman."

The notion had not occurred to Urrell, although there were times when he thought of the youngest woman of his tribelet, she of the chaplets of berries and the small breasts beneath her summer cape. The memory did agreeable things to him; but nothing more.

"Me? But you have no woman, Agaratz."

Again silence. That remote expression that betokened an area of Agaratz's life not open for revelation.

"Where are women, Agaratz?"

"When hot weather, we go to *mor*, to place tribes meet. There girls."

"Where?"

"Far, far. We take things for trade."

"Don't you want a wife, Agaratz?"

Deep silence. Urrell shifted uneasily. But then, as though to clear up something difficult to explain to a child, Agaratz spoke:

"When *konkorartz*, not for womens."

He did not expand and Urrell knew best not to ask. Their silence was relieved by Rakrak whimpering for food, most unusual for her.

They ate honey – humans and wolf – that night, after nuts, herbs and meat. Urrell, whose turn it was to cook, strove to invent variants in their fare. The near smile on Agaratz's face told Urrell his efforts had not gone unnoticed. Then he watched as Agaratz went to his stores and returned with what looked like a stick or a tube with small holes bored along it.

Agaratz squatted by the fire, the light illuminating the long face and russet sideburns, coarse reddish hair hanging down past his ears. But for the translucent intelligence of the eyes, almost yellow in the firelight, the hunched figure with the thin hairy leg and its cloven foot might have been some odd woodland mismade animal rather than a man.

Agaratz turned the tube one way and another, squinted down the hollow centre, put an end to his mouth, while Urrell watched and waited. Swaying gently Agaratz blew into the tube. A sound such as Urrell had never heard, or could ever have imagined, rose from it. Then another and another.

The lad sat enchanted. Even Rakrak pricked her ears. The flute carried its notes beyond Urrell, far into the gallery, yet entering into him in a sensation so new that he shivered. Agaratz's fingers moved up and down the tube, stopping and unstopping the holes as he blew, swaying more and more, playing without looking, to Urrell's surprise. Instead, the player's eyes seemed to be fixed beyond their cave, their small ice-bound gulch in a cliff-face overlooking the vast prairies where summer flocks of bison and herds of ponies filled the horizon as far as the mountain land of mammoths and huge cave bears. Urrell's skin fristled. He felt like soaring, hurling spears vast distances, leaping hills.

When Agaratz stopped playing the melody went on running through Urrell's whole body. He nodded and skipped to it, possessor of something never-to-be forgotten, of a turning in his life, of a precious thing that he wanted for himself. This skill he must master. "Agaratz, teach me that."

"One day. If you can."

If he could? He could, and he would. Nothing would stop him, not even travelling to the land of the mammoths. But he knew there was no use in asking; Agaratz might show him the very next day or perhaps next spring.

Other things occupied his mind. "We go fish."

"Fish? Where?"

"Nani."

The river would be frozen over. Urrell felt loth to ask how they could fish through ice. He would wait and see.

As it was to be an expedition of several days and nights, in cold that froze to death any creature caught in it lame, lost or hungry, Agaratz displayed his skill and foresight in the preparations for the trip, one he must have made often before on his own, thought

Urrell, who took in every detail, only too aware, since his frostbite, of the dangers of the great cold.

Agaratz dragged out the travois used earlier in foraging expeditions for nuts, seeds, bulbs and the like. He dismantled the bison hide from across the cave entrance and thawed it by the fire, before piling on it extra pelts, food, weapons, tools, fishing lines and bone hooks. When all was ready to his satisfaction, with Urrell's help he broke through the snow wall to get the bundle and travois out and on to the snow-drift just below the lip of the cave. On the travois he fixed the hide with its contents, handed Urrell packets and poles, then slung a line over each of his shoulders and they set off.

"Wear all furs, Urrell. On face too."

He draped a fox fur across his nose, fur inwards, and Urrell did likewise. Both pulled down fur caps over their ears. Rakrak trotted beside them as they issued from the gulch on to the hard snow of the open lands. In the windless air their breath froze. They moved slowly, deliberately, lest breathing in too sharply might freeze their lungs. They took frequent turns to pull the travois.

Urrell, unused to the silence of deep winter, his mouth and nose muffled, made no sound. Nor did Agaratz. They spoke in signs. Rakrak, too, conserved her strength, wolf-like, with the easy trot of her kind. They were alone in the world, three figures in the emptiness – a hunchback, a wolf and a youth – on their way to the river Nani and its waters gliding to the sea beneath thicknesses of ice and snow. Urrell stopped wondering how they would catch anything.

Far out in the open the snow depth grew shallower. Winds and blizzards had driven it towards the cliffs leaving patches where grass showed through, forage for reindeer, or snowdeer as Agaratz called them. When they passed groves and spinneys, the surface bore signs where grazing animals had sheltered and pawed through the snow for withered grass, leaves, pine-needles, anything to eat.

"See, snowdeers," said Agaratz, half muffled.

The cold was so intense that the air scarcely carried the sound of his voice.

The Nani's belt of trees afforded more cover for animals, now as in summer, evidence of life that surprised Urrell, accustomed to all beasts as well as humans migrating away from these wastes before the long winter. Hoof-prints, droppings, streaks of urine, told of grazers and browsers remaining behind. Spoor of big cats showed that they too remained. It was good to be wary and armed, thought Urrell. Yet Agaratz, intent on his purpose, ignored these tell-tales and plodded on. Only Rakrak showed interest, reconnoitring and sniffing such proofs of living things in a sterile world.

"Stop here," mumbled Agaratz when they arrived at a spot among trees he plainly foreknew. "Build shelter."

Using the downswept boughs of a fir as a roof, he and Urrell made a shelter from poles left from previous visits. Through these they pleached fir branches, laid the bison hide over and scraped snow against the sides to freeze in place and make it wind-tight. They scraped the ground bare inside, then lined it with more fir branches and twigs. It looked quite cosy to Urrell. When Agaratz had found several fire-blackened stones and made a hearth, their shelter was ready.

They ate a handful of nuts, chewed bison fat and got ready for the next task. It was past nightfall, but in the whitish gloom of winter their eyes picked out everything, helped by a shy moon in a still, clear sky.

"Take, Urrell." He was given flint hand-axes, some rough boards and wooden scoops.

Agaratz stepped out on to the snow-covered river at a bend Urrell remembered from earlier visits, recognising the trees. There had been a deep pool where they were standing. Agaratz scraped snow away till he reached ice, a patch two handspans across. "Now work, Urrell." Work it was, as they picked at the ice with their axes and antler points. Soon, hot inside his furs, Urrell suffered thirst. He knew better than to suck snow in such weather. Later they would melt some in quaiches by the fire, dropping hot stones in, a tiresome business but the only way to obtain water. Rakrak would have some too, though in the manner of her kind she fended for herself, seldom needing to drink.

By the middle of the night they had chipped a good way down, lying on the snow to do so.

"Tomorrow finish. Catch fishes and get water."

Under their fir tree, its branches lit from their fire through a smoke vent in the roof, they braised meat. Snow they melted by the fire in wooden vessels that Agaratz dug out of their hiding place. They were black with smoke and age, larger than anything Urrell had ever seen. "Who made these, Agaratz?"

"Olds, Urrell."

Urrell must have looked uncertain. He repeated, "Made by olds. Olds men."

"How did you get them, then, or your folk?"

"They give. Now gone."

That was it. Urrel knew better than to ask further.

They each ate a piece of honeycomb, Rakrak sitting on her hunkers for a share, before they crawled under fir branches for the night, fully clad, drawing every spare pelt they had over themselves. It was warm enough. During the night Agaratz rose several times to replenish the fire and Urrell sensed that he expected something but by morning, when Urrell wriggled out of his lair, he noticed nothing new. All was quiet, no sound of beasts moving despite the evidence of animals they had come across on their way to the river.

Agaratz grilled meat, sending savoury odours wafting into the tree overhead, tickling the nostrils of both lad and wolf as they waited for it to be done.

"Today wolfs come," said Agaratz. Urrell must have looked blank. He added: "Rakrak know."

Rakrak, eating, seemed more interested in her food than the arrival of her kind.

"But what wolves, Agaratz? How do you know?"

"I know. I tell. Come for fishes."

Muffled in their furs, they set off to their hole. Agaratz dragged a short, heavy log with him. Both got down to further chipping.

At a distance a herd of reindeer passed, their antlers forming a frieze as they raised their heads to survey these two humans out in the open scratching in the snow, then, surmising they were no threat, back down the frieze went to ground level to paw and scrape for whatever lay hidden and edible underfoot.

"Soon see snow oxes too, Urrell."

Not sure what they might be, Urrell said nothing, too cold to talk.

They had scraped and chipped till midday when Agaratz stood up.

"Break ice." He up-ended the log and Urrell saw its purpose: to batter the ice plug they had been chipping away. It took several blows, with all Agaratz's might, to break through the ice and reveal the dark water running beneath.

Into it Agaratz dipped a scoop and brought up a mouthful of water. "For you," he said, passing the vessel to Urrell with a faint grin on the ice-stubbled face. Urrell sipped the water, ice-cold, savouring the liquor, so different from melted snow. They drank thus, in turns, very slowly lest the coldness numbed their face-bones and froze their mouths. Rakrak had hers too. "Now fish, Urrell."

Urrell watched as Agaratz unmittened his hands and showed

him how to weight the lines with stones, bait the hooks with scraps of meat and skin, and drop them into the hole. There were two lines, one apiece. They crouched on the ice and waited.

But not for long. Urrell felt a tug, and with it the excitement only the fisherman knows at contact with his unseen quarry. He jerked his line and his first fish was hooked. It came up through the hole and flapped on the snow, a foot-long beautiful thing.

"Give to Rakrak."

He did. An ancient observance, something unspoken? Henceforth he, Urrell, would know.

Rakrak took the fish, placed a paw on its head and the other on its still flicking tail and picked at it as at a bone.

The next fishes both humans ate raw, tearing at the taut skins almost before they ceased to twitch. Then they set to and in the space of two hours had caught enough char, chub, trout and other fishes unknown to Urrell, and to Agaratz only in his own tongue, to form two piles on the snow. It was easy work, the fish biting readily, to Urrell's surprise, and he soon learnt to let the fish hook itself before tugging at the line. Despite the cold this hunting was so engrossing to Urrell that he noticed nothing until Agaratz nodded across towards the bank.

"See. Wolfs."

Slinking out of the trees the silvery shapes of Rakrak's pack came out on to the ice. Urrell recognised the pack leader and Rakrak's mother, and others of her siblings despite their winter livery. Rakrak ran to meet them, rolling on her back to her father, then prancing greetings to others in a ceremony new to Urrell. This accomplished, the pack advanced and squatted round the fishermen, expectancy on their alert faces.

The big lead male came up to Agaratz and they sniffed as Urrell remembered from their meeting in the ravine.

"Urrell, give fishes to wolfs, like me."

He took fishes and handed one to each wolf in turn as they came forward in an order of their own, and withdrew to eat their prize. It fell to Urrell to feed the mother and siblings of Rakrak. They touched noses. The she-wolf's eyes met his, held them, and he glimpsed, or thought he glimpsed, deep in her bluish depths another's gaze. Startled, he glanced up at Agaratz. The hunchback was looking at him, part wistful, part absent.

Old Mother, Old Mother of the Mammoths.

He rued then his forgetfulness of her. Now he would remember.

When each wolf had eaten its fish – a dainty morsel rather than a meal – they raised their muzzles and joined their pack leader in a long, musical call, again a new one to Urrell, to which Agaratz and Rakrak responded in unison. Then they turned and left, disappearing the way they had come through the woods.

"Wolfs now help hunt," said Agaratz.

As he had seen scant game, despite tracks and droppings, Urrell wondered.

"Hunt? Hunt what, Agaratz."

"*Mammurak.*"

"Oh!" It was a moment before he realised the tease.

"No, Urrell, not *mammurak.*"

Those three nights spent by the Nani Urrell determined should stay in his memory.

The days remained dull counterparts of their nights. Through the overcast sky a faint, far-off sun glimmered, doing nothing to lessen the intense cold. Life, apart from their threesome, seemed to have fled. From the hole, which refroze overnight and had to be re-broken, they pulled a never-ending harvest. Some they baked, some they gnawed raw; most Agaratz packed in bundles till their catch outweighed what men and travois could carry. Urrell wondered how Agaratz intended to transport so much.

"Now hide fishes, Urrell."

He beckoned to Urrell to help him carry the frozen bundles to the foot of a massive fir, one broken off halfway up and regrown where a branch had become the new lead shoot, forming a saddle. On this platform Agaratz proposed to cache their surplus fish.

With a bundle strapped across his shoulders he swarmed up the tree, using every knurr of the deeply creviced bark and every foothold on downsweeping boughs, as if from memory. He was soon down again for another parcel, prepared by Urrell. In less than an hour all surplus fish was stashed beyond the reach of passing scavengers.

"Perhaps see lion," said Agaratz.

"Lion?"

"Old lion. Die soon."

They had neither seen nor heard lions, and few other beasts. It was almost too cold to wonder what Agaratz was talking about. Urrell felt as if he had only half heard the words so had half forgotten them in the preparations of breaking camp, dispersing the shelter poles and hiding the hearth stones when he stopped, immediately alerted by snuffling and whimpering from nearby brush.

"See, Urrell, lion come."

They both stopped and watched as a lion, weak and thin, limped out of the undergrowth and squatted twenty paces from the humans and the wolf. It was a lioness, her winter coat matted and shaggy, and she was starving. "You feed, Urrell. Give fishes."

Urrell hesitated. Agaratz urged, but seeing the lad still wavering he took a fish himself and placed it before the lioness then stepped back. "See, Urrell, hungry, hungry." The lioness, with a little pounce, seized the fish and crouched to crunch it, giving out little gurgles of contentment.

"Come, Urrell, give food." Agaratz beckoned him over.

Much as Urrell trusted Agaratz since the meeting with Rakrak's wolfpack, his confrontation with the bear and his judgement in so many matters, he still wavered. But Agaratz's insistence won and he sidled over, within a hand's touch of the animal. She, intent on her food, ignored him.

Agaratz handed him another frozen fish. "You give, Urrell." He dropped it by the lioness and saw how thin she was under the mat of winter fur.

"She come with us. Or die. Too cold for her hunt."

"Take the lion?"

"Yes, you see. She come."

"But Rakrak..."

"Rakrak know."

When the last fish was scrunched and swallowed, the old lioness rose and followed them to the campsite. Rakrak sat watching. She made no move of acceptance or resistance, the lioness acting likewise.

"How did you know the lioness was coming?"

"I know."

"But how?"

"My people know."

"But tell me *how*, Agaratz."

"One day you know too."

The cold left little energy for discussion. They muffled up, each slung pouches across his shoulders then took up a handle apiece of the travois in a gloved hand and the long trudge home began.

Beyond the trees they found their own tracks and followed them back over snow frozen hard enough to bear their weight. Apart from the criss-criss of the trailing travois poles on the snow crust all was silence. Rakrak led, the lioness brought up the rear.

Their first stop would be a clump of small trees, one of the few features in the expanse and which Urrell knew had a watering-hole in better weather.

It was over two hours before either spoke when Agaratz unmuffled to ask: "Urrell, you know big forest deers?"

"Big deer?"

"Very big. Like big horse, with wide, wide horns."

"I know fallow deer, red deer, reindeer but like a horse, no."

"I show you."

Urrell turned his head to scan the snow, no easy matter in cold-stiffened leatherwear, furs, headgear, muffler. He saw nothing.

"No Urrell, I *show* you."

The tone, the emphasis, puzzled Urrell enough to make him swivel his head, in its casing of furs and neck gear, to see Agaratz's expression. Only one cheek and one eye managed to peer round his ear muffs to see that his companion's expression was its frequent, slightly absent self.

"I show you deers, Urrell," he repeated, "I *show*."

They were a few spear-casts from the grove when he said, "See, Urrell," and pointed ahead.

In and around the trees milled a herd of huge deer-like creatures, on long ungainly legs. Most striking was the immense spread of their antlers, greater than any Urrell had ever witnessed, even among the biggest elks. There was something horsish about them. As he watched the strange animals moved into the grove and through it.

"What are they, Agaratz?"

"Big deers, from great cold, from land of *mammurak.*"

Urrell pulled harder on his end of the travois, eager to draw nearer, though Agaratz made no effort to speed up. Neither Rakrak nor the lioness seemed to have noticed anything.

By the time the little group reached the trees, the travois

lowered and pouches dropped, the deer had vanished. Urrell hurried through the firs and aspens eager to find traces of their passage, curious to check whether their feet were hoofed or cloven. But he found nothing. Beyond the trees the snow lay untrampled and empty to the horizon.

Agaratz was twirling the fire-stick when he came back.

"Agaratz, where have the horse-deer gone?"

No answer. "Agaratz – the deer?"

At his impatience Agaratz raised his eyes from what he was doing, with their mischievous glint Urrell knew too well.

"They far, Urrell, far, far. Land of ice," adding as if by afterthought, "land of *mammurak.*" And half rising from his crouch over the fire-log he pointed the fire-stick north, to the land of mammoths.

Old Mother's memory flashed before the youth's mind, as vivid as a childhood smell recaptured, vanishing before he could seize it, ungraspable as mist between his fingers. He strove to recapture the vision. She came back, but fainter, and each time still fainter, until the woodsmoke from Agaratz's new fire brought him back to the present. Soon the smell of thawing fish grilling amid the resinous odours of burning pine-needles would occupy his attention, while Rakrak and the lioness gnawed their fishes, still frozen hard, as they might have crunched bones. The sputter of the fire and the sounds of their eating was all they could hear in the stillness of the snows.

"Eat then rest, Urrell."

They slept for an hour, propped against trees for fear of freezing had they lain on the snow. As Urrell dozed off his last memory was of the lioness with her head on her forepaws, snub face as close to the fire as she dared, contented at last. The sight of her carried over into Urrell's dreams, where Old Mother appeared to him with the scarred and battered old face of the lioness, yet perfectly recognisable, and so vivid that he would remember the vision for long after. When he scrutinised the lioness on awakening he thought he descried something of Old Mother's remembered expression when she cackled with pleasure. He would say nothing about the dream to Agaratz: it would be his own to keep, a sign.

CHAPTER 17

"Soon reach cave, Urrell."

Exhaustion dulled him. Ahead the line of cliffs showed, renewing Urrell's strength for the home stretch.

Home it was. Never had he felt a homecoming like this, unlike the shifting camps of his boyhood where he belonged to no-one. They had merely been places to cadge scraps, to creep up to the fire for warmth when the men were absent, to be cuddled by childless old women and to listen to their stories.

Sight of the cave mouth as they rounded the gulch entrance drove all thoughts of the giant elks from Urrell's mind. They were another of Agaratz's sleights, to be understood one day. Fire, food and sleep prevailed.

Rakrak shared his mood, speeding ahead to be first into the cave. The lioness trotted behind as though familiar with this way all her life. A little coaxing from Agaratz and she jumped up and into the cave. Agaratz unknotted the bison hide from the travois and tipped the bundles of fish on to the snow.

"Later dig, Urrell."

Together they dragged the hide up and hung it back across the mouth of the cave, then repacked the snow wall. "Now foods."

The fire lit, Agaratz prepared a homecoming feast: collops of bison meat were soon searing on a bed of embers. Onions and garlic, nuts and honey came out. The lioness stared into the flames, her snout twitching with pleasure at the smell of roasting flesh and hot garlic. Deep in her chest Urrell heard a sound new to him – the low rumble of a lion's purr.

"Piura happy."

"Piura, Agaratz?"

"Piura is lion."

"You know her name?"

"My people lion people."

The statement did not invite questions and Urrell asked none. He would think about it and ask another time.

Meanwhile all four crouched as close as they could to the fire, warmth feeding into their limbs, its light glowing on Agaratz's shelves and stores, picking out the black entrances to galleries beyond where further piles of objects were stacked. All was familiar now, and comforting.

Hot fat dribbled down Urrell's eating face, greasing his tunic. He caught Agaratz's amused look at such gulping. Whatever his own hunger, Agaratz ate carefully, sparingly, cat-like in his cleanliness; Urrell felt gently rebuked for his slummocking. Beside him, Rakrak and Piura feasted in the manner of their kind, Rakrak the more meticulous as she scrunched everything to the last bone, Piura messier, her teeth worn down, a fang broken, daubing her face and whiskers with fat whilst purring and growling with pleasure. Urrell saw her eyes meet Agaratz's and her gaze soften in a communication between the two that left him out. He was struck by how alike their eyes were, hers slightly the lighter.

Agaratz of the lion people.

For comfort Urrell patted Rakrak.

That feast, with honey and nuts to finish, would remain in his memory as the seal of their clanship – men and beasts. Piura's matted fur, thawed and warmed by the fire, smelt. Urrell's own face smarted with dirt, exposure and cold-spreathe. He touched his nose and cheek, felt the crust of grime and chapped skin, and wondered how Agaratz showed no signs of the cold they had been through together. He felt as unkempt as the lioness. His leathers warmed and felt greasy. Black lines criss-crossed his palms and he imagined what his face must look like now in the pool at the spring where he had admired his own reflection last summer.

Drowsiness overwhelmed him as thoughts like these mingled with memories of his past, of the girl with the budding breasts and berries in her hair.

When he awoke Agaratz was binding a spearhead. For all Urrell knew, the hunchback had not slept at all. Rakrak lay alongside; Piura by the fire twitched in dreams of her own.

"Ah Urrell, time go see *mammuraka.*"

Urrell, though suddenly alert, said nothing, mammoths or not. The elk vision, the untrodden snow beyond the clump of trees, was too recent, too like a dream for him to rush forward a second time. Was this another of Agaratz's tricks?

"You come, Urrell."

He took up several torches of resinous wood, lit one and led the way. Urrell fell in behind and Rakrak astern. Piura remained asleep.

At the fork to the privy Agaratz bore right, down the main gallery where Urrell had never been nor thought to go. Agaratz's torch lit smooth stone walls to the roof. Soon the gallery widened. On one side Urrell made out vast stalactites in a forest of stone, from floor to ceiling. Further on the torchlight hinted at a frozen river, or a series of cascades in stone pouring for ever into the interior of the earth. Instead of exploring these Agaratz moved towards the other, plainer cave wall and held the torch aloft, steadying the flame in the airless atmosphere, to show Urrell something.

"See, Urrell."

At first he saw only the flat wall, with its cracks and discolouring, but as he came nearer and Agaratz tilted the torch, a procession of faint engravings showed up as a frieze such as Urrell had never beheld before: a line of mammoths processing into the cave, shimmering with the tremor of the torch flame, intent on their journey. Why the engraver had drawn his scraper so lightly across the stone, in a single perfect line, then touched in hints of the shaggy coats, Urrell did not think to ask himself. Their creator had perhaps meant them so, never to be seen again as they journeyed eternally into *mamu*. He was silent with awe.

Agaratz was silent also, absent in thought.

A whimper from Rakrak in the shadows brought him back.

"Did you draw them, Agaratz?"

He must have heard the question but the answer was long coming.

"From old, old time," and he rolled his free hand over and over in that gesture of a measure of how long ago. Then, by way of after-thought, "When great ice."

Urrell's interest, he must have known, would be roused. Was he teasing the lad? He went on, "Then olden mens. All time ice."

"Your people, Agaratz?"

"Not. Before my fathers."

He moved on, torch aloft. Urrell noticed how he hugged the smooth wall, as though he knew the way, till the stalagmites and stalactites lay behind them and the gallery narrowed to less than a man-wide gap. He stopped when the torch lit a row of palm-sized red dots at face level. Before Urrell's wondering eyes he paused and muttered something in front of each, addressing the dot or the rock, and then moving to the next. At the end of the row Urrell watched him dab a new dot in red ochre from a pad in his belt. To this he muttered also.

Farther on the passage inclined and widened, then steepened sharply so they slithered and sent gravel rattling ahead of them into the dark. Somewhere in that dark the rattling vanished.

Urrell was to see why: the passage stopped on the lip of a swallow-hole, a black chasm beyond the range of their resin light. Agaratz was exploring the rim, his unconcern comforting. From boyhood Urrell had heard how folk lost in caverns never came out, sucked into unimaginable underworlds. One slip by Agaratz, the torch dowsed or dropped into that hole, and death of the fearfullest kind would be theirs. He gripped Rakrak. Meanwhile Agaratz had found what he was looking for, sticking up over the rim of the pit – the tip of a fir tree. It was another climbing pole, like the one in the honey cave, as old, perhaps left there by the same honey-seekers. Agaratz intended to go down it. He handed the torch to Urrell as he lowered himself over the edge and felt for a foothold. His mane of hair was level with the rim when he found one. He reached for the torch.

"I go down, Urrell, and light for you. Rakrak stay." And down he went, hand over hand, the pole flexing till he stood in a small pool of light at the bottom.

"Come, Urrell. Safe."

It did not feel so. Urrell gingerly lowered himself over the edge, clinging to the quivering tip of the fir tree, his leg swinging in search of a foothold. At last his foot found a snag thick enough to bear his weight. He looked up at Rakrak's intelligent face faintly lit from below and began his descent.

By the time he reached the bottom and stood on the sandy floor Rakrak was invisible. He called to her and she responded. *Rakrak, wolf spirit.*

There was no way Urrell could guess how big the chasm bottom was, or where it led. Beyond their circle of light all was blackness. Agaratz peered intently around until having found some bearing known to – or distantly recalled by – him alone, he set off. As they went Urrell made out footprints on the sandy floor, tracks of others going in the same direction, the owners of the fir-log perhaps, the honey men. He tugged Agaratz's arm to show him the tracks, with their splayed toes and heavy outer-foot impression.

Agaratz shrugged. "Olds mens, Urrell, make these."

They all led the same way. Beside them Agaratz added his own distinctive club foot imprint in the sand, as fresh as those of the long-gone 'olds mens'. Urrell, intent on looking down and around within the pool of light from the torch for more signs of those earlier folk, had not noticed what the light showed ahead when Agaratz stopped.

Stacked in a jumble against the farther wall of the pit lay a pile of tusks – mammoth tusks. Urrell held his breath.

"Olds mens put here." Then, turning aside, Agaratz said: "Look, Urrell," and holding the torch as high as he could he walked with it to one side. "See." Perched on a boulder, guardian of the tusk hoard, with one long tusk still in place, was the skull of a huge bull mammoth. In the torchlight its gaping eye-sockets glowered at the intruders.

Urrell froze. Agaratz, however, approached the skull and addressed it much as he had the mammoth drawings in the painted cave, intoning in a language unknown to Urrell, appealing, pleading. When he had finished, Agaratz remained silent in front of the skull, the only sound in the huge space around them being the hiss of burning resin from the torch. Whatever Agaratz awaited did not happen.

"We take tusk, Urrell, but quick."

As Urrell remained rooted to the spot, he added, "For flute."

In his practical way, changing from incantation to tool-making, Agaratz handed the torch to Urrell while he chose a tusk from the pile. This done, without another glance at the guardian of the hoard, he shouldered the tusk and gestured for Urrell to lead the way back along their tracks to the climbing pole.

"I go up," with which Agaratz swarmed up the tree trunk into the gloom above, almost in haste. The long swirled tusk over one shoulder seemed to be no hindrance. Only the quivering of the trunk betokened his progress to the top. When Urrell heard Rakrak's greeting, it was his turn.

Till now, the presence of Agaratz had kept his fears at bay. To make things worse, the torch was burning low, drawing the circle of darkness closer round him. He hardly dared turn his back to the chasm. Carefully he edged round the trunk to scale it up the under side. His arms almost managed to encircle it, one hand grasping the torch, feet scrabbling for holds. His free hand found a grip just as his feet swung away, leaving him suspended within reach of anything on the pit floor. In a flurry of panicking effort he hauled himself round the trunk and, using his legs, scissored himself up over knurrs and stumps, scratched and cut, towards the safety of Agaratz and Rakrak. He glanced down. Was it a glimpse he caught of forms in the half gloom closing in on the foot of the bole? With a little shriek he flung the guttering torch at them. As it hit the sand, sending up sparks, he knew he saw heavy-browed faces looking up at him just as they vanished back into the dark, things as surely seen as those glimpsed from the corner of an eye yet invisible head-on.

Those last few lengths of the fir trunk he shinned up in a frenzy, by touch, till he almost shot over the rim, grasped by Agaratz and hauled over to lie quaking by Rakrak, ashamed at his own panic and the insides of his leathern breeches, warm and wet.

Rakrak licked his face.

"I fetch light. Wait." Agaratz swung down the bole, retrieved the glowing stump and was back up in what seemed a trice to Urrell, still face down on the ledge. Agaratz twirled it back alight and from it lit a spare torch, shouldered the tusk and led off up the incline. To Urrell bringing up the rear, gripping Rakrak's fur, his moccasins slipping on the gravel, it felt as if the presences were pressing up behind him, mocking his fears. Not till the narrow passage and its dots, at which Agaratz paused as before to mutter words, did the sense of being pursued lift from Urrell.

And not till they were back in their cave, the fire still alight, Piura dozing in its warmth, Agaratz busying himself with fish and bison meat, did Urrell feel himself truly safe. To one side, the tip of the tusk caught the firelight, a reminder that this had not been one of Agaratz's tricks; while his own scratches and wet trews were real enough.

"Agaratz, how did you know about the tusks?"

Agaratz went on with his tasks. After a longish pause, as an adult answers the unanswerable questions of a child, he said: "Fathers know. Fathers' fathers tell. My father tell me."

Urrell removed his leggings and skins down to his breech clout to scour himself clean with handfuls of grass dipped in snow water and ashes. As he did so he noticed several toes were discoloured under the filth.

"Agaratz, my feet."

Agaratz came over and looked intently at their condition.

"Uh-huh."

He beckoned the youth to sit on a stone while he went to his stores for remedies. Urrell watched him grind bulbs and herbs with a pebble on a flat stone, adding honey as a binder. This paste he applied to Urrell's toes, dabbing it on with a twist of moss, his touch as delicate as a girl's. Then, to Urrell's surprise, he said: "Eat," handing the stone pallet with the remainder of the paste to Urrell. It tasted vividly of its herbal ingredients, some flavours familiar to him, some strange, the honey making the whole palatable.

"Now cure," said Agaratz but not before intoning a low chant with his hands over Urrell's head, who noticed nothing but felt better, even a trifle euphoric.

"Agaratz, I know some plants for medicine. Tell me yours."

"I tell, but you not know." And he reeled off a litany of names in his own tongue, or perhaps the tongues of others, not one meaningful to Urrell.

"But you want to know?"

"Oh yes."

"I show."

To Urrell's delight, Agaratz, in expansive mode, fetched his pouches and bags of simples and laid out the contents on skins, naming them as he went, so that the strange names took on meaning. Urrell would remember them every one, as he knew he was meant to, and their uses.

"This garlic, for cure ills of neck, this iris of the rock for throat, this for sick stomach, this…" The list went on and on.

Many of the plants Urrell recognised without knowing their uses, so he remained keenly attentive to Agaratz's explanations.

When he was shown some brownish globules and lumps of a tinder-like substance he had to shake his head.

"Is juice of tree."

"Sap? Resin?"

"Uh-huh. Grow long, long way." Agaratz dropped a globule on a hot stone by the fire, incensing the air. Urrell sniffed, overcome by the perfume, pursuing its wisps with greedy nostrils, never able to suck in enough as it faded away.

Next a blackish fungus, unremarkable. "Is…"Agaratz sought a word "…like *perretjikac*. Few times grows. I know place. Too much kill."

At last a black piece of rind, from a nut, he explained, from *intchaur*. "We get from place of bear."

"Walnut! Green walnut rind."

"Yes, juice good for skin, for teeth."

"Will you show me these plants, Agaratz, in summer?"

"I show. Now I show you make pipe and music from…" the mischievous grin, "from *mammurak* tooth." Urrell's eyes followed his finger to where the tusk lay at the edge of the fire-glow. He thought he saw it quiver, then he looked closer and it appeared to writhe, its point directed straight at him. His hair prickled. *The hole under the overhang. The rank weeds.* He blacked out.

CHAPTER 18

Agaratz was holding Urrell sitting upright when he came to, shivering with chill but clear-minded. Nothing had changed in the cave. Piura dozed, snout to the fire; Rakrak crouched, head on paws, her eyes on him.

"You better now, Urrell."

Indeed he felt fine, cleansed, smooth. He had been through something, and was disconcerted to find everything the same. He glanced up the gallery, into its blackness: there was nothing to cause concern. Agaratz had dragged the tusk closer to the fire, that was all.

"You help, Urrell. First watch."

Agaratz marked off lengths and scraped and sawed with flints at a line he had traced round the tusk. Urrell could not see how the fossil-hard ivory would ever be cut. Every few strokes Agaratz was obliged to stop and sharpen his flints by knapping and flaking them. It was the most tedious of tasks.

"Now burn."

Urrell could only look enquiringly.

"Yes, burn. You see."

To prepare for this he placed resin globules on a hot stone. With a bone pick he smeared the result round his shallow cut, lit a spill from the fire and, as Urrell slowly turned the tusk, Agaratz burnt a ring round the ivory. The scorch did not go deep but he repeated the operation time and again, all that day and the next, scraping out any charring till the encircling cut began to show. Only when the incision was deemed deep enough after the two days' work did Agaratz lay the tusk across two stones and strike the weakened spot with a heavy flint hammer. He smote it so smartly the single blow snapped off the end of the tusk cleanly. Urrell applauded.

"Give me hand, Urrell." Urrell held his hand out. Agaratz measured the span of the lad's hand along the severed length, plus a half handspan more, stained the place and, apparently satisfied laid it aside for later. It was time to eat and rest.

Several more whole days were to be spent cutting off the span-and-a-half length of ivory, to be followed by burning and drilling out the core. Agaratz would leave the work aside a while, cook or do other chores, but always returned to it with a sort of relentlessness unfamiliar to Urrell. Under his direction, Urrell took turns at the task. All this time they remained confined to the cave.

"Now for ghost."

Urrell wondered but remained silent.

"*Mamu*, Urrell, *mamu* of *mammurak*."

He squinted down the now hollowed ivory tube, blew into it, and tapped it with a lop-sided antler implement that Urrell had noticed hanging up. To Urrell, quietly expectant, nothing seemed to be happening.

"Now catch *mamu*."

Agaratz marked five dots, with great care, along the piece of tusk, dots that reminded Urrell of the dots on the rock-face to which Agaratz had chanted on their way to the hoard of tusks.

Now began the drilling. A bone awl, tipped with flint, twirled between both palms, was aimed at the first dot on the length of ivory. As he drilled Agaratz kept up a low chant, again reminding Urrell of those dots on the cave wall which had sealed off whatever lay within the cavern from whoever dwelt without. There were no words to the chant. It was not speech as Urrell knew it, nor one of the tongues that Agaratz seemed to know but was sound from otherwhere. He was wondering if Rakrak or Piura understood it when it was his turn to twirl the awl.

His palms grew sore from his stints rubbing the awl back and forth. By the time Agaratz was satisfied with the holes and the sound they made when he blew down them, ten or twelve nights must have gone by. As each one was completed he poured honey in it and muttered, "For Mamu." Still Urrell waited to see what the outcome of this would be. Nothing Agaratz had undertaken so far occupied the adolescent's attention so wholeheartedly for so long.

Agaratz's final step was to fashion a bone insert and fit it painstakingly into the narrower end of the tube. When it was in place he signalled to Urrell that an important stage had been reached, and that they were to make ready.

They groomed themselves, Agaratz by combing his hair and mane, singeing the ends and attending to his nails, while Urrell scoured himself with tufts of grass and dried herbs dipped in snow water to scurf the grime from his body and counter the smell of smoke and sweat that hung around him. With a brand he burnt off his fuzz of beard and was pleased how soft his face felt from weeks under shelter. Indoor life and good rations had also let Rakrak, and especially Piura, grow sleeker in their winter coats.

A ceremony was about to begin. Urrell waited, his only experience being the coarse cavorting of hunters of his clan after a kill, and some swaying and stomping by younger women in time to chants and clapping, usually when the men were absent.

Agaratz stripped down to his loincloth. He placed the pipe in the centre of the floor with both hands, as though it were a great weight, signalled to Urrell to stoke the fire with bundles of twigs and kindling to light up the cave, and then began a slow dance round the tusk. His shaggy shoulders and hump, one leg ending in its cloven foot, danced in projected shadow on the cave walls before Urrell's mesmerised eyes, and those of the watching wolf and lion. As he jigged, Agaratz chanted an invocation, reciting a tale it seemed, in words that meant nothing to Urrell, yet which drew him in, part of the dance.

Then it happened: Urrell saw the shadow move along the cave wall where the hump-backed human's shape had been – huge, tusked – and he leapt up, casting off his jerkin and leggings to enter the dance in a mimickry he would never be able to recall later. He was outside himself. The chant seized him. How long he danced he would never know either. Old Mother appeared to him – *he saw her, as from afar, veiled in a haze that nothing he could do would disperse.*

She vanished as the trance lifted. He looked around. There crouched Agaratz, still in his loin-clout, by the fire, pipe to mouth, making sounds that Urrell felt he had always known yet had never heard till now.

"For thee, Urrell. Thy pipe."

He took it in both hands, like an offering, watched intently by Agaratz.

"You *mammurakan* now, Urrell."

He felt caught up in the sense of expectancy of a ceremony not yet completed. Something would be revealed. As he stood there undecided, still holding the tusk, warm in his hands, he felt it stir and wriggle as though trying to free itself from his hold.

He felt impelled to put the end to his mouth, as though the pipe knew its own way; his fingers found the holes of their own accord, and he blew. From the tusk came sounds as from a huge distance, bearing him along in his favourite dream of soaring through the air over all earthbound things. The sounds made him dance to exhaustion, round the hearth, round Agaratz, Piura and Rakrak, playing as he went, till he recovered and saw the circle his feet had left in the hard dirt of the cave floor.

CHAPTER 19

Provisions had dwindled in the weeks they had stayed indoors. Their bison meat was all but gone; much of the fish eaten. Nuts, roots, grains – things that Agaratz doled out as treats – were low too. The hungry weeks before spring were drawing in, while winter continued as raw as ever. Often wolves called, driven near the cliffs by scarcity. A fox had taken to sniffing at the bison hide across the cave entrance, enticed by food smells. To Urrell's surprise Agaratz lured the silvery creature close with scraps until it came daily and daily grew tamer, eating from his hand.

"Is lame, Urrell."

It was. Starving drove it to beg. Urrell, too, fed it, watched by Rakrak, head tilted. In his clan a poor scavenger like this would have been pelted with stones and bones – Agaratz's action delighted Urrell, and he recalled the young woman and her pet squirrel.

"Will it stay, like Rakrak?"

"When warmer, find mate, Urrell. Not for us."

That evening, as they gnawed bones, Agaratz said: "Go for fishes, Urrell. Piura stay. Rakrak come. Help."

"Help how?"

"Perhaps hunt."

"Hunt? Nothing to hunt now, Agaratz, is there?"

"Snow-deers perhaps."

Before dawn they set off, dragging a travois, Agaratz pulling, Urrell behind with spears and thongs, Rakrak scouting about, pleased to be out of the cave. They made good time over the hard snow. As Urrell had thought, game they saw none. The seasonal transhumance had swept all life away to milder parts. Yet here Agaratz survived. It puzzled Urrell and he had once asked him: "How did your people live here, all year, in the cold, without game?"

"Not so cold then, Urrell, big ice long way," and he had waved his hand into the distance, northwards.

They arrived at the foot of the bent fir of their fish cache. "Make fire, Urrell, I fetch fishes." He climbed up, despite his thick moccasins and the cold, gripping the bark till he reached branches and thereafter the ascent was easy. As Urrell rummaged out the hearth stones and assembled kindling from low-lying fir boughs, Agaratz dropped packages of frozen fish and scrambled down after them. They feasted with the abandon which comes from recent dearth of food, scrunching whole rudd, char, daice, roach, half-cooked, deliciously fresh, in the pine-scented air with the cooking smells from grilling fish eddying round them. Rakrak joined in the meal. Not another creature in their empty universe seemed to notice them as they lay back finally, glutted and content. They rested a long while like that till it was time to pack the travois with bundles of fish for the return journey. Before they left, Agaratz sneaked off to look at their fishing hole, now frozen over but clearly visible. He seemed to commune with it. Urrell wondered if he was performing some private ceremony, as he did so often to mark events and places according to a calendar of his own.

They made such good time back, taking turns to pull the travois, that the fire was still warm when they arrived, with Piura huddled by it. When she rose to greet them, stiff from age and inertia, Urrell grabbed her head and nuzzled her, *his lioness, Piura*. Then she and Rakrak touched muzzles.

Soon the fox appeared, peeking round the hide. It came half way in for a fish, only to scuttle away with its prize. Urrell looked out to see which way it went: up-gulch. There would be its den, its own place, to eat at leisure, later to raise cubs.

With food assured, Agaratz set to carving lengths of tusk into disks, drilling and honing them to make necklaces and ornaments, while Urrell practised on his flute, between helping, perfecting melodies that Agaratz hummed to him. He was discovering a skill in himself revealed by the mammoth flute, by Agaratz, which allowed his spirit to soar and wander. Agaratz slyly approved. Now he, Urrell, was impressing his master.

"Play *mammurak*, Urrell."

"*Mammurak?* How, Agaratz?"

Agaratz laid down what he was polishing by the light of a resin torch stuck in a cleft overhead. He stood, circled and began a low buzzing sound, his slow gyrations throwing a shadow on the cave wall that, to Urrell's eyes, grew and shrank by turns. The chant rose, the gyrations went faster, the shadows heightened and shifted, while in Urrell's grasp his flute felt warm, a prelude to something happening. All a-quiver he waited. The tusk seemed to move – he could not be sure – and with a sort of elation he joined Agaratz. Putting the flute to his lips, he discovered sounds coming from it that were not his own, though his breath blew them, his fingers formed them. They matched and underscored the chanting of Agaratz as it rose into animal trumpetings, snarls, gurglings, expanding a line of music unbidden by the flautist whose role appeared to be to jig to the sound and blow into the instrument, piper and pipe one thing. He was one thing too with Agaratz. He would remember little of that night when he danced the mammoth before the attentive eyes of wolf and lion, Piura growling low, under her breath, as a lion might in the presence of so mighty a beast.

They danced and made music to exhaustion, slept where they fell and when Urrell woke Agaratz was already at work carving.

120

The foxy glint in those yellow eyes told Urrell he had travelled somewhere only Agaratz knew. He had crossed – been led across – a boundary.

"You play *mammurak*, Urrell. Mammoth now" – he pointed at the pipe – "in there."

Never before had Agaratz said anything like that. Now he, Urrell, the lone youth, could summon the mammoths.

Old Mother, would that she had been there.

CHAPTER 20

In a lull in the weather, a hint of spring softening the air, Agaratz said in his sudden manner: "Go dance *mammurak.*"

"Go where, Agaratz?"

"In *mammurak* cave, Urrell. You take flute."

"Ah."

There would be no point in asking more. In his own time, Agaratz would lead the way.

It was two nights later when he did, as though a propitious moment had arrived, noticeable only to him.

Agaratz took torches for them both. From his collecton of pouches and bags he gathered an antler with a hole drilled in the shank. This he hung with a thong from his belt. He also produced a deer thigh-bone drilled to make a pipe, stuffed it into a belt pouch with several bark boxes that Urrell knew he used to store herbs and dried fungus for his medical potions and poultices. They donned heavy outer garments, Agaratz gathered embers into a fire-box and off they went, both Piura and Rakrak of the party. Even the lame fox tagged along for a while.

They turned left, hugging the cliff, the direction whence Urrell had come that first day. He expected a long march and determined not to forget a single landmark, memorising each tree, jut, fissure. This time he would not be left facing blank rock. Even so, alert as he was, Urrell was to be confounded when Agaratz vanished into the cliff a few paces ahead of him.

Look as he might, Urrell could not see where Agaratz had gone. Low brush grew thick at the cliff foot, which he shoved aside to look for an opening, but there was only a long vertical crevice little wider than a hand's span, certainly not big enough to disappear into. He was wavering there, scanning the cliff in the dark, when a faint, teasing tune seemed to come from the rock, through the crevice, mocking him for not finding a way in.

He listened, wondering if he had really heard the elfin sounds. They paused then began again, apparently from lower down where the crevice widened enough to allow nothing much bigger than a fox to get in. Into this he was meant to crawl?

The rank weeds. The women far down in the meadow.

He brushed aside his boyish terrors. Headfirst he wriggled into total darkness, the flute music egging him on – Agaratz must be close ahead – comforted by Rakrak creeping behind him. Piura, too big, would wait outside. On his elbows he slithered and dragged himself forward along the muddy tunnel as the music drew nearer. Not far and he shot into a torch-lit chamber where Agaratz crouched playing his deer-bone flute, absorbed in his music-making, a shaggy figure in a pool of light, oblivious to all else. Rakrak followed Urrell, stood up and shook herself, breaking Agaratz's absorption.

"Ah, Urrell."

Urrell hesitated. He felt an intruder. Agaratz, mud-free and dry, compared with Urrell's muddy elbows and leggings, and Rakrak's mud-caked paws and belly, seemed to be the denizen of this place into which they had blundered from the outside world.

Agaratz resumed his playing. As Urrell's eyes adapted to the torchlight he looked eagerly round the chamber walls for engravings and paintings: they were blank. Without stopping his music, Agaratz signalled Urrell to come and squat in front of him, in the light. Rakrak followed, sat on her hunkers, looking at both. The piping went on, a monotony of notes, sequences, pre-melodic tones, thin whistling sounds from the deer-bone flute that Urrell felt no desire to join.

This went on a good while, part of something Urrell felt would be revealed. Finally Agaratz rose, freed one hand from the pipe without ceasing to play, unhitched the antler on its thong from his belt and before the watching eyes of youth and wolf whirled it in time to his playing as he began a slow, stomping dance round the torch, stirring the air so that his shadow flickered on the smooth walls of the chamber. The performance went on and on till the torch began to gutter. Urrell followed Agaratz's look and nod to his pouch and took out a new torch, which he lit from the stump of the dying one, all this without Agaratz stopping playing, dancing and whirling the antler. He evidently set store on ceaseless movement and music. Why, Urrell no more knew than how Agaratz had managed to vanish into the cave and appear in it dry and mud-free.

Still the dance went on, never gathering tempo, almost stately, Agaratz pivoting on his goat foot, shaggy shoulders bare of tunic, which he had laid by his pouch with his outer garments. Urrell seldom saw him so lightly clad.

Then, so suddenly that Urrell, lulled by the monotony, scarcely had time to notice, Agaratz was back to his squatting position and the music had stopped, though it seemed to float on in the air. This time Agaratz opened his pouch himself. From bark boxes he took contents, like jerked meat but which Urrell saw was dried fungus.

"Chew, Urrell."

"For *mammurak?*"

"*Mammuraperritxac*, Urrell. Eat. Good."

It did not taste bad, just a little acrid, and tough. These words were the nearest to an explanation Agaratz had ever come, perhaps because no words existed to say what he wanted, or none that Urrell knew.

Urrell chewed and swallowed the woody fragments. They roughened his throat.

This done, Agaratz produced bundles of dried herbs, roots and seeds. These too were chewed small and swallowed. Although Agaratz ate his share, Urrell surmised that he did so more to encourage him, Urrell, than from any need of his own.

After a short pause, he said: "Now blow, Urrell."

Urrell, on his mammoth-tusk flute, blew as bidden. He started a melody of his own, waveringly, till Agaratz joined in, picked up the line of music and expanded it, leading Urrell on in ever greater confidence as he started to move in time to his own playing round Agaratz and Rakrak, round the torch and its pool of light. He noticed the resinous smell of the torch as never before, sniffing with delight. Crevices, knurrs, flaking patches on the half-lit cave walls leapt out; every hair on Rakrak's coat grew discernible; pouch and garments revealed creases made by the identity of their user and wearer. He felt he could touch his music in his head.

Slowly this clarity blurred. No longer were Agaratz and Rakrak so present.

His mind drifted to the shelter under the overhang, huddled women; Blueface; the brook; rubbish where he scavenged; Old Mother looking up, her eyes blinking through smoke, gone before he could speak; his trip over the moors; hawks; the bison with the trapped hoof. When he came to the present he felt giddy, ill, retching as he jigged round, unable to play and following only Agaratz's music.

New visions started up – dim distances, lakes and forests, herds of bison and horses stretching to the horizon, groups of aurochs, musk-oxen, a giant bear, followed by beasts he had never seen, with shaggy fur, stripes, scales, strange horns and snouts, giant fangs. They slank into his vision and back out into oblivion. None of this frightened him. He felt – intensely – that this was leading somewhere.

By now exhaustion was taking over. His gyrations dwindled until he sank to the floor, accompanied by Rakrak's whimpers of concern. He could not see her clearly, unable to focus his eyes, but felt her fur and warmth, fondled her ears and was soothed.

This was the prelude to another phase. He felt better but weak. Lights in his head shifted and shone with the phosphorescent gleam of rotten wood, the elf-light he had sometimes found in the forest. It seemed to get into his mind's eye. He was rising shakily, bidden on by Agaratz's incessant playing, when he saw them – there, in front of his eyes, in single file, at a slow loping stride of their own, came the mammoths. They were perfectly clear on the cave wall, alive. He stopped dead in his excitement.

"*Mammurakan, mammurakan*, Agaratz, *mammurakan!*" He could only croak the words, his voice hoarsened by the fungus and roots chewed, retching, slipping into Agaratz's language as the only one fit for such an event.

Agaratz's response was to continue playing while he rummaged in his pouch with one hand. He drew out pieces of charcoal.

"Draw, Urrell, draw *mammurakan.*"

Impelled by Agaratz, who for once showed urgency, Urrell guessed exactly what to do. The music from Agaratz grew wilder, longing, mournful as Urrell drew the outlines of the mammoths with long, sure strokes, seizing their movements, using excrescences to emphasise here a shoulder, there a domed head, instinct with an artistry he could never have explained. He drew at speed. The column strode by on the stone for him. Its lead animal, an old cow, watched him with her small, reddened eye. As he caught her oblique glance, for the time of a glimpse it turned golden, like Agaratz's, then back to ill-tempered ochre – he might have imagined it but he knew he had not. He drew till the frieze extended across the lit surface of the wall to the edge where darkness began and the beasts filed away into the mountain. His frenzy of drawing only stopped when Agaratz's piping ceased.

He subsided to the floor.

"Now I paint, Urrell."

Holding a lump of greasy blacking, and balancing on his club shank with the delicacy of a bird, Agaratz underscored Urrell's outlines, picked out features, touched in the shaggy flanks, hinted at the sweep of tusks, till the mammoths stood out in the torchlight.

With reddle he doodled a deer and a pony, beneath the frieze, neither larger than a man's hand, both ones Urrell recognised – animals from long ago, before he had met Agaratz.

"Agaratz, how do you know that deer, that horse?"

But already Agaratz was gathering up their things to leave.

Old Mother, were you that lead cow?

CHAPTER 21

When Urrell revived he was deep in the pine-needle and bracken litter of home cave, huddled with Rakrak. Instantly wakeful he expected the torchlight, the mammoth frieze he had drawn, but as instantly knew he was mistaken. Wrapped in a pelt, he lay with Rakrak's forepaws solicitously on him, as though she had been waiting for him to come round. A strong smell of body sweat issued from the fur wrapping when he stood up, teetering on the springy litter. He felt thin, feeble, and could not understand why he was in such a state at all.

He parted the hangings of the alcove. Agaratz was at his usual place, by the fire, carving by the light of a torch, with Piura curled on some old furs as near the embers as she could without singeing herself. The air of the main cave felt chill after the sweaty wrap in the alcove.

"Ho, Urrell. Good. You much sick. Now better."

It was a longish speech for Agaratz, yet did not reveal why he had been ill, how he had got out of the mammoth cave or back home. He knew then, and he knew firmly, that the mammoth cave had not been an illusion, one of Agaratz's tricks: it was graven in his mind. Nothing Agaratz did was going to fool him this time. With a determination that surprised him, he decided there and then to put the matter out of his mind, away from Agaratz's reach, so that later, when he was better, he would return alone and find the cave, squirm back in and rediscover his frieze, his very own frieze. Agaratz would not foil him this time.

"Eat, Urrell."

He shuffled to the fire, still in his pelt wrap, his legs trembly, body shivery, but his mind unwontedly clear and bright.

Hot venison lay on the slab. Agaratz had hunted while he lay comatose.

He wondered how long he had lain thus. Instead of asking he bit into a hunk of meat and with it chewed a whole head of garlic. There were onions and scallion bulbs laid out too as though expecting his arrival. The concert of flavours held his full attention. Some nuts and seeds, autumn's last offerings, were also set out. He munched on, deliberately, methodically, making up for lost time to fill out the hollows in his body. No thoughts of mammoths, caves, fungus-food or wild dances entered his mind, or if any did they were dismissed as fast as they came.

No, this time Agaratz would not learn of his resolve to retrace his steps.

On a frame he saw his leggings, jerkin, skins and even moccassins hanging where Agaratz must have put them when he had fallen ill. They were the same old worn and greasy things, creased with use. However, he realised there was something amiss with them; not a trace of the mud he had wriggled through in that funnel to the rock chamber remained…

While Urrell devoured his food, half out of his pelt by the fire, Agaratz left the cave. When the bison hide was lifted, Urrell could see the snow was half gone – during his sickness winter had moved into the short spring of the north. How long must he have lain senseless since that foray to the mammoth cave?

Agaratz returned with a pouchful of mushy snow.

"Urrell, now need clean. You stand."

He stood, two handspans taller than Agaratz, a lanky youth turning into a man.

Agaratz nodded, approvingly. Then with handfuls of snow and

tufts of fern and dried grass he scoured Urrell's flinching body from top to bottom. There was no let up. With a woman's skill he scrubbed away a winter's grease and dander, enlivening Urrell's blood till he glowed.

"Now dress, Urrell."

Instead of his old leathers Agaratz handed him a new set of garments, cut and sewn while he had been unconscious – a tunic, kirtle, leggings, cap, moccassins – all assembled and adorned here and there with quills and tassles, as for a special occasion. He donned his outfit, its soft inner leather pleasurable on his newly scoured skin, a suit of clothes made to mark a turning point in his life in the unspoken scheme of things by which Agaratz lived.

Within days Urrell's strength returned. They went on brief outings, mainly to gather green stuff, shoots of herbs, the first bulbils of the allium plants that throve in pockets of earth where the snow first melted away. Overhead, skeins of geese honked on their way to elsewhere. Soon herds of bison, horses, flocks of deer and wild sheep would pour back over the plains for the summer grazing, calving and plenty. Their main occupation was carving. Agaratz seemed in haste to make as many necklets, pierced disks, antler points as time allowed. He decorated shoulder blades, femurs, antlers, horns with scenes and designs from a world unknown to Urrell: lion and deer entwined, bison running with aurochs, strange flightless fowl sometimes, bears and tigers, and creatures that Urrell had never heard tell of, even in the fearful tales recited by tribelets in those winter quarters by the sleety sea. When asked, Agaratz gave them names that meant nothing to Urrell. They might have been drawn from a bestiary of another time, known only to his mentor.

One evening, when Agaratz took his pipe and played, Urrell looked about for his mammoth flute, inwardly surprised for not having given it a moment's thought all these days since his illness, as though it had been a figment of the mind, or part of a mammoth dream. He began to look for it along the ledges, under piles of objects heaped against cave walls, like a dreamer pursuing something forever just out of reach, a finger's length ahead of his clawing grasp, beyond the tip of recollection. While he was searching thus, in mounting exasperation and panic, he distinctly heard Agaratz play the notes of the mammoth dance. He glanced at Agaratz, to be met with that teasing sidelong look, the yellow eye mischievously mocking, akin to the glance of the lead cow in the frieze he had drawn. Then the notes were gone and Agaratz was looking at him.

"Now you play, Urrell."

"No pipe, Agaratz."

"Pipe with tusk."

And there it lay, among lengths of unwrought ivory, jostling its kind.

And there along its length was a line of mammoths that Agaratz had etched for him, so delicately, each animal no bigger than a thumbnail, yet perfect. At their head, the cow led. Urrell fondled the flute, handled its shape, blew into it gently to recapture his music but although it gave him notes, played true, made music, the flute would not surrender to him that wild dance which he knew he would only ever recapture in the mammoth cave.

CHAPTER 22

Their winter stores were now truly low, Piura's lean flanks tokens of scarcity, Rakrak's quiet hunger a reproach. Even the lame fox no longer visited. Hunger had driven Urrell one day to scratch about in Agaratz's pouches for remnants of stores while their owner was out foraging. In one he came across several handfuls of grain, dried hard as grit, which it occurred to him to kibble with a pebble on a slab of stone. While he was doing this some water spilt over the meal. He scraped it up with a bone flake into pellets the size of thrushes' eggs which he ranged on the slab. As he had often parched and roasted nuts, he placed his doughy lumps in the embers where they hissed a little before giving off a most savoury aroma. He was engrossed in doing this when Agaratz returned. A smell of baking dough hung in the air.

Urrell's activity gripped Agaratz's attention. No cat watched a fledgling more keenly than Agaratz followed Urrell's demonstration of how he had ground the grain and mixed it with water before baking the result. He pulled a lump out of the fire and tossed it from hand to hand, blowing on it till it cooled enough to be broken open, and gave half to Agaratz. They bit into the charred crust and into the moist, doughy centre with delectation.

"You make new food, Urrell. Good, good."

There was admiration in Agaratz's voice. Urrell felt a new pride that he had been able to show something to his all-knowing mentor. They ate all that batch and then emptied every bag and pouch down to the last dusty seed to make enough cakes so that Rakrak and Piura could join in feasting on this manna of Urrell's devising. It would be another day he never, ever, would forget.

"Agaratz, we hunt soon? Herds must be coming?"

"Yes, we go. But careful. Hunters follow herds."

Urrell remembered the hostile group and Agaratz's feat when he had saved Rakrak from their spears. His wariness must stem from many such encounters over the seasons as Agaratz had struggled to survive on his own.

"Best set traps, Urrell."

"Traps?"

"Traps. Like hunters use for bison. I make; you see."

The hint of a grin said, 'You may make dough-balls, but I can do things you know nothing about.'

Agaratz went out again on an errand linked in some way with these intended traps.

Soon after, Urrell went out too. Snow remained in pockets in the lee of cliffs, in dells among the trees, but everywhere else plants grew, freed from the grip of ice, while still the geese honked overhead on their own travels to lakes beyond the land of mammoths. Youth and wolf, bodies skinny from winter, scoured woods and plains for anything edible.

Urrell saw far out on the prairie a dark tide of advancing bison, the harbingers of the herds that would be following as the snow fled. No lone hunter could hope to spear one in such a dense mass of beasts. Only when groups broke off to browse in the woods might there be chances. Till then, his best hope was small game rendered unwary by interest in mating.

They entered the fir-line, Urrell listening for the clucking and crowing of big fowl displaying in leks, favourite spots where cocks strutted to attract their hens. With luck he might down one with a shot from his stone-thrower. When he found such a lek, hens camouflaged among the herbage clucked and flew off, sending up a puff of wings, alerting the two capercaillie-sized cocks they had been admiring as they jousted in their brilliant spring plumage. A fine roast lost. Later, he could return to snare one of the performers with springes that Agaratz wove with such skill from splints and horse-hair twine.

In a wide arc through the woods Urrell and his wolf trotted on, noting tracks of deer, hearing wildcat snarl, glimpsing game down glades well out of spear-cast. By a brook Urrell found cresses; Rakrak snapped at mice and froglets. Fingerling trout, gudgeon and other small fry swam abundantly in the clear water, small fare but good if they could be caught. Urrell remembered his boyhood skills and followed the brook till he came to what he wanted, a pool large enough to harbour good-sized fish yet shallow enough to empty by digging an outlet. Rakrak entered into the fun, scratching with gusto, till between them they had lowered the level of the water enough to strand fish.

Urrell beat the water with a switch to drive them into puddles where Rakrak splashed about catching as many as she could, gulping them whole, while Urrell scooped more out for himself and threw them on the strand until he had enough bigger ones to fill a pouch and tiddlers to chew raw there and then.

They were noisily engaged in this, oblivious to everything, when instinct warned man and wolf to fall silent and turn: standing on the bank overlooking the pool were two hunters, whether hostile or not Urrell was never to know for, with the certainty that precedes thought, he hissed, "Zass, Rakrak," and the wolf was up the bank and at the men before their astonishment could turn into fleeing legs, a wolf's fangs at their heels.

Nothing like this had ever happened to them and they fled, not knowing that Rakrak chased them more in fun than in anger.

Enough it would be for the legend of the fisherboy and his wolf to spread round campfires, and grow in the telling, for many seasons to come.

On their return to the cave Agaratz was already back, the object of his errand visible in the pile of osiers that he had been out to cut. Urrell's fishes and cresses were welcome, but Agaratz listened with unwonted intentness to Urrell's account of the two hunters and their discomfiture.

"Bad mens." He did not elaborate. "Now I show how to make traps."

Round a framework bound with thongs he wove osiers into a wickerwork box. The withies, being last year's growth, were tough yet supple. Agaratz left a gap in the top, a sort of slot, where Urrell surmised that an animal's hoof would snag, as the wounded bison's hoof had been tangled when he first met Agaratz. But he still did not see how such a device could help to secure prey.

In two days they had made four between them.

"Agaratz, why not use bane on spears?"

"Not make now. Only when *perretarrec* ready."

During a lull in their activities, Agaratz downed his carving tools and said, as though he had mulled over a decision, "Urrell, I show you *poodooec.*"

Agaratz selected several spears from his arsenal, ones Urrell had never seen him use. They were blackened with age.

With them they descended into the gulch. Against a spot on the cliff face Agaratz up-ended a half rotten log and chipped a blaze on it. "That man," he explained.

Urrell must have looked mystified.

"Bad man. Soon come bad mans, Urrell. You need *poodooec* for their *poodooec.*"

They went back about forty paces. Agaratz chose a spear,

weighed it, eyed the mark and in one smooth movement cast it straight at the blaze.

"Now you, Urrell."

He did as bidden, chose a spear, weighed it, took his aim and with all his young hunter's skill threw it at the log. It struck the cliff half an arm's length from the mark, not a bad shot at that range, it seemed to Urrell.

"Not *poodooec,* Urrell. You look."

This time Agaratz picked one with a series of deer engraved in a spiral down the shaft, so blackened and worn as to be shadowy. Urrell noticed that Agaratz took this one with his left hand. He watched as Agaratz weighed the weapon and appeared to think at it for a few instants before he lofted it and as smoothly as with the previous one, but left-handledly this time, sent it flying true to the blaze where it struck and held beside the first. Urrell could not retain an 'ah' of admiration.

Urrell's next try went closer but he knew it was skill, not whatever Agaratz called *poodooec,* that had guided his arm.

"Urrell, *think* bad man, *think poodooec,* and not miss."

He handed the next javelin to Urrell and stood behind him with his fingers on the butt, as though to help propel the missile. "Now throw." The javelin quivered in Urrell's grasp as, with absolute certainty, he lofted it, with Agaratz moving in unison, his arm working with a will of its own, and sent it flying with total accuracy at the target where it lodged alongside Agaratz's two.

"See, Urrell – *poodooec.*"

They retrieved the spears and tried again. And after that again and again. Whatever his hits, Urrell knew they were luck or skill but never whatever it was that Agaratz called *poodooec.* Not once did the shaft quiver again for him nor did he sense that feeling of foregone accuracy he had had in the throw under Agaratz's guidance.

If Agaratz felt disappointment in his disciple he did not show it whereas Urrell allowed frustration to surface, for the first time since he had known Agaratz. This certainty of aim that the crookback's powerful shoulders appeared to transmit to the javelin, to a stone thrown by Agaratz if he chose to, lay just beyond Urrell's reach. Once more he sensed that it had something of dreams about it, of a knowing that lay just beyond his touch.

CHAPTER 23

With the lengthening days, game returned by land and air, filling the sky and woods with sounds and calls. The air grew scented. Insects teemed so that each stride roused clouds of grasshoppers and flies from the grass. Worst were the swirls of gnats.

Into this world Urrell and Rakrak roamed, sometimes overnighting in simple bivouacs against a tree. However far he went Urrell never wandered beyond sight of the scarpment that was now home to him. In it somewhere strode his mammoths, forever marching into the mountain. Strive as he might he could not find their entrance. Spring seemed to have wiped out the memory of winter. Each cleft and cave he explored led nowhere. His careful mind-set of what the entrance looked like fitted nothing he found. In his searching he wandered as far as the cliff hollow where he had eaten with Agaratz that day they first met. He approached warily, as Agaratz had done, but nothing stirred in the undergrowth or among the saplings that looked more grown than he would have expected. He had to push his way through them into the hollow. Inside nothing showed signs of occupation by man or beast. The ledge where Agaratz had kept food, as though in anticipation of his coming, lay bare and it was hard to believe that here the hunchback had amused a quailing boy with animal mimickry and handstands. He remembered the climbing pole Agaratz had thrown back into the undergrowth and looked for it. Nothing remained amid the well-grown young trees. Rakrak entered into the fun, fossicking about for whatever it might be her master sought.

"Gone, Rakrak, all gone."

Then, on a sudden resolve, he set off further along the cliffs, to the spot where he had watched the bison, the hunters and had come face to face with Agaratz.

The fir trees were much as he remembered them, boughs sweeping to the ground, each huge tree big enough to hide a tribe under its skirts. Beyond the firs, however, the glade where he had spied on the hunters was now so overgrown that he would have been hard placed to see them, and might have blundered into them. He looked for the spot where in his hunger he had gnawn the cast-off bones from the hunters' meal. A return of his boyhood fear held him back. The glade was strangely silent, not a bird singing or even a butterfly fluttering past. He looked at Rakrak but she remained unconcerned, so he gathered his courage and moved out of the firs, as he had that time, to the spot where the bones had lain scattered. No sign of the hunters' hearth remained nor the stone on which they had sketched the bison.

A coldness hung over the spot. Of a sudden Urrell picked up his spears and set off at a fast lope into the firs towards home cave, hastening his pace as he went, feeling pursued. Rakrak trotted by him.

… below him he saw once more the combe, the women berry-picking…

He ran and ran on the springy pine-needle floor of the forest till his breath gave out. Only when familiar sights appeared did he slow.

When youth and wolf arrived at the cave it was empty and cold, the fire out. Urrell felt the ashes – they were dead. Piura was nowhere to be seen. Neatly stacked nearby were two more wickerwork traps. It was as though Agaratz, in his sly humour, had made them to mock Urrell's trip into the past. Piura, with the better weather, had perhaps ventured out too. Not for a long time had Urrell felt so lonely.

He looked for his flute, found it and played a little, half solace, half the nagging wish to recapture the music of that night in the mammoth cave. In it lay the key to finding the elusive place itself. His flute played true, entering into his mood, its notes floating in the cave and drifting into its depths, drawn to the black chasm where the Old Mens dwelt with their hoard of tusks. Normally he never thought of the pit. He knew it was cut off from him by the red dots and the engravings, placed there to seal its entrance from the outer world, yet the flute was hearkening back to its origins, trying to draw him with it. He swayed as he played, stomping slowly round the dead hearth. In the deepening gloom the outer mouth of the cave showed lighter against the sky. His excitement grew, he felt he was recapturing the half-remembered dream-like night when the mammoths came to him. The music drew from the cavern's depths a breath of air as cold as off an icepatch in summer. Rakrak whimpered. The flute distinctly moved just as a figure appeared against the cave entrance and startled Urrell into silence. It was Agaratz, back from the hunt.

"Ha, Urrell, play flute. Good."

How much he had heard, Urrell could not know. But the cold vanished. In one hand Agaratz held two wildfowl by the neck and in the other his weapons and a pouchful of something he handled with care.

"Eggs, Urrell."

He had found clutches of wildfowl eggs, beautifully speckled, and caught two of the parent birds as they brooded.

"Light fire, Urrell. Time we eat."

"Where is Piura?"

"Piura here soon."

Agaratz asked nothing about Urrell's adventures, leaving Urrell almost sure that in some way he knew, however much Urrell practised blanking off his mind.

"Agaratz, where did you hunt these?"

"By river. Soon we go. Much eggs and fishes."

The prospect of a joint hunting trip calmed Urrell's mind. He twirled the fire-stick till the tinder smouldered, glowed and lit a twist of grass. In a trice the fire was ablaze. Only then, in the glow, did he look closely at Agaratz's traps: the bindings were twine, exactly like that given him by Old Mother with her necklace and whose retting process she had taught him and he in turn had described to Agaratz. It had been something Agaratz had seemed to value and not to know. The boy had felt proud. Now he saw that Agaratz must have known all along and this was his way of saying so.

They roasted both fowl and ate them with Rakrak. Agaratz set aside some 'for Piura'. It was a feast. The eggs they cracked and ate raw or, if part-hatched, buried in embers and baked. They were on these when Piura crept in, exhausted from her sortie, and slumped by the fire. Agaratz fed her. She must have gone far, on her old legs.

The two men finished off with green shoots, bulbs, herbs and a remnant of honey.

"Why the traps, Agaratz?"

"Help catch bison."

"Are we going bison-hunting alone?"

"Only for one, for pelt and meat. Rakrak wolfs want meat."

At the sound of her name, Rakrak cocked her ears.

Urrell's fear that Rakrak, a fully-grown she-wolf, might rejoin her pack or seek a mate resurfaced.

"Will Rakrak come?"

"Yes, she hunt bison, like wolf."

"But she may run off with the wolves."

"She stay. I tell her. She now Urrell's wolf. Tomorrow go river, Urrell. I show you go on water."

The bison hunt was for later.

Their expedition was to be a long one, to judge by Agaratz's preparations. They were to take their travois, laden with spears, fishing lines, fire-making things, bags and pouches. He produced axes and adzes Urrell had not seen before. They were made from big flakes of the beautiful flint that Agaratz called *sakarrik*.

Next day, as they followed the now familiar route across the grasslands, Urrell could see the vast herds of game moving north; and in their wake the beasts that preyed on laggards, calves and strays. Overhead circled vultures and eagles, ravens and crows.

Not far from the herds, as both of them knew, travelled bands of hunters, ahead of their women and children, as they followed the yearly tide of animals to the summer grazings. Those must be the 'bad mens' Agaratz was wary of.

Rakrak's senses helped. She warned of big cats before they got close and her presence frightened off inquisitive predators more than once. Piura, bringing up the rear, must have disconcerted them even more. The long-haired lions that followed the herds cocked their heads above the grass as they passed, Agaratz amusing himself addressing them in Piura-talk, in which Piura joined, teasing them till they got up and ambled grouchily away from the man-wolf-lion circus going past.

At the river, Agaratz turned upstream. Full of meltwater the river ran dark and smooth between its banks, high into the rushes where waterfowl nested and Agaratz and Urrell had splashed to retrieve ducks brought down in their previous hunt. This time Agaratz was intent on other things.

He stopped at a small creek sheltered by birch and sallow carr.

Rushes grew taller here than lower downstream. Agaratz downed pouches, and Urrell the travois. Agaratz plainly knew the spot. Hearth stones were dragged from the bushes, a fire lit and food was soon cooking. While Urrell handled this task Agaratz reconnoitred the banks and came back with duck eggs and freshwater mussels.

Placed on embers, the mussels opened. The iridescence of their mother-of-pearl insides delighted Urrell. In one he found a small pearl and showed it to Agaratz, who held it delicately, rolling it between finger and thumb and naming it in his own language, then returned it with an appreciative nod.

"You keep, Urrell. Girls like."

He now surprised Urrell yet again. From a small wallet he took out several fish-hooks carved from the very mother-of-pearl Urrell had just been admiring in the mussel shells. With the hooks went fishing lines plaited from the long hair of horses' tails.

"For to fish, Urrell. But first go on water."

He showed what he meant – half afloat, half beached among the sallows, lay a thing Urrell had never seen before: a construction of poles and logs lashed together with thongs and strips of bast. It was his first view of a raft.

Agaratz set to with Urrell dragging more, drier logs from the woods around and when he had as many as he thought needful he showed Urrell how to cut last year's dry reeds with a flint knife and bundle them. They only stopped to have time to fish for supper, using mussel for bait, and soon had as much as they cared to bake or eat raw and share with Rakrak and Piura. The cooking smells attracted a fox which came and sat with them for its share, reminding Urrell of the lame one they had befriended that winter. It seemed to know Agaratz who treated it, as he often did other animals, with humorous familiarity. He had shown the same insight when he had collected Rakrak from her pack. Like *poodooec,* this ability to empathise with the animal world was something Urrell knew he could never match.

"Tomorrow, make float. Now sleep, Urrell."

The next few days they spent cutting and adzing logs to renew rotten parts of the raft. Using withies they bound in the new poles till the raft met Agaratz's satisfaction. Then he showed Urrell the purpose of the bundles of reeds by lashing them round the outer edge of the craft, as floats and fenders. Once pushed and shoved into the water of the creek it floated high and true. They moored it to a tree and went off to fish for supper, as Agaratz intended to go afloat next day. Whither they were going he did not say but Urrell guessed an egg-hunt was intended.

During the night a panther or lion snuffled round the camp, attracted perhaps by Piura's presence. They added dry sticks to the fire to make a blaze, Agaratz made noises and the beast slank off.

They cast off early, Rakrak a little hard to coax aboard but once aship finding the adventure to her taste. Only Piura would not budge. They left her on the shore, Agaratz soothing her with promises to pick up her up on the return journey, or so he explained to Urrell. He left her a pile of food, knowing a lion will hang around a supply till it is eaten before moving off.

Agaratz had cut two long poles. With one he punted the raft into the stream while Urrell tried with the other. It was some time before he got the knack and assisted Agaratz against the current. It was very slow going. Late in the day Agaratz steered the raft into an inlet among giant trees and tied up. Blackened stones attested to regular use of the spot for campfires. While Agaratz fished, Urrell and Rakrak explored the woods. They saw the bark of saplings frayed where stags rubbed their antlers and heard larger beasts crashing about in the depths of the woods. Wild strawberries were ripening. On their way back, Rakrak darted into the bracken and came out with a fawn in her jaws. She had killed it cleanly and brought it still warm to Urrell. He patted her head and they quickened their pace back, Rakrak bearing her prey.

At the camp Agaratz was already baking fish and opening mussels. He had also caught some crayfish by hand. Despite Agaratz's pleas of a cub beseeching its mother for food, Rakrak would not yield her fawn to him, but took it to Urrell.

"See, your wolf, Urrell."

They dined off the tenderest of venison, baked fishes, mussels, crayfish and strawberries by the mouthful.

It was the fat time of year, when food abounded, furs grew sleek, young were born and nestlings flew. Day merged into day.

"Tomorrow be at island, Urrell."

The line of cliffs towards which they were slowly propelling their craft must have been an outlier, thought Urrell, of their home escarpment, or perhaps its continuation as it swung in a wide loop. What he could not guess was how the river got through the barrier.

Later next day this grew clearer as they worked their way round a long bend in the river and the cliffs came into sight. There was a gap parted by a solitary crag with a dark patch on it. The cliff line continued into the distance until it merged with the horizon. Only ahead, both sides of the crag, were there breaks through which the current ran.

"Egg place," said Agaratz, nodding at the crag round which wheeled thousands of water fowl, more than Urrell had ever seen in one place, even by the sea. He saw now that the dark patch was the gape of an immense cavern.

The current, forced through narrows, ran strongly, twisting and swinging the raft, which took all Agaratz's strength and skill to edge slowly into the lee of the crag where eddies swirled. Rakrak cowered amidships, ears flat. Their poles were finding increasing depth while the current snatched at them with a malice of its own.

"Now, Urrell, now," and with a supreme effort both drove the raft under the lee of the rocks into a pool of still water with a little shingle beach, hidden from view even from half a spear's cast away. Agaratz jumped ashore and pulled the raft up, Urrell and Rakrak only too happy to follow. Evidently Agaratz knew the spot and exactly what to do. Urrell's legs trembled as he stood on the shingle. He felt queasy from the effort and tension and it was a while before he could do much, leaving the unloading of the raft to Agaratz who piled such contents as they had higher up the shingle and manhandled the raft above the water-line.

"Now go for eggs," he said.

He knew his way up the wet, black rocks, white on top from guano. Overhead sea and waterfowl wheeled and squawked at the intruders. Nests were everywhere.

As they climbed Urrell was mightily surprised to find the birds quieten rather than grow noisier. It was as though they recognised Agaratz or he possessed some power over them or they knew he was no threat, or all three. Despite the plentifulness of eggs, the strain and hazardousness of the voyage by raft to collect them seemed to Urrell to be disproportionate. Could they be the sole purpose of the trip? He waited to learn what it might be.

His first surprise came at the manner Agaratz collected eggs on the way up. He took one egg only per nest, groping under the unresisting bird, often replacing the egg without explanation, stroking the bird's neck and making soothing sounds. There was no pattern or choice of species: all contributed. Soon his and Urrell's pouches were full.

They had reached the flat upper part of the crag by then.

"Now cave, Urrell."

This would be the huge cavern he had seen gaping from afar,

approached by a rough path. Large as he expected it to be, Urrell was still taken aback by its looming height.

"Many flying mouses, Urrell. Leave pouches here, with Rakrak."

From just inside the entrance, overhead and into the cave, he saw what Agaratz meant. Bats lined the roof and walls of the cavern. Their droppings lay in drifts, in places half up the walls. Strange colourless insects scurried about in the gloom over the mounds.

"When big ice, Old Mens live here."

Urrell looked around, half expecting to glimpse slouching shapes. He wanted to ask why they were there. What was the reason for the egg-collecting. But somehow the sheer size of the cavern, its rustle of bats and insects, silenced him in awe. His unsaid questions were part answered when Agaratz volunteered, "Then my fathers come."

"Your people lived here, with the Old Men?"

"After Old Mens." He rolled his hands over and over in that gesture for immemorial time past, then added, "Old Mens go with ice."

Now Urrell was all attention. His own thinking surprised him. Something in him seemed to take over as he heard himself ask: "How could the Old Men live here, or your fathers, with the river?" He meant the stream running both sides of the cantle of cliff on which they found themselves.

"Big ice then, Urrell. No river. River under ice. Mens walk on ice."

After an explanation this long, Agaratz fell silent and they slithered on into the cavern over mountains of bat dirt, disturbing myriads of the faintly luminous beetles which fed on it. Overhead an incessant low squeaking announced the bats. Light from the huge cavern mouth filtered in just enough for them to make their way deep inside. At the very limit of the light's range, in near-dark, Agaratz stopped and began scraping about in the dung.

"See, Urrell."

He saw, or rather felt. There was a harsh, dry surface; then he felt coarse bristles.

Old Mother. Beneath the droppings lay a mummified mammoth, or part of one.

"Agaratz, *mammurak!*"

"*Mammurak.* Die when big cold. More inside." He pointed into the vast black gulf of the interior.

"Did your people kill the mammoths, Agaratz?"

His voice, half grown man's, quavered.

"No, no. Old Mans hunt mammoth. But mammoths come and die here when big cold. No foods."

Then, as though that was that, Agaratz spun on his club foot and started back to the entrance.

"Go see fathers."

Urrell tingled with excitement. The touch of a mammoth! Now what else was to be shown to him? He sensed it would be something extraordinary as he followed Agaratz back over the mounds of droppings, their droppers starting to squeak more loudly overhead in readiness for the dusk flight. At the entrance they picked up their pouches full of eggs and moved to a side entrance, one of several which Agaratz plainly knew.

"Light fire now, Urrell, eat and rest."

To do this they had to return to the raft and their belongings for tinder and supplies. It was dark by the time they camped. There was too little fuel for much of a fire. They ate fish they had brought and sucked several eggs apiece near the cavern entrance where Urrell was soon to view one of those sights which mark a life to its end – the dusk flight of clouds of bats into the sunset as the wildfowl were returning from a day's foraging far away, their pouches and maws heavy with fish for their brooding mates.

Agaratz was withdrawn, Rakrak subdued. Only the rush of water far below broke the silence once the waterfowl had subsided into rest. Urrell re-felt and relived the sensation of touching the mammoth. Agaratz had vouchsafed him something, a precursor to more? He had not been able to recapture the music of the mammoth frieze, to find his way back to it; and it had slipped beyond his grasp for ever. This time, whatever it was, he would be alert to it, note the markers back to it and its retrieval, never again to be baffled by a blank cliff.

When it was dark, a clear night with stars but no moon, Agaratz bestirred himself as Urrell awaited the next move.

"Bring torches, Urrell."

"Can Rakrak come?"

"Rakrak come."

Urrell lit a torch from the fire for Agaratz, took spares and followed. They entered the cavern, shutting out the stars. In the stillness the rustle of insects running up and down the bat hills was clearly audible. Faintly he could hear the plash of the river on a rock, an aural bearing to the outer world, but soon that too would vanish with the starlight.

Their pouches of eggs awaited them in the side cave for collection as Agaratz led the way up an inclined tunnel, gravelly underfoot as of an old watercourse. This soon opened into a domed chamber so big their torchlight could not light the roof clearly but only illumine the nearer reaches of the walls. Urrell looked for signs of engravings – nothing. What took his eye instead was the floor of the cavern. As far as the light of the torch carried it was littered with heaps of stones.

Agaratz stopped, stuck the torch in the nearest cairn and with fluent speed stripped down to his breechclout, revealing the hair-covered hump of his back, oddly out of place next to the powerful arms and torso, as though they had been assembled from two separate beings, much as the two legs, though familiar enough to Urrell, might have been taken for those of a beast and a man joined at the crotch. Yet this was not what surprised Urrell but that the massive torso, arms and waist had been streaked with dye or reddle while scarifications marked forearms and chest. Agaratz must have prepared himself for the trip in some solitary ceremony, as would have been his custom over the years that he had dwelt alone. It marked the importance he accorded the egg-gathering trip.

CHAPTER 24

Watched by Urrell and by Rakrak, Agaratz dismantled a cairn stone by stone till a slab appeared. This he gripped at the edges, the lift straining his powerful arms.

Urrell, determined this time not to be cheated, would have wished to take the torch and shine it into whatever the slab hid, but he held back in awe. Something in Agaratz's behaviour and the solemnity with which he treated whatever he was doing warned Urrell that he was witnessing a central event in the hunchback's world, and that he was meant to witness it but not to intrude.

Agaratz straightened, took the torch to light the gap under the slab and said: "My father."

A bundle lay in the hollow, a mummy, the legs tucked under. Looking closer Urrell made out a shrivelled face with dishevelled reddish hair on the skull. A spear lay by it, of an ancient sort like some Agaratz possessed, as well as a flute like the one Agaratz had carved for him, Urrell. Would his be his own funeral flute, when the time came?

All around, beneath their stones, Agaratz's people lay, with their flutes and spears, awaiting each year the visit of their own kind from the land above, from Agaratz the last of their kind to see the sun.

Agaratz broke an egg and smeared the yolk on the mummified face. Rocking on his hunkers he keened in a note almost beyond hearing. Rakrak lowered her ears and cowered. His dirge done, Agaratz replaced the slab and piled the stones back on top, then moved to the next cairn and opened it in the same way. A dried face, the hair longer, necklets and ornaments of bone and shell revealed a woman's finery. Urrell guessed she was Agaratz's mother, whom he seldom mentioned. Agaratz broke an egg, adding red ochre for a woman, and keened again, in a different note. Urrell helped to rebuild the cairn unbidden, and went on to help with the next, and the next, as the night wore on. Their torches burnt low and were renewed, until a score and a half of tombs had been opened and closed again after the ritual egg-wash. From the delicacy with which Agaratz touched their faces and the sorrow of his lament Urrell knew they had been family members he had known in life and that he recognised their features in death. He seemed tireless. For the many other cairns of remoter kin he simply broke an egg on each, with an incantation. Old shells strewn everywhere spoke of earlier times, of bygone ceremonies held by Agaratz's forebears over their own dead, whom they had long since joined under those very cairns.

When they issued from the funerary chamber into a dawn chorus of birds, the bats had already been back on their roosts for some time.

Agaratz resumed life as if the night had not happened, but he would eat no more eggs from the island nor touch the wildfowl. Instead, they lived off their stores and off fish caught in the pool at the shingle beach, along with mussels, some bigger than any Urrell had seen before but, to his disappointment, empty of pearls. On the crags Agaratz showed Urrell a samphire-like plant that made crisp eating.

This way they stayed for several days and though Agaratz did not say so, Urrell sensed that the delay formed part of their visit, as if to keep the dead company for a while. Most of the time Agaratz left him to his own devices. With Rakrak he explored every cranny on the ait and sat for hours watching the water slide past. On one of the days he made himself a bundle of torches from rushes and the grease of a dead waterfowl. Determined to revisit the mammoths, lest they too were a trick of memory, he set off into the cavern. Overhead the bats formed their rippling, squeaking mass, dimly discernible in the rushlight. Underfoot he scrambled over mounds of droppings and rocks fallen from the roof, disturbing the translucent insects which teemed on the ever-renewed detritus of the cave floor. He found a young bat that had fallen from its perch. It was quite unafraid and fastened itself to his tunic like an emblem, ate insects he fed it and was content to travel with its benefactor on his mammoth-quest.

Far into the cave where the roof gradually sloped down and bats did not venture he stumbled on huge bones. Shreds of hide hung from them. The massive shapes lay where their owners had huddled in death. Urrell's weak light threw shadows of rib-cages on to the rock face, shone on whitened, domed skulls, heightening the eye and tusk sockets. These were not the remains to which Agaratz had led him. It was a while before Urrell realised no tusks lay about. A cold shiver ran down his spine, as a spider might, when he remembered the hoard in the pit; his fear and his flight up the pine trunk; Agaratz's humorous nonchalance as he swarmed back down to retrieve the torch Urrell had dropped in his fright. Not a memory he welcomed. Now he, Urrell, disciple of Agaratz, would fear no more, and with an effort of will he quelled his terror and forced himself to approach the bones. Even by the glow of his sputtering rushlight it was evident that tusks had not been wrenched or broken from their sockets. They must have lain loose with age when the Old Men gathered them for their hoard, in the times when the ice bridge allowed access to the island. Urrell felt proud to have thought this out for himself.

"Come, Rakrak."

Before leaving he tore off a shred of hide as a keepsake, as a token of the mammoths' existence.

Near the entrance, Agaratz, stripped to his breech-clout,

shoulders and torso streaked with reddle and guano, crouched in a circle of eggs, some dabbed with ochre, some not. He was chanting and rocking, his low chant aimed at each egg in turn.

Although Agaratz went on regardless of his presence, Urrell knew that this farewell, staged at the entrance of the cavern as he returned from his private mammoth hunt, was partly for his benefit: Agaratz meant him to hear this call to his people and his yearning to join them in the land beyond.

The ceremony filled Urrell's breast with foreboding. Urrell the foundling lore-bearer, bereft-to-be in the icelands.

Old Mother. Those tuskless mammoth bones.

CHAPTER 25

Their return downstream took only a few hours. Agaratz steered from the stern, using his pole to keep the raft inshore, surprising animals drinking along the banks. It amused him to see how startled they were at the sight of logs drifting by with a cargo of humans and a wolf, and even more so when they heard themselves called in their own voices from the flotsam. Some stopped in mid-flight, a paw raised, heads turned. Agaratz mimicked the calls of each beast without moving his mouth, throwing his voice in a way Urrell could not make out. Another skill worth learning.

To their amusement a bear followed them along the shore bandying growls with Agaratz, convinced there was a bear aboard the raft.

A thrush-like bird landed on Agaratz's shoulder, in answer to his whistle.

"I feed when sick," he explained.

Urrell wondered if his bat would know him if he ever returned to the island of the dead.

"Soon see hunters," Agaratz warned, as though he was announcing sunset. He steered closer inshore, away from the farther bank.

Urrell watched out for them. How did Agaratz know? Was it the same as he had foreseen Urrell's own approach that day, and come provisioned for a starving lad? His musing was broken by a javelin striking the log by his foot.

"See, Urrell?"

Agaratz pointed at the trees opposite till Urrell, as keen-eyed as any hunter, made out the tiny movements that the canniest stalker makes. He saw the movements but not the movers. Soon they were out of range. Agaratz examined the shaft of the javelin, reading the incisions that ran in a whorl from tip to butt, snake-like.

"Who are they, Agaratz?"

"New peoples, Urrell. Follow bison and fight. Come from hot lands, far."

He seemed unconcerned. The javelin lay on the raft for Rakrak to sniff, its stone tip chipped from the impact.

"Agaratz, what shall we do with this spear?"

"*Aztamakil*. You keep for owner."

"The owner?"

"Yes, when you meet."

"When shall we meet?"

"Soon. You see. Not good mens."

Urrell left the matter there but determined to be wary.

At their starting point Agaratz floated the raft into its hithe among the sallow carr and rushes. With practised ease he camouflaged it so well that Urrell had to look twice to see it. Piura awaited them, hungry but well. She nuzzled them all three in turn, rubbing her scarred old head even against Rakrak. They made something of a feast from food cached, caught a salmon and bivouacked for the night.

"We stay a while, Urrell. I show you swim."

Urrell's home folk had always shunned water, afraid of water sprites and monsters that dwelt in deep still pools. Urrell had grown up among them, folk who never went further than a shallow paddle. Agaratz showed no such concern.

Next day he bound two bundles of rushes as floats for Urrell then both stripped down to their breech-clouts and waded into the creek, the icy water numbing Urrell's legs. It did nothing to

Agaratz, who ducked right under. He swam as animals swim, dog-paddle, but fast with the power of his shoulders drawing him through the water.

"Like this, Urrell."

Urrell strove to overcome his apprehension and hide it from Agaratz. Soon he got the knack but the cold chilled him to the bone and he had to get out of the water.

"I warm you."

Agaratz rubbed Urrell's shuddering body from top to bottom with handfuls of ferns till his skin glowed, then scoured the remains of red ochre and guano from himself. The cold of the water had not affected him.

In the three days they spent by the river Urrell became so adept at swimming that he ventured out of the creek into the main current with Agaratz, drifting with it, even crossing to the far bank at a bend before returning obliquely across the current and landing far downriver. He slowly grew inured to the cold. Rakrak trotted along the bank with Piura and all four walked back up-shore to camp.

"Good to know swim, Urrell. Escape bad mens."

"Can't they swim?"

"No. They afraid water."

Like Urrell's people. Another difference with Agaratz's folk, safely asleep on their island.

CHAPTER 26

Home cave was there, waiting. Urrell had half hoped, half expected the lame fox to be waiting too. All the trees and bushes, whose every twig he knew, stood where he recalled them, remembering each detail with his hunter's eye. In his short absence they had grown; new plants sprouted from fissures; the forest had edged a few strides into the savannah. He glanced at Agaratz, but Agaratz showed no sign of noticing, nor Rakrak of unease.

Would the climbing pole be in its place among the bushes? It was. Together with Agaratz he pulled away the weeds entangling it and set it up. Inside the cave, all lay as it had been left, yet not till the fire blazed and food was cooking did Urrell feel the emptiness disperse and allow him once more to feel at the centre of daily certainty and recurrence. He wanted to speak to Agaratz about this sense of unease but could find no words to express it. Instead he fondled Rakrak's ears and noticed for the first time silvery hairs on her snout.

"Soon time to go big meet, Urrell."

"Where, Agaratz?"

"Long way. Go river. Walk much." The statement left a pause in the air, as unspoken thoughts rose in Urrell's mind.

Agaratz went on: "Many days we walk. Peoples come. Much dance. Fight. I go with my father, now Urrell go with me. Find you woman, Urrell."

Softnesses glimpsed under the tunics of girls nagged at Urrell's imagination and stirred him.

"How, Agaratz?"

Women were traded, swapped, paid for with bride-price. Urrell had nothing.

"Take *xerratxis*, tusk, necklaces." Agaratz indicated the store of mammoth beads and trinkets he and Urrell had wrought so long and carefully.

"Find pretty womans, Urrell. You play flute, for they dance. I talk to fathers." He made the trafficking sound straightforward, part of the passage of the seasons.

Then, having made this announcement, he seemed less than anxious to set out, letting days slip by, as though expecting a propitious moment, much to Urrell's impatience. One morning that looked like any other, he said: "Tomorrow go."

They spent that day and much of the night repairing and assembling bags and pouches, straps and spears, binding all with thongs to the travois. Their choicest flint heads, ornaments of ivory, needles, fish hooks, a roarer and flutes were packed, whereas few provisions were needed, for the world lay under summer's plenty. They would forage and hunt as they went. They slept well, rose early, ate and set off, Rakrak scouting, Piura bringing up the rear. The sounds, sights and scents of their gulch as they left it for the open plains tugged at Urrell with a sentiment that a period in his life was over and another beginning. His strength, his hair, his body were now nearly a man's, his spear-cast as far and as accurate as it would ever be.

They travelled in leisurely stages across the plain, aslant the range of mountains that Urrell had first seen at the end of his boyhood trek across the moorlands on his way, had he known, to Agaratz. To him this new journey was a continuation – he had but to follow, as a tree grows, a body develops, a herd moves.

When the sun was hottest, they rested, lolling in the grasses, amid the flowers of summer and the innumerable insects of the grasslands. Clouds of gnats swirled about, filling eyes and nostrils, biting bare skin, Urrell's at least. Agaratz was untroubled. They tormented even Rakrak's muzzle, Piura's ears and her old eyes. She pawed and rubbed her head in despair.

Agaratz grinned. "You not *poodooec*, Urrell."

"*Poodooec?*"

"For gnats."

"How can you be *poodooec* for *gnats*, Agaratz!"

"You see."

Agaratz rose and gyrated round Urrell and the two animals, humming like a swarm of midges, his visage intent, repeating the slow stomp a dozen times and ending it by placing a hand on the head of each in turn. His humming ceased. The gnats went on swirling but henceforth kept a spear's length away from them all.

"How do you *do poodooec*, Agaratz? How do you know?"

"From long times. My people know. You know too."

But how, how? This latest spell was at one with the accuracy of Agaratz's javelin cast; with that stirring of the flute in Urrell's hand when he had captured, or been captured by, the music from another plane; with the mammoth cow in the cave as her herd lumbered past his drawing hand, mocking yet knowing, teasing him to draw and understand. If this trip was a stage to that understanding, to his own *poodooec*, as the herds of bison they skirted knew their *poodooec* and returned without fail to their very own grazing each year untaught, he, Urrell, would travel to the very heart of the icefields to find his.

Food was easy. Agaratz, for all his skill as a hunter, seldom slew if other food abounded as it abounded now: roots, berries, grubs, clutches of eggs, hives of honey... Urrell observed how Agaratz took only one comb from a hive, a few eggs from a clutch, muttering words that Urrell memorised without understanding and mimicked when he found a nest, to Agaratz's approval.

160

"What do the words mean, Agaratz?"

"Mean *poodooec*."

"Which language, Agaratz, your people's?

"Alls languages." Then he added, "Like speak Old Mens and Olders Mens. My father teach."

"Teach me, Agaratz."

Several days out, far into the sea of grass scattered with island copses, Agaratz pointed. "We go to see bison meeting."

Herds had been streaming slowly by along the horizon, under circling crows and vultures. Bands of horses came closer, sometimes towards the two humans to stare. Wolves they saw too but though Rakrak stood alert she showed no desire to join them. Piura's kind they saw in prides from time to to time, a woollier variety of lion. From the remains of their kills Piura and Rakrak had meat.

Agaratz changed course and turned towards the herds and the far-off mountains. They left their travois to be able to trot more easily through the high grass, kicking up showers of insects at each footfall, flushing partridges and great bustards that ran away before them, Rakrak in pursuit, more in high spirits than in hope of a capture. At the end of a long day, the land became undulating, the first swell of the distant mountains. They had been moving parallel to an immense herd of bison grazing their way north. Urrell had never seen so many. The ground trembled with the drumming of their hooves. When Agaratz and Urrell slept for the short summer night the vibration of the ground had not ceased at dawn.

"Soon there, Urrell."

By mid-morning they were. Over the rim of a low bluff they saw before them a vast hollow in which milled thousands of bison, the air thick with dust. Animals were frisking, tails erect, males and females alike, rolling in the dust sprinkled with their own urine, bulls jousting and mounting cows.

"See, Urrell, here bisons find womens. Many more places." He pointed towards hazes of dust in the distance where other encounters were happening. Agaratz's eyes gleamed. "*Poodooec* for bisons," he said.

"Agaratz, where do the mammoths go for this?"

"Far, far. When old time."

"Old time?"

"When old mens. When all cold, big cold."

He rose and began the mammoth dance Urrell remembered so well from their first meeting. As the mimic dance became the mammoth, cold fell round Urrell, a cold so intense he stood still, eyes seeing beyond Agaratz and the gambolling bison in their dusty heat haze.

Agaratz stopped. The spell broke. Urrell watched beads of sweat on the backs of his hands melt. Drops on his downy upper lip thawed. He had clenched his hands in the sudden cold. As he unstiffened them, a little pool of mushy snow lay in each palm and slithered on to the grass at his feet. When he looked up, Agaratz had already turned his back on him to watch the bison.

"Now go," said Agaratz.

They returned to pick up their travois, following the trail of grasses bent by their footfalls on the outward journey, a track as easy to read as spoor in snow. Rakrak chased grasshoppers; Piura brought up the rear.

CHAPTER 27

For days Agaratz led, Urrell second and Piura third, Rakrak scouting and sometimes slinking off to explore a movement that caught her eye. Not another human marred the world. They skirted huge herds of bison and droves of horses. Caribou-like deer appeared and stared at their little group. Wolves and woolly lions grew commoner as the tree-line of the distant mountains sent out spinneys and even small woods into the grasslands, harbingers of a vast green army. None of this concerned Agaratz. After each detour round herds he resumed his line of advance aslant the mountain range.

Berries, fungus abounded. Raspberries, bilberries and other fruitlets throve in endless quantities, often showing where bears had brashed and combed their branches in orgies of feeding. If they met bears, Agaratz would exchange grunts with them and part amicably. For the brief summer nights they stopped and ate wherever they were, sometimes lighting a fire to braise fungus or cook the small rodents that teemed everywhere, lemming-like, and when roasted whole were passable fare. Rakrak and Piura ate theirs raw, on the hoof, snapping them up as they went.

By now the vast mountains were drawing nearer, if obliquely, looming larger, their peaks and valleys, crags and ghylls, huge screes growing clearer. On the lower slopes, forest clad everything. Higher up, those streaks of whiteness that had so intrigued Urrell he now saw was ice snaking down from the snowy peaks into the valleys till it reached the tree-line, where it ended.

From following the range at an angle, at a point that to Urrell looked like any other, Agaratz changed course and made straight for the mountains. He knew Agaratz's sureness of direction better than to wonder why. It took them two more days of travel, now in driving rain and sleet, taking turns at pulling their sodden travois, to reach the first foothills where Urrell saw that Agaratz had aimed for a gap between two outriders of the range which formed a glen that one would have needed to know existed in order to find it. A river ran along the middle, smooth and dark and fast. When Urrell drank from its water it was ice-cold. Firs grew down to both banks.

Behind them spread the sunny grasslands, their innumerable herds, the circling swirls of prey and carrion fowl overhead, showers of insects at every footfall, drifts of berries, whereas ahead stretched, it appeared to Urrell, endless tree-bound gloom and the spongy pine-needle floor of the forest. Into this quiet, cool world Agaratz strode, leaving Urrell to drag the travois over roots and mossy boulders. To their left ran the river, never far, sometimes glimpsed, then coming into full view where the glen narrowed to little more than a clough and they travelled almost along its bank, the forest silence unbroken by any ripples from its rapid current. That night they bivouacked beneath a fir that towered above in search of whatever light there was high above the gulch at the bottom of which centuries earlier its seed had first rooted.

"Big tree," said Agaratz, tapping a massive ridge of bark. "Old mens tree."

As he did not elaborate, Urrell busied himself with trying to light a fire while Agaratz circled the tree, climbing over the buttresses of its roots, examining the fissures and crevices of its bole, Rakrak tagging behind him.

"Why old men's tree, Agaratz?"

"When small tree, Old Mens here."

"Then mammoths were here too!" Old Men and mammoths went together in Urrell's vision of things.

CHAPTER 28

"Old mens slay mammoth, Urrell. Then big cold time end and mammoths go."

"Go where? And the old men?"

"They follow mammoth." He waved a hand vaguely in the direction they were going, upstream into the mountains. Agaratz's manner was listless, which heightened Urrell's attention, aware as he was of every flicker in Agaratz's moods and movements.

Agaratz circled the tree. Its needles were of a sort new to Urrell. It appeared to be a singleton, a survivor from a previous age. It might have known the mammoths as they streamed past on their last journey. Urrell's mind awoke to all this as he followed Agaratz round the vast bole.

"Agaratz, when did you come this way?"

"I not come."

"But you know the way. You know this tree."

"I know, yes."

"How, but how?"

"From old fathers. From old mens before. They know." Then turning his yellow eyes on Urrell's own he concluded: "Now Urrell know."

He took Urrell by the hand and laid it on the bark, cracked so deeply that a man's hand might scarcely fathom its fissures. Deep in some were objects that Urrell first thought were stones caught up as the tree had grown, but then recognised these to be offerings embedded in the trunk, from long ago.

Agaratz started a chant full of harsh glottals, rasped consonants

165

alternating with crooned vowels, none of it intelligible to Urrell; nor were the sounds like any of the other tongues that Agaratz sometimes used. While the chant went on a chill rose, as from the river, summer fell away and Urrell shivered. He would not swoon this time: he would let the *poodooec* work whilst he kept his wits about him. He clung to the reassuring roughness of the bark as the cold intensified. Under his summer tunic and leggings his body juddered and his teeth clattered. The huge tree rose overhead as all around the landscape of the clough changed. Gone were the fir trees. Only stunted taiga grew dotted with thickets of dwarf birches and willow. In the unbearable cold, Urrell strove to keep alert, clinging for dear life to the tree trunk, his eyes blurring so that his vision, impaired, hardly took in the movement of three figures as they appeared at the bottom of the clough, coming his way. They were three squat men, swaddled in furs, carrying short spears, their gait shambling but steady, almost a slow trot. He heard in the distance, beyond the men, a massive trumpeting and as he went under from the cold his last thought was *mammoths*.

"You better, Urrell?" Agaratz was crouched by a fire chafing Urrell's hands and face. All he said was, "You sit by fire. I make warm."

Agaratz stoked armfuls of brash and twigs on the fire till it blazed, lighting the criss-cross of enormous boughs over their heads. Burning twigs from the ancient tree gave off a fragrance that confirmed it was of a kind Urrell had never before encountered, and yet he felt he knew it. He sniffed hard. The harder he tried the remoter became the recollection of its scent.

"Look in fire, Urrell." He looked and saw flames running through a scene of brush and stunted firs, followed by human figures waving spears and torches, urging the fire on. Beyond the men he saw what appeared to be the purpose of all this – for, trunks raised, a herd of mammoths lumbered ahead of the flames and their tormentors. Just as suddenly the scene vanished and Urrell jerked out of his bemusement to catch Agaratz's sly girn, and the impish light in his eyes.

Neither spoke. Urrell felt himself overcome by a huge weariness. He lay down and slept by the fire, on needles dropped over centuries by the giant overhead, Rakrak to one side of him, old Piura to the other.

The air grew chillier as they approached the ice. Outlying patches of snow lay in hollows and the heights above the tree-line were often white. Yet in the river valley it was warm by day, and in the stretches of mountain-meadow between the firs flowers of all kinds bespeckled the grasses. Most were new to Urrell. If he stopped to examine a bloom, a bulb or a fungus Agaratz gave it a name and commented on it as:

- good to eat, Urrell
- that one, medecine for bones
- that leaf, you eat if belly hurts
- That wort – he pointed carefully in such cases – that wort kill even bison.

Once shown a plant, Urrell would never forget it. Life teemed in these grassy gaps in the forest. The grass rippled with movements of rodents which Rakrak and Piura pounced on as they went.

To amuse Urrell, Agaratz mimicked the calls of birds, getting them to flutter over his head, even settle on his shoulders. Urrell also tried, imitating the calls as truly as Agaratz and yet, for lack of some quality of sound, he only roused the curiosity of fowl but not their trust. They drew near but not near enough. It peeved him not to match Agaratz's powers.

"When shall we reach the great ice, Agaratz?"

Their river valley and its green-black current seemed to go on for ever, a world of its own, where wild creatures unsure of humans did little to avoid them. Bears, often fishing, they avoided. Rakrak's presence was enough to deter the curiosity of panther-like cats and leopards, and to startle away deer. Once they nearly bumped into an auroch, alone in the woods, but he was as surprised as they. Neither Urrell nor Agaratz unsheathed a weapon all day, as berries and fruit abounded and the nests of waterfowl were easy to find. Some evenings they fished in the fast stream. Their two companions fended for themselves from the endless provision of small animals they caught. At night they camped under a fir, dry even after heavy rain, lit a fire to light the tracery of branches above, liernes of an arboreal vault, and slept in peace.

In this way they had travelled unconcerned for about a dozen days, in short stages, when the valley began to narrow. In a mist of rain and drizzle, round a turn, they came to the ice. It blocked their way. No fragments, no moraine littered the glacier's approaches: it was a total surprise, to Urrell at least...

CHAPTER 29

What next? Urrell, from behind, could not see Agaratz's face to discern his reaction to the wall of ice. Without a change of speed, pouches swinging, spears at the trail, Agaratz carried on ahead, impenetrable though the ice looked to Urrell. Nor did there seem to be a way up the sides of the valley and over the ice.

They were near enough to the wall for Urrell to feel its coldness before he noticed that the river, issuing from under the ice, had carved a tunnel somewhat larger than its flow needed, as though it had been bigger in the past. It was to this that Agaratz strode.

"Leave travois here, Urrell. Take things."

They loaded themselves with bags, skins, food, weapons and their stock of ornaments and their pipes. They had food enough for men, wolf and lioness for several days. Beyond that Agaratz would know. "Rakrak carry some," he said and called the wolf.

With thongs he tied a load on her back, whispered in her ears, and all were ready to move on, Piura, unburdened, padding last. "Too old for load," said Agaratz.

The river had worn the ice smooth and left a gravelly bank the width of a javelin along its edge. This they entered, lit dully at first from outside but soon utterly dark.

"Rakrak go first. You hold this, Urrell," and he handed him the end of a thong tied at the other to his own belt. He hitched another to Rakrak's pack as a leash and spoke to the wolf, who pricked up her ears and set forth leading the tiny caravan into the blackness.

Old Mother. Urrell's boyish fears welled up, but soon evaporated.

It felt warm under the ice, almost snug, in the total dark. Only the footfalls of their moccassined feet on the gravel, and the occasional purl of the river water, broke the silence. He had full faith in Rakrak and Agaratz ahead; behind him he could touch Piura's ears as she followed close, a rumbled purr in response to caresses. Soon he was sweating under his burdens.

The air, unless he was imagining things, seemed not so much milder to Urrell as denser. Far from being completely still, as in caverns, he thought he felt movement in it.

Perhaps the current drew air along as it ran. The sensation increased the farther they went till Urrell felt sure something unusual lay ahead. When they stopped for a rest and snack Urrell voiced his curiosity.

"You see, Urrell, soon see."

Soon was relative. They stopped twice more before the darkness began faintly to lighten. Rakrak pulled at her leash and the pace of the file hastened. The light increased from translucence in the ice, thinning as they advanced into warmer air at a stumbling, eager gait, till they burst into a wide ice-free area, a bowl with ice-walls all around.

Their river, now more a big stream, ran across it, wisps of mist rising from its surface.

"You touch, Urrell, touch water."

He did. The water was luke-warm, and the mist was vapour condensing like a man's breath on a frosty morning. Urrell's astonishment so amused Agaratz that he went into one of his rare chuckles. Sitting on a boulder, he was shrugging off his packs and pouches as he shook with mirth at Urrell's reaction. Urrell, a trifle abashed and puzzled, loosened his as well, then unburdened Rakrak. She, to add to his surprise, ran about, frolicking, tail erect, in a joyful release under the effect of this strange place, so he joined in and they scampered about over the gravel and among the boulders till tired out.

"Now we eat, Urrell." Agaratz drew out strips of dried bison meat, the jerky kept in the bottom of bags as iron rations, or to celebrate. All four gnawed their way through this bark-hard food, sucking the nourishment that no berries, no roots or shoots could provide for exhausted bodies.

This done they unrolled pelts on the ground between two boulders and slept pell-mell the sleep of the weary for a full twelve hours.

It was dark when Urrell woke. Agaratz was sitting on a boulder, outlined against the ice-wall beyond. Rakrak poked her head from under a pelt and crept out. She licked Urrell's nose, a new familiarity. Piura, last as ever, rose and stretched.

"Urrell, we eat and go on. Follow river."

They chewed dried berries, nuts and a few strips of jerky.

"Soon plenty foods, Urrell."

Skins rolled up, bags slung they set off, the wolf leading. The gloom had a clarity of its own, setting off boulders and stones against the paler bed of shingle and pebbles that lined the combe floor. They followed the waterway, as before. On either side towered the cliffs of ice, in places closing in, even arching overhead. In this silent world the only sound came when the current swirled round an obstruction.

"Growing warmer, Urrell." They dipped their fingers in the stream, the water now quite warm. "Soon be there."

By first light – less dawn than decrease in dark – the ice-walls had widened and they entered a shallow basin-like expanse, dotted with pools and lakelets. Vapour rose from several.

"You watch, Urrell." They had stopped to look. Urrell did as bidden, expectantly, but observed nothing unusual except for steam. Soon, however, he was to be rewarded: a pool bubbled, plopped and fell still again. He glanced at Agaratz to see what manner of trick this might be, accompanied by its tell-tale grin, but Agaratz was watching the pool as steadfastly as he had been, so he resumed his own scrutiny.

Agaratz plainly knew something was afoot. Urrell's expectancy turned to unease. Tales of water-beasts told round the fires in the cold nights by the sea which had made him shiver with fear in his boyhood tugged at his mind now. Even Rakrak and Piura were attentive.

He was therefore taut with alertness when the bubbling renewed itself and whatever lay beneath the water, angered, impatient, tore itself free and hurtled into the air, hung cliff-high in the pale light, and as suddenly collapsed in a froth of foam and seething water before Urrell's astonished eyes, and vanished below. Urrell glanced at Agaratz. The golden eyes were gleaming with excitement. That instant Urrell knew, and knew with perfect insight, that Agaratz had never viewed this thing, in life or vision, and had not known quite what to expect. His all-seeing companion, who had known the route hither, unerringly following a memory from another time, nevertheless crouched in awe before this wonder.

Urrell's love of his mentor was nowise diminished, but grew. Master and pupil had shared an event neither understood.

As though continuing a previous conversation Agaratz spoke:

"Old mens come here long, long time past. Here *mammurak* come. Place have much…" He searched for a word to convey what he meant, for which perhaps no language had a word, certainly not Urrell's. "Is like caves; great *poodooec*. Like when you see mammuts, Urrell."

Meaning half-dawned between them. The silence of this eery, empty spot, its pools, the ice-walls hemming it in, weighed on Urrell.

Old Mother, was this your land of the mammoths?

Agaratz said: "Catch food."

Nothing catchable met Urrell's eye but he followed Agaratz to a big boulder, of sarsen-stone size, in the lee of which Agaratz set down his bags to camp. Urrell did likewise. Piura, thirsty, was sniffing at a pool but loth to lap.

Agaratz selected salmon spears and a leister and led Urrell to their nearest pool where Piura was now suspiciously sipping the surface.

"See, Urrell." The pool was ice-water clear, each pebble of the shingle bottom visible. "Touch, Urrell." The water was agreeably warm. As he touched it he jumped back – the water had moved and a swarm of creatures twitched and swam away.

"Good to eat, good to eat!"

Good or not, Agaratz was not in pursuit of these. Instead he made for a larger pool which acted as headwater of the stream they had followed all the way. Here Agaratz showed Urrell large grey fish swimming against the current. With ease he forked one, then another with the leister, tossed them on the bank and brained them with a stone, reciting the words, in his own tongue, he used whenever he slew a living thing from need. The surviving fishes ignored him.

"*Poodooec*, Agaratz?"

"No. Fish not see. Look." He showed Urrell the rudimentary eyes of his catches and it was evident they were blind.

"Live like in cave, Urrell, under ice. Eat those things when they leave pool." He wiggled his forefinger in and out to imitate a shrimp swimming. They were the creatures, translucent in the water, that Urrell had disturbed. The shrimps teemed in the warmer pools, whereas the fishes, explained Agaratz, preferred cold water so they swam upstream to the outflow to catch unwary crustaceans.

Urrell stared round their stony surrounds for any sign of fuel with which to cook their catch. He caught Agaratz's eye and its mischievous twinkle. "Follow, Urrell." He went to the pool where they had witnessed the geyser. He was unconcerned, so Urrell followed with Rakrak. There Agaratz ran a thong through the gills of the fishes and dropped them into the water.

"Urrell, water cook fishes."

It was true. The water in the pool was seething hot, quite still on the surface and bottomless, shimmering below as if constantly welling up yet never overflowing. They had been there a while parboiling their fishes when the bubbling began in the centre. Urrell started up and backed off, with Rakrak, eyes fixed on the phenomenon, while Agaratz went on crouching, his stiff club leg a little askew, holding the thong.

"Not danger, Urrell – not yet."

Only when the bubbles subsided, as though gathering strength from the deep, did Agaratz pull up his fishes and join Urrell, a full spear's cast away. If Agaratz felt this was safe, Urrell decided he would too. They had a good view of whatever was to happen. As they waited they gnawed their half-boiled fishes, one apiece. Rakrak was eating the heads and remnants by the time the pool bubbled again, built itself up and whooshed a column of water and steam into the air, held it aloft the time of Urrell's pent up breath, and let it crash back, foam a while and lie still once more. It was the replica of the first blow they had witnessed.

"Like this all the time, Urrell, since…" he rolled his hands over and over, "since olds, olds. Ancients come here, for *mammurak*. Before ice." As if to remind Urrell, he took a few steps of his mammoth dance.

"Did your people come here, Agaratz?"

The wistful expression, the one he had seen at the burial island, was answer enough. It was always so when he asked Agaratz about his origins, his forefathers and his singular existence. Perhaps these were things that could not be uttered, as men's things might not be witnessed or spoken of by women; nor, as he knew from boyhood eavesdroppings, might men see such women's things as where and when they gave birth, or the ceremonies with which they accompanied their moon-bleed.

Suddenly, as if to compensate for his evasiveness, Agaratz volunteered: "Soon see *mammurak, mamu-mammurak*, Urrell."

"*Mamu,* Agaratz?

"*Mamu.* Like deads, Urrell, but not deads."

"Is that *poodooec*?"

"No, not *poodooec*. Is like dead but not dead – is *mamu-orrak*."

There must be no other way of saying that. He would have to wait and see what it was.

Now it was time to catch more fish, for Piura, for Rakrak, for themselves, for a fish feast by the seething waters of the magic pool.

CHAPTER 30

The pools, Urrel discovered, varied in temperature, from scalding hot where the geyser leapt at intervals, something to which Urrell grew accustomed but never indifferent, through to near seething, hot, warm, luke-warm and cold. As the air near the pools never fell below freezing, despite the ice of the glacier, they went about their fishing, resting and exploring at ease. They bathed in the warmer water, Urrell naked, Agaratz with the breechclout he never removed and Urrell never thought to ask why. Rakrak and Piura, loth at first, entered into the spirit of the fun and disported themselves in their own ways.

Here Agaratz taught Urrell how to dive deep and find shell-fish, crabs and crayfish under rocks in the bottoms of some of the pools. He had been right – there was food galore for all.

This way they spent days. "Get strong, Urrell. Eat much." Meanwhile they explored every part of this enclosed place, hemmed in by high ice walls, its bottom strewn with stones and boulders. The only other living things, above water level, to share the place with them were flocks of waterfowl that came and went, feeding on whatever it was they caught in the pools. Their calls and honking from beyond the ice announced their arrival, the only sounds in the silence. They were nearly tame and some answered Agaratz's mimick calls so well that they came and ate from his hands.

When Agaratz announced: "Now time to see caves," he did not explain but took a few things and led off towards the ice-face to a spot where the overflow from several hotter pools cut a low tunnel under the ice. Into this Agaratz stooped, paddling in the hot water, his moccasins round his neck. Urrell followed. At a word from Agaratz, the wolf and lion had remained behind, at the pool edge.

Soon the passage widened and heightened into a chamber. Urrell's eyes accustomed themselves to the bluish gloom. "Wait, Urrell." Agaratz had brought his fire-making bow-drill and some tinder and with difficulty managed to ignite a few pinches of the tinder in the hole of his fire-log, enough to light a resin torch. It smelt delicious. However, its light revealed nothing, just ice walls smooth as salt.

"No, Urrell, look down." There, as Agaratz held the torch aloft, lay giant bones strewn around, on and under the ice, the results of a unimaginable catastrophe, a massacre, no two vertebrae linked, skulls tossed anywhere, a vast dismemberment. He guessed what Agaratz had meant by *mamu-mammurak,* this graveyard of mammoths.

"What happened, Agaratz, what happened?"

"Old mans hunt. Hunt much. Hunt *mammurack otelosey.*"

"*Otelosey?*"

"*Otelosey.* Till none left." He made frenzied stabbing movements to illustrate.

Holding the light up Agaratz led Urrell among the bones, searching for something.

"Ah, look Urrell." He held up a spearhead, a heavy chunky one, unlike anything Urrell had seen before, cruder than any he had ever handled. It had once been the tip of a short stabbing spear to finish off fallen beasts, wielded by someone with shoulders powerful enough to drive this blunt point through the hide of a mammoth's belly. More of them lay scattered about among ribs. To Urrell's surprise, Agaratz, his all-knowing Agaratz, examined them with the keenest interest, stroking the coarse chipping of the flint and basalt with girlish fingertips, suggesting to Urrell that by this action he was drawing from the points their story, their strength, absorbing their potency, that which he called *poodooec*. So intense was Agaratz's attention, his shaggy mane of reddish hair hanging down his head and shoulders against the light of the torch, that Urrell knew better than to interrupt. In the total silence, the bones lay around unthreateningly. There was no hostile feeling towards either him or Agaratz. It was as though the bones had been lying there awaiting their coming.

Then, in the innermost recesses of his ear, Urrell heard his tune. It was tiny, clear, from a great remoteness.

"Urrell, look."

In the ice wall of the cavern a frieze of mammoths, full height, was visible, frozen. The lead cow's little eye returned his gaze. He saw even the coarse hairs of her flanks and ran, stumbling over bones, to touch them. His hand met the ice: she was gone.

"We go now, Urrell."

They left the way they had come.

Outside Agaratz made no comment as he donned his moccassins. It was back to their routine of fishing, feeding and making a paste by pounding shrimps which Agaratz packed into pouches with salt-like rime scraped from the edge of brackish pools near the hot springs.

These occupations left Urrell ample leisure to range about the combe, exploring every crevasse and cleft in the ice faces, keen to find any more traces of ancient folk and their quarry. But he found no more mammoth remains, search as he might, only evidence of tool-making by their persecutors. These, some complete, some half made, many botched and cast aside, spoke of long residence by hunting groups in earlier times, the Great Cold in Agaratz's words. He brought back samples of his finds to Agaratz, who merely nodded, his interest apparently sated by their visit to the mammoth ice-cavern earlier, where he had absorbed all he wished to know from the bones and weapons strewn there.

However, Urrell's disappointment must have touched him. "Look, Urrell," he said and took a sizable pebble from the many lying around, selected a small boulder, and in a few deft blows chipped and flaked it into a core, then taking another pebble shattered one against the other to make a crude hammer-chopper. With this he flaked the core into a spear-head indistinguishable from the ones they had found. The whole process took a matter of minutes. It was as if one of the ancient stone-knappers were directing Agaratz's hands, transmitting to them the skill of generations.

"You do, Urrell." He handed him the pebble-hammer. Nothing could be easier. Yet try as he might, and try he did, Urrell could not reproduce spear-heads with the authenticity that sprang so naturally from Agaratz's hands. His spear-heads were workman-like, yes. But he knew in his inner self that whereas the spear-head flaked by Agaratz would have flown true and pierced the toughest mammoth hide, his own would have mis-flown, mis-struck and bounced off.

This apart, they did little else than fish and eat, men, wolf and lion, battening on the easy pickings, though Urrell sensed that Agaratz was distrait, often lost in thought, as though they were marking time or awaiting some signal.

One morning, the air warm from the advance of high summer, Agaratz came alive again, his old puckish self. "Now ready to go."

"Go where, Agaratz?"

He seemed a little taken aback, as though expecting Urrell to know what he meant.

"Go to meet peoples. For mens meets womens. For, for... ceremonies."

"Which way, Agaratz?" Urrell felt able to ask, part of the decision-making, a near full-grown man. He could see no way forward. A long trudge back down the ice-tunnel seemed the only way in or out.

"Follow sun, Urrell." That meant ahead, against the further side of the combe and the glacier face. He helped to pack, noticing that Agaratz was taking especial care to bundle everything compactly, winding all their thongs into a single coil which he slung across one shoulder. He laid out a large pelt and tied thongs through holes to make a sling which he folded with unusual care. This and the rest done they loaded up and set off towards the ice-cliff to a spot Urrell had skirted during his explorations. A pool of hot, smelly water lay there. It stank of rotten eggs, he thought. Its outflow ran under the ice-face, where it had cut a low opening. To this Agaratz led them.

The opening was hardly more than wolf high. Encumbered as they were they would have to stoop to get in along the outflow with their faces just above the stinking water to reach a ledge inside.

CHAPTER 31

Urrell bridled, wolf and lion wavered.

"Only way, Urrell."

Agaratz led. It took some shooing and persuasion by Urrell, bringing up the rear, to get Piura to follow Rakrak into the water and under the arch.

Once inside, while wolf and lioness shook themselves dry, Urrell looked around. Several fissures rose as chimneys in the ice, rather like the water-worn swallow-holes he was familiar with in caves. The same effect of meltwater had caused these, he thought, or an extinct geyser. "Old mens use," Agaratz said, as though reading a half-formed question in Urrell's mind. "Not high," he added. "In old times, much bigger." If he meant the pool, or the chimneys or even the ice-face, was not clear or important to Urrell: how to get up was. The sides of the biggest chimney seemed very smooth.

Agaratz unrolled a pack and selected an antler pick and a stone-bladed adze from his tool kit. He wound the coil of thongs round his shoulders and waist. "I go up, Urrell, send down thong, you tie pouches and I pull up, then Rakrak. You tie Piura in skin –" he pointed to the large pelt with eyelets round the rim " – and when you come up we pull Piura." Upon which he started up the chimney, chipping finger- and toe-holds with the adze, hooking the antler pick into these and other crannies, bracing his back and knees against the ice and worming his way up, the powerful shoulders hauling and the club foot seeking the least purchase. It took him quite a while. Ice flakes rained down as he chipped his slow way up. Finally, "Now, Urrell," and the uncoiled thong ends came down to be tied to pouches and bags, hauled up into the gloom and the job repeated until all equipment and belongings were aloft. Urrell stood half in the smelly water all the while. When it was Rakrak's turn, he tied slings under her, coaxed the creature into the water and steadied her as Agaratz, somewhere above, pulled her up hand over hand. Next Urrell baled Piura in the pelt, threaded thongs through the eye-holes so that she could not wriggle free, should she try, and shouted up to Agaratz that he was ready to come up himself.

Agaratz, anchored above, let down a line which Urrell hitched to his belt, so that by using the footholds, bracing himself as he had seen Agaratz do, plus with the hunchback's powerful grip on the line, he reached the ledge where Agaratz crouched, their goods piled around him. The last task was to haul up Piura. She was too big for the chimney unless pulled up head and forequarters first. Once this manoeuvre was managed she helped herself up by clawing at the surface of the ice, making things far easier for her hauliers than Urrell had expected. Her rumbled purr as he rubbed her head told Urrell of her happiness at not being forsaken by her pride.

"Make light, Urrell." In the gloom Agaratz found his fire-making implements and with that deftness Urrell felt he would never equal, had soon lit a torch, revealing a passage leading from the ledge into the ice. Waters long past must have worn it and then cascaded down the chimney they had just climbed. Without comment they loaded up, even Rakrak shouldering her pack as usual, and set off along the passage as it slowly ascended, Urrell hoped towards daylight.

They emerged well enough on to the glacier surface at a crevasse, into late daylight, and by following the crevasse eventually came to the surface of the ice-field. They were on top of the glacier. Across its ribbed surface, Agaratz leading, the others in single file, they tramped with care. Agaratz was looking for something in the featureless white in the long summer dusk. It was a depression in the snow-field, as though the ice had caved in. To this Agaratz headed. "Soon find new river, Urrell."

They did. At the bottom of the snowy slope a funnel-like hole led to a river under the ice, a river flowing away from them, one warmed from hidden springs somewhere along its course. Soon they were once again on a ledge in total blackness, following a fast-running current.

"Rakrak lead," said Agaratz. He tied a thong to her pack and ran it back past himself to Urrell who had himself tied a line to Piura behind him. Thus, trusting to Rakrak's instinct, they moved on in single file. Here the air was clammy, faintly smelling of brimstone from the stream. When they stopped to eat Urrell tried the water and found it distasteful. They sucked chips of ice instead.

"How far, Agaratz?"

"Two days, Urrell."

"What will there be?"

"Land, Urrell, like before, then, how you say, *weald*, big woods, to land of other mens, land where *mammurak* live long ago. You see."

"Did your people live there Agaratz? Was this their homeland?

"Before great cold come, my ancients live here and where we go too. Many places."

"How do you know the way?

"I remember."

"Did you come with your father?"

"I remember." He tapped his head. "I know from fathers, from old time."

Urrell, aware of the migrations of bison, deer and horses, of waterfowl that rose in huge flights when it was time to leave, as they had always done, guessed what Agaratz meant.

Towards the end of the second day of their trudge, broken only by stops to nap and eat, the ice became thinner overhead, translucent; shortly, they issued into a jumble of broken ice and a stony plain. Across this their river headed purposefully, vapour rising from its tepid water, and as it was going their way they followed it.

The long summer days enabled them to travel twelve hours with only brief stops. Two more days and they entered scrub that yielded to birch carr and then pine forest. Urrell sniffed the resinous scent with pleasure. They cut poles to make a travois, and a small one for Rakrak.

"How much longer, Agaratz?"

"About seven days, Urrell. We see hills and then come to place."

"Why are there so few animals in these woods, Agaratz?" They had seen only a few musk-oxen from afar, glimpsed wolves, foxes, hares. Overhead flew the usual scavengers.

It was an empty wilderness compared with their home range in the grasslands. Agaratz, in a hurry to arrive, made no attempt to hunt or forage but relied on their stores, supplemented with berries and wild fruit they found on their way. They did not even light campfires. Piura, on short rations, kept up as best she could, her ribs beginning to show.

"Urrell, long time ago in this land, many animals, in time of old mens. Animals gone."

"Gone?"

"Like mammuts: no more." As they reclined, Agaratz, with the facility that so amazed Urrell, drew on flat stones a succession of beasts, some familiar, many not. Several had woolly flanks; one a single horn; huge bears; tiger-like and panther-like predators with fangs of unbelievable size; strange fowl, one flightless; as well as rodents big and small; immense owls and eagles, all drawn from a phantasmagorie, a recollection, that left Urrell in wonderment.

"You saw these in cave paintings, Agaratz?"

"No, not caves."

"Where then?"

"I not see them. They no more. Gone with old peoples."

"But Agaratz, how can you draw them?"

He remembered the engraving of his own great bear, one like those Agaratz drew now.

"Urrell, when you have *poodooec*, you *see* too."

"How can I have *poodooec* Agaratz?"

Agaratz fixed his gleaming eyes on Urrell's. The lad held his gaze.

"Not yet, Urrell. Not ready yet."

Any more questions would be fielded likewise. Any annoyance, any impatience, he felt, would go unanswered.

Four days farther on their river met outliers of a range of hills and turned aside to flow elsewhere. They left it, not without a little tug at Urrell's heart. Agaratz, on its banks, chanted a brief farewell to the current that had been their companion and guide for days.

They now entered slopes clad with the forest trees of Urrell's boyhood, oaks, ashes, beeches, elms, walnuts, and an understorey of hazel nuts and elder, hawthorn and crab apples, with nuts and fruit ripening. Wildlife abounded again. Hinds in herds, led by stags, trotted off at their approach, aurochs lurked in deeper glades, lynxes stared at these strange bipeds, the wolf and lion, and slank off to ponder such oddities. He thought he glimpsed the woolly horned creatures Agaratz had drawn but said nothing lest Agaratz's grin gave away yet another trick of his. His companion was in a playful mood. He mimicked the calls of a doe with fawn till one came within arm's length and only started off when she espied Rakrak. An owl landed on his upheld wrist. To Urrell's alarm he enticed a she-bear with cubs to eat a piece of jerky from his hand, her two cubs warier than mother, keeping a little away, and Urrell, to Agaratz's amusement, farther away still, aware of a she-bear's fury at the slightest hint of a threat to her young. It was an idyllic scene, made more so by the delicious thrill of fear down Urrell's spine.

It seemed to whet Agaratz's sense of fun.

"You like to see animals come, Urrell?"

"Oh, yes."

"We go a little farther and I show you." As so often, he left Urrell wondering.

CHAPTER 32

L ater that afternoon they came to a clearing, a dell in the forest, one of those areas where the trees seem to have held off encroachment to allow the grass and flowers a patch of their own. Urrell felt that Agaratz knew the place. A brook ran across it. Butterflies flitted about in the sunlight and Rakrak, suddenly skittish, once her pack was off, gambolled about and ran in circles. Piura settled down to watch.

"You see, Urrell, Rakrak knows is good place."

They threw off most of their apparel, along with their packs, and Urrell lay in the herbage, basking and chewing grass stalks. He looked as Agaratz rummaged in a pouch; he pulled out not something to eat but his flute.

Urrell sat up.

Agaratz began to play. Warming to his tune he rose and circled, the limp from his bare club foot noticeable, a short cape and trews his whole attire. As the music quickened, filling the glade, Agaratz circled faster to it. Urrell leant on an elbow listening, half-expecting something unusual to happen, while Rakrak continued her excitement and gambols.

He had been so absorbed by the music, by the intenseness of the sounds which thrilled him to his hair roots, that at first Urrell did not notice they were no longer alone. Creatures were appearing from among the trees. First several deer edged out, bunched as though to give one another courage. Other animals followed, ears pricked towards the flute player. Urrell kept quite still. Out crept foxes, badgers, wild boar, more deer, cattle of a sort unknown to him, smaller than aurochs. All these drew closer, intent on the flute, in thrall to the sounds.

Rakrak squatted by Urrell, her skittishness gone. Agaratz circled. The least pause in the stream of notes might break the spell. On it went. A panther, drawn by so much easy game, padded out of the shadows and Urrell, expecting it to leap, half stirred to warn Agaratz, thought better and lay back in the grass. It did no more than push itself forward to observe the source of the sounds, then plopped down to watch and listen. Other beasts appeared: several lionesses, woollier than Piura; a pair of true aurochs; and forest bison, shaggy coats moulting. Urrell noticed birds alighting on branches, attracted by the sight and perhaps staying to listen. However, it was when he saw the massive shape of a he-bear, upright at the wood's edge, head and round ears cocked inquisitively to the ring of animals, that he knew he was witnessing a sight beyond anything Agaratz had ever conjured before, or he might ever witness again. Mammoths could not have stunned Urrell more.

The performance went on and on, the music echoing animal calls yet transmuting them so that although Urrell made out within the line of melody sounds familiar to him from forest, grassland, heath and hill, they were such as to slip from memory no sooner heard. Were he to blow his own flute a year on end he knew that he could never recapture those sounds.

When Agaratz let the notes dwindle away and slowed to a stop in his circling, some animals shook themselves, some stretched, a deer pricked its way forward to sniff the flute in Agaratz's hand. Agaratz himself went about among the creatures, stroking one here, tickling another one's ears there. Urrell watched as panthers let him approach. Even the he-bear made no threatening movements before lumbering back into the forest. In ones and twos the animals drifted away, as though loth to return to their lives in the woods.

"Now hungry, Urrell. Eat." He looked worn. As he put the flute back into his pack, Agaratz gave Urrell a little grin, a 'you see, no tricks' look, and they settled down to pemmican and berries.

"We stay here, Urrell. Good place. Soon we meet people."

"Which people, Agaratz.?"

"Many. Some bads, some goods. You see. Be careful. I tell Rakrak and she watch."

Agaratz lit the fire that night using only the driest sticks, to avoid making smoke, something he had not bothered about during all the days of their long trek. Urrell was reminded of the wisp of smoke he had seen from the scarpment, when still a boy on his long, lonely journey. The wisp had meant humans, but peril as well, yet it had led him down into the fir forest in search of company, to the bison hunters, and then to Agaratz.

Any wisp of smoke now might draw hunters too.

However, they slept untroubled, trusting to Rakrak's watchfulness. No one, nothing could have crept up on her unannounced.

They broiled jerky for all four in the embers next morning, supplemented with white mushrooms that studded the grass by the brook. Urrell found patches of wild strawberries which they crammed into their mouths by the handful.

"Two days, we arrive," said Agaratz. "Many mens, womens." Urrell felt a rush of joyous anticipation: he was beginning to yearn for the squeals and glances of girls, the tales of old men and women, the sound of voices, the smells of a camp, the company of young men against whom to measure himself.

CHAPTER 33

Over the brow of a low ridge, clear of the tree-line, their little group looked down on a vast natural bowl, crossed by a river. A line of rocky heights blocked the view in the distance. He could see a cavernous opening, and several smaller ones, in the face of the rock line. Scattered about were clumps of humans. Fires smoked. Urrell scanned the scene as far as he could see, and it looked to him as if all the folk in the world were assembled there. Never before had he seen so many people, not even when his tribelet joined other clans to overwinter by the sea on shellfish, carrion and seaweed.

"See, Urrell, big moot. Only come when long years."

What 'long years' were he did not ask, so engaged were his eyes on the scene below.

"Come Urrell, come."

They gathered up their bundles, pouches, sling-bags and weapons and loped down the grassy slope. From other directions other arrivals were approaching the riverside, choosing spots and making camp. Agaratz went straight to one of the few trees, an oak, by the river, as though he knew the place already. The orderly way other groups did the same, heading for one spot rather than another, like migrant fowl to old nest sites, left Urrell feeling odd-man-out, with a feeling of 'what next?'

Nothing happened. Agaratz lit their fire, sending Urrell to scour the outlying parts of the combe for fuel. Children and elders foraged alongside him, but Urrell, wary of so many people, shunned all contact.

Two or three days went by in this way, as more groups and family parties arrived and slotted themselves into the settlement. The river was rich in fish, freshwater crabs, crayfish and mussels. Overnight, edible mushrooms appeared in the grass. Raspberries, whortles and small sweet plums throve on the outer slopes of the combe and the open country beyond. The delicious woodland strawberries abounded. Urrell found thickets of hazel and groves of walnut, their nuts coming into season. He brought back pouchfuls. One day he found a hive in a tree hollow. With his boyhood skills he smoked out the bees, filching honey while leaving enough not to destroy the hive – that much he had learnt from Agaratz – and returned to camp with his booty to find Agaratz in deep conversation with a young woman.

She was comelier than the general run of females he saw in the camps, or the giggly maidens he encountered while berry-picking who fell silent as he went past with his wolf. This one looked him straight in the face. He had a sense of recognition, one which occurs perhaps twice or thrice in a lifetime, of knowing a stranger beforetimes. It might have been her eyes – they bore a family likeness to Agaratz's. With them she looked quizzically at him, a faint mockingness as of pre-knowledge, or perhaps Agaratz had been speaking about him to her, so that he felt clumsy before her. But the mockingness was not disdainful, rather the look he had seen in kittens, cubs, young creatures engaged in tumbling matches, even in the roguish grin of Agaratz himself.

She turned to speak to Agaratz, in a language that differed hardly from his, many words of which Urrell had learnt but not enough to follow rapid speech between two native speakers. It was the first time he had ever heard it spoken between two persons. Agaratz's features shone with pleasure, whether from what was said or from hearing his own tongue, or both, Urrell could not tell, nor tried. It did not concern him; and yet he knew it did.

"This Guimera, Urrell. I think woman for you."

It was put in Urrell's language. She was not to understand, although she no doubt caught the drift of Agaratz's brokerage. Her eyes smiled, as much a come-hither as no-you-don't, neither arch nor coy, yet all of these in a glorious amalgam that left Urrell suddenly red and blurting, reduced from the manliness of the young hunter to a blattering fool. Or so he saw himself. Oddly, he did not mind a bit. It was all part of this meeting he found himself in, of this new place of people, brakes full of berries, nut groves, gaggles of girls picking fruit. On impulse, he offered her the leathern pouch of honey he had brought back. With a little bob, she took it, looked in and dipped her finger into the liquid gold. As she licked the honey, her eyes rose to meet Urrell's and he saw in them that mocking playfulness he knew from Agaratz, the herald to some performance, some mimickry, some prank to astonish him. But none came. Instead she smiled, said something to Agaratz and was gone. With his honey. She had not been a dream.

CHAPTER 34

Though he plied Agaratz with questions about the girl in the days that followed he could learn little, only that by some chance Agaratz had stumbled on people from a remote clan akin to his own in language and appearance. Whence they came he either did not know or would not tell. Nor where they were camped.

The girl's smile remained a fixation in Urrell's mind. He took to ranging around in search of her, edging up to groups and encampments hoping for a glimpse of her, or of folk who might be of her people and a clue to her whereabouts, but she had vanished.

"You see again, Urrell, you see Guimera, but not before dance."

"Dance?"

"Dance for maid girls. Now eat, Urrell. You get strong for fights."

"What fights, Agaratz?"

"Fights when young mens wrestle, throw, run, to show how strong."

He mimicked the competitions, even ordeals, young men were expected to undergo. Urrell had been noticing youths larking about more than usual, practising spear-throwing, lifting stones and running with them, performing feats of strength, wrestling. They must be preparing. The boys of his tribelet had talked about trials too, fearfully. To fail them meant banishment from the clan, to starve alone in the forest. "Show me, Agaratz."

They found a secluded spot, a little dell, where Agaratz's lessons might not be overlooked. From falls and twists of those brawny arms Urrell was soon bruised and aching. It was days before he could remain upright from his mentor's hug and thrust. He soon realised that strength alone was not enough, that Agaratz was teaching him skills and feints no other youths practised when he watched them, and his confidence grew. He learnt to use Agaratz's power in mock attacks to yield before him and throw the attacker, nimbly sweeping his feet from under him, or, if down, launching his foe overhead with unexpected leg moves only Agaratz could invent. He would be able to hold his own.

Next came marksmanship with javelin, throwing-stick and missiles. Urrell recalled his early javelin-casting lessons. Since then hunting had honed his skills, yet still Agaratz insisted on practice, striving to convey that sense of certainty when the weapon knew its mark, as in dreams. Urrell could not capture it, only sometimes in response to a sudden movement, when he was paying least attention.

His wanderings among the camps, looking for Guimera and her kin, were not always welcome. Several times he fought off youths bigger than himself and but for Rakrak's snarls might have come off worse. It did not stop his searching. At the very edge of the encampments, where the poorest and weakest groups huddled, he came across some strange people, shaggy and short-limbed, who shied away from his friendly gestures. They pointed at Rakrak; he signed she was harmless. Their weapons were cruder, less well made than his or those of other groups. Their shelters sketchier.

He was drawn to them. When not foraging or practising his skills with Agaratz, he took to visiting their camp and squatting with them. As their trust grew, they tried to speak to him, crouching face to face and parleying with series of clickings, snorts and guttural coos. They also made a range of whistling sounds. Urrell noticed that when one of them wanted to speak to him, he stared straight at him, as they did between themselves. Their eyes were unusually deep-set, filmy, and often greenish. It was as though they needed this eye contact in addition to speech. They reminded Urrell of the three squat figures he had espied in the cold, from the great tree.

They grew to like and expect his visits. He brought them little gifts of game, a honeycomb, crayfish. They greeted him by pressing noses face-to-face and staring into his eyes. The men's ragged whiskers and hair smelt stale and the message those opaque greenish eyes sought to convey remained untransmitted. He wondered if Agaratz would understand, but for the first time felt loth to ask – these people were his discovery, and he would explore them. Besides, Agaratz spent long whiles away, between training sessions, on what he did not say. Lulled by these thoughts, in the unchanging warm weather of late summer, Urrell lived from day to day without much thought of the trials ahead.

During one of these visits to his ragged friends Urrell determined to penetrate into their minds. They, in turn, appeared to wish to respond. Urrell squatted in front of an elder and locked gazes with him. As he stared into the old man's rheumy eyes a picture formed deep down in them, as though Urrell were prying into an ancient vision in someone else's memory, resurrected from ages past. In an icy landscape of vast slopes, dark shapes moved, too small at first and distant to make out. The harder he stared the closer they came, till he recognised the woolly flanks of a huge kind of bison, of musk-oxen and then, farther away, the unmistakable outlines of hairy mammoths. Tiny human figures trailed behind them.

"*Mammurak!*" He jumped up, breaking the spell. The old man's eyes emptied. It was too late to recapture the vision, to Urrell's bitter regret. Had those humans been hunters, or worshippers of the mammoths? Could this old man, indeed all his folk, connect to the mammoths in a memory held in common by these silent people? Urrell had heard of some men who could summon fishes out of the water, and as a boy had once seen an old man call the seals to the shore to be slaughtered. Could these people call up mammoths?

Something of his thoughts must have connected with the elder. The old man rose and went into his hutch. He came out holding a length of hide, a sort of belt, one end of which he handed to Urrell while he grasped the other.

He was expecting something to happen. Both waited. As they did so, Urrell felt the thickness of the hide and its coarse stubble of shaven bristles. As he wondered at it, the air grew cold around the encampment, the old man mumbled and clucked in the manner of his people and stared with a greenish intensity at Urrell, the misty, empty eyes lighting with new power, drawing Urrell away from where he was, into a coldness remotely recalled from the episode at the huge tree.

Later he could scarcely recreate what happened as he froze in his summer apparel. A vast distance traversed, behind the elder and a group of his clan. They travelled into the ever-colder, ever-farther, ever-vaguer elsewhere. Urrell's awareness grew fainter but he hung on to it, knowing he must not let go, as a man knows he survives in the cold by dint of consciousness.

His reward came. Through snow-dazzled eyes he saw, he knew he saw, within a stone's cast of him, a group of massive animals, darkly outlined against the surrounding whiteness. His companions went towards the mammoths and his last memory was of them trudging in the snow behind the huge creatures as the animals lumbered away.

When he came round he was curled on the ground. He got up and looked around for the camp, for the elder and his folk. All had vanished: hovels, hearths, people.

In his hand, he held the strip of hide. This he would reveal to no-one, not even to Agaratz. It was to be his alone.

*****

Meanwhile, Agaratz seemed to have a quest of his own, absenting himself without a word for days. He would not answer Urrell's tentative enquiries, only saying, "Soon see."

He was loth to spy on his mentor, even wondering if he was meant to or not. By chance he got his answer when, out foraging in a remoter part of the combe's rim, he stumbled on a sight that struck him still, making him hold on to Rakrak's fur lest she rushed forward: it was Agaratz. He was stripped to his breechclout, face and limbs streaked white and red, his rusty mane dishevelled and hanging down his humped back, his ears and cheeks. He was intoning the same lament which Urrell remembered from Agaratz's long farewell to his dead kinsfolk in the cavern on the River Nani. He was addressing them again, but why? Was he about to rejoin them? Fear rose in Urrell's whole being, of possibly becoming an orphan once more.

Whether in answer to the lament or not – he would never know or ask – the ground shook. A powerful tremor nearly knocked Urrell off his feet. He knew these occurred and remembered a severe earthquake when he was small that had brought down sea cliffs and cantles of rock from crags. Old women had told the boy that the Great Bear in his cavern underground had woken and shaken himself. Even as a small boy he had found that unlikely. He had never sought an explanation from Agaratz, the all-knowing, any more than he asked what shooting stars were meant to be, or do, flashing across the night sky as he gazed at the stars. Some things were not known or meant to be known.

During the tremor Agaratz had remained motionless in his posture of supplication, the lament rising.

Urrell edged back and returned silently to camp. He noticed that the rock face over the biggest cavern bore new cracks and that one or two slabs had detached and were being cleared away.

CHAPTER 35

One day activity started round the grassy open space in front of the cavernous openings. For the first time Urrell noticed men entering and leaving the caves. They carried in objects taken from shelters round the green and returned empty-handed. When he tried to see what they were doing, old men in strange furs, carrying ceremonial wands, barred his approach and shooed him and other youths away.

When he asked Agaratz, he only got the same "Soon see".

And soon he did. A long horn blast next dawn announced the start. From every shelter and hollow girls wended their way to the green. Urrell wanted to follow.

"Only young womens, Urrell, this day."

He watched them stream over the green into the caves, to the blare of horn-blasts, and waited for them to come back out again. They did not. Nothing else happened all day save the ceaseless horn-blowing at the cave mouths, performed by men in furs with stag antlers on their heads, led by one adorned with the horns of a bull. That night the blaring continued and the maidens remained confined. No-one in the camp slept, fires blazed, groups sat round them, eyes on the green.

At dawn the maidens streamed out, to more blares on horns. They were almost naked, bodies streaked white and red, hair hanging down, faces haggard. A huge shout rose across the encampment, mixed with yells and ululations, as much from women as from men. Urrell noticed that Agaratz remained silent. As suddenly as they had begun, the shouts died down. The horn-blowing stopped and all fell quiet.

The tall man, he of the bull's horns, made to look taller by his headgear, took the lead with a blast of his long trumpet, followed this time with several notes, a sort of tremolo, which had the effect of setting the girls into a circular dance, one behind the other, holding hips. A group of old women began a monotonous rhythm tapped out on drum-like hollow logs, accompanying the feet of the maidens. This went on and on. From his distance, Urrell could not make out whether Guimera was among the begrimed, painted figures jigging round and round.

The dance proved the only event of that day, and continued until exhaustion set in, the circle of girls dwindling as dancers fell from weariness, sprawling where they tumbled, or gasping on their hands and knees in the grass, hair hanging down. By dusk there remained but half a dozen maidens still shuffling round and Urrell imagined he saw Guimera as one of them in the shape of a taller girl with tawny locks that straggled over her shoulders on to her painted breasts.

As suddenly as it had begun, the tap-tap of the old women ceased; the horn was blown; the exhausted girls, those still upright and their sisters who got up or were helped up by one another, re-entered the cave mouths for the night. The throng of watchers dispersed to their shelters, fires and food.

When Urrell reached his shelter, Agaratz was already enlivening the embers to grill bison meat he had traded for beads from neighbours who had had a good hunt. Of what might occur on the morrow there was no hint, but whatever it was to be Urrell vowed to himself to get nearer to the green, through the crowd, to see Guimera. Outside, there was a sense of anticipation in the camp. Rakrak slept beside Urrell, her head on his feet. Piura gently snored nearby.

Nothing happened next day, only tension hanging in the air, an aftermath of excitement from the dancing of the girls, the blaring of trumpets, the drumming, the horned men. Agaratz looked wary. "Keep Rakrak and Piura here," he said.

Gangs of youths, with the high spirits and the pack instincts of young males, roamed about looking for fights. Wrestling challenges ended in injuries and spear wounds were not uncommon. Stones flew. Misrule reigned.

Amongst all this a gang of tall men, swarthy and bedecked with beads, came round, upsetting shelters, bullying and purloining, in search of someone or something. Agaratz, at his cooking, looked up. "Watch, Urrell. Spears."

Both recognised men from the tribe that they had crossed on the grasslands. They must have heard of a hunchback or of a youth with a wolf.

Agraratz laid out his spears, signing to Urrell to do likewise. He heaped pebbles beside his stone-thrower, three short throwing javelins with the spear-thrower, and a cudgel inset with flints at the knob-end which he had just made, a weapon new to Urrell. Satisfied with these preparations, he stood up to watch the progress of the oncomers. Shrieks from shelters, shouts and cries, signalled their advance.

The tallest, the leader to judge from feathers strung in his hair, noticed Agaratz first, pointed with a spear and yelled to the others, who came out of a shelter they were ransacking, its inhabitants fleeing downhill. The men advanced up the slope towards Agaratz and Urrell. There were six of them. Agaratz showed no concern, merely stooping to pick up a pelt and wrap it round his right forearm as a shield. "Do too, Urrell." As Urrell did so, he shooed Rakrak back into the shelter for safety. Piura, by the fire, crouched and watched.

When they were within range, Agaratz held his spears aloft and brought them down points first, a sign of non-aggression, only to be met by a yell of derision. Agaratz gestured to Urrell to do as he did: he laid down the long spears and picked up his spear-thrower and short javelins. Urrell's, with its rim of tiny mammoths, felt warm, ready for action in his grasp, a true weapon.

Two spears flew close and now Urrell saw the purpose of the wadge of pelt: with it Agaratz fielded the missiles, snapped the shafts as he had done before, and threw the pieces at their foes. Then it was Agaratz's turn. Urrell was to see another side of his mentor. The yellow eyes blazed at the spearmen advancing up-slope, never a good tactic for missile warfare. Agaratz set the butt of a javelin in the dub of the thrower, singled out the tall man and in a long arc of his left arm, using all the power and leverage of his shoulder, hurled it. The man continued forward as though the javelin had missed. Even Urrell thought it had. Then he fell on his face. His fellow warriors paused, looked uphill, looked at their leader, and fled. Timid people who had been peeping out of their shelters started to creep out. A boy shouted he had found the javelin farther down the slope and ran up to Agaratz with it, proud of the blood on his fingers. Urrell realised that the javelin had not only hit its target but gone through the man's ribs and beyond.

Agaratz turned back to his hearth and cooking.

Around the corpse huddles formed to stare. From there they drifted up to Agaratz and Urrell, making an uneasy half-circle, others packing in behind the first arrivals. Several tendered small gifts, a lame old man stepped forward, spoke and made an obeisance, an old woman prostrated herself followed by others who beat the ground with the palms of their hands and wailed. At this Agaratz left his cooking to acknowledge their attention, leaning on a spear, flanked by Urrell, a wolf and a lioness.

Urrell wondered what he would do next. Mimick animals? Do handstands? Pipe?

Instead, Agaratz stepped forward, raised the woman and went

up to the crowd, touching each member in turn as though pacifying a herd. When all were quietened he waved them away with both arms. They turned and went back to their fires. Several men, led by the old man who had spoken, dragged the body away.

It was a golden afternoon. Word of Agaratz's feat must have travelled fast. Small knots of men and women came to look at him, standing humbly a little way off. What they sought Urrell could only guess – some kind of solace, a sense of wonder at the survival of such a strange being, for everyone knew the fate of babies born hunchback or malformed.

Agaratz, after his spear-throw and the calming of the crowd, seemed weary and somewhat shrunken to Urrell's eyes.

CHAPTER 36

In dribs and drabs the maidens had left the cavern to return to their family groups. Urrell did not see Guimera come out. She must have slipped by when he was out foraging with Rakrak. Although he searched among the shelters, wherever he dared, alive to the hostile clan whose leader Agaratz had slain, he could not find her or whatever group she belonged to. She had vanished.

When asked, Agaratz waved a hand. "You see. Now not."

Little knots of people went on hanging about their shelter. They stared at Agaratz, at Urrell, at the wolf and at the lioness. Shyly some brought offerings, gifts of food, objects to trade, and in return Agaratz showed them his stock of beads, amulets and carvings in bone and ivory for them to wonder at. Nothing Urrell saw from others could vie with the craftsmanship of his objects, yet Agaratz looked at each offering with interest and encouragement.

A woman brought a sick child. Agaratz took the child, felt it and muttered over it, rubbing its belly with a paste of his making. Urrell watched as it seemed to improve. The rumour of a healer ran round the camp and soon others with ailments, wounds, sores, even fractures, trooped to be cured, patched or blown over.

He turned none away. Urrell observed that his concentration of mind, chants, hands laid on the sick and smoke blown over some of them wore Agaratz down. After he had laid hands on an ill person, muttering under his breath, sometimes kneading a back or a limb, he would appear diminished, would need to rest back in the shelter. It was entirely new behaviour to Urrell who, as though in response, felt surges of energy enter him as Agaratz tired.

"You touch, Urrell."

The patient was an old woman bewailing aches in her middle. Urrell acted as he had seen Agaratz do. He laid her down, placed both hands on her midriff, and concentrated, eyes closed. He wondered what would happen. As he did so, Agaratz came from behind and placed his own hands on Urrell's shoulders, pressed down with them, accompanying the pressure with an incantation. In moments Urrell felt a warmth run through him, down his arms and into the woman. She ceased her moaning and went limp.

"Now you *usashin*, Urrell. Heal sicks."

Urrell's arms ached slightly and his shoulders felt stiff. A momentary weariness overtook him but then power seemed to flow back through. He felt a need to play his flute and to recapture the melody from the mammoth cave that had so enraptured him, oh so long ago.

"You play, Urrell. Pipe ready." There it lay by his couch, not where he remembered he had stored it in his innermost pouch. The ivory was warm to the touch – warm as from another hand. It came alive as he blew, tentatively, fingering the holes, creating notes, and he felt that he was being strengthened in order to extend its range, and to be at one with many things, even with mammoths.

Since the revelation of Agaratz's healing powers seldom a moment passed without gawpers hanging round the shelter, expecting who-knew-what, watching and staring. At Urrell's first notes these now drew near, some waving to summon others from a distance, heralds of an event. In a trice Urrell had an audience. Scarcely aware of their presence, he was borne away by the sounds issuing from this warm, living ivory thing that he held and handled and which willed him to sway and jig to a compass of its own, not his.

It must have been quite a while. Returning as from a trance, Urrell noticed with a little shock that he must have moved whilst he played, for the grass was trampled in a circle. He remembered nothing. Squatting in front of the lodge were numbers of people from other shelters who shook themselves as the music ceased, released as the animals had been when Agaratz played to them. They got up and drifted away, while one or two shyly approached to see the pipe Urrell had been playing, as the deer had done with Agaratz.

"Good," said Agaratz. "You play *mammurakan-a*. If mammoths, they come."

Nothing Agaratz had ever said to him equalled that. He fell into the sleep of the weary and did not wake till hours, nights, whole days perhaps, had elapsed.

It was then he thought of the strange ragged folk in their outlying camp, with their knack of evoking mammoths. His strip of hide was real enough. Would they have reappeared, as they had vanished? They might like him to play, he thought, so he took his pipe. He knew the way perfectly well, yet when he got to the campsite nothing remained. Their shelters, their very untidiness, had vanished as though they had never been. Rakrak showed no interest, or sniffed around as she might have been expected to when a group whose scent she knew had decamped. Urrell observed that even the grass was unruffled: nothing and no-one had ever been there that his eye could discern.

He said nothing of this to Agaratz on his return.

CHAPTER 37

Whatever was to take place before the main cavern hung fire. Urrell saw now how the cavern roof was fissured, and was surprised he had not noticed before. Agaratz seemed listless, as though waiting for events to unfold. Since the maidens' dance, the whole camp site had gone quiet. Wherever Urrell now wandered with his wolf among the shelters the inhabitants acknowledged him. Was it his pipe, or the power in the healing hands of Agaratz, that accounted for his prestige, he wondered? Some came to him with ailments, as they had gone to Agaratz, mostly children and old women who seemed to have most faith in him. When his healing worked he knew it by the ache in his body, the weariness, as though the patient's pains had transferred to him.

One night Agaratz pointed at the near full moon. "Cave for mens soon."

The initiation ceremonies, the contests, anything else Agaratz had hinted at would be about to begin. Urrell felt confident, despite trepidation before the unknown, confident that nothing could best him now – Urrell the music-maker, the healer, the apprentice of Agaratz the master-healer and master of *poodooec* who was initiating him, little by indirect little, into his mysterious abilities. He thought of Guimera and the thought of her gave him strength and added purpose. That night both Piura and Rakrak cuddled up to him as never before.

A pre-dawn blare on a hollowed bone trumpet from the biggest cave summoned the young to its gaping maw. From lodges and hollows across the wide combe youths and boys shuffled down to the green in front of the cliff face. He of the horned headgear directed them in, helped by other elders clad and muffled in skins. There was quite a throng already entering as Urrell slipped in behind them, stooping a little not to be noticed. He was older and taller than most.

What to expect, none knew. Fearful tales recounted by old men, wont to redouble the content of their own far-off initiation rites, were no help. The boys and youths crowded together for comfort, in the grip of a fear which no bravery, no crowing, no boasting can allay – the fear of an unknowable yet inevitable ordeal to come.

Urrell's eyes soon accustomed themselves to the interior. Caverns, he realised, held less fear for him than for most of his companions due to his visits to caves with Agaratz. Despite which, this cavern astonished him. In size, judged by lights placed in crevices and on ledges all around, it could easily have swallowed Agaratz's funeral cavern along with the cave of the honeycombs. The light came, Urrell saw, from little clay lamps like those cave painters used – a wick burning smokily from the edge of a puddle of fat in a palm-sized holder. The air reeked of them. Several hundred pairs of frightened eyes flickered to right and left at the impenetrable blackness overhead; at black gaps where other caverns led off from the main hall; at what unimaginable horrors and trials those caverns held; at things no quivering mind could conjure with, any more than a sleeper can control the nightmare that engulfs him.

They were herded by figures dressed in skins, complete with animal heads, antlers and claws. Some wore pelts of creatures no-one had ever seen. Each guardian carried an antler swinging by his side from a thong in his belt, a pierced antler such as the one Urrell recalled from the hoard of ancient objects Agaratz stored in their home cave. He had wondered then at its purpose. Here they seemed to be some kind of a symbol of power, perhaps a power itself packed with *poodooec*. As though in answer to these thoughts, the leader stepped on a rock and started to whirl his antler overhead on the end of its thong, swooping it within a finger's breadth of the cowering heads bunched in front of him. The instrument whirred through the air, ever faster, ever nearer, driving heads down till a tine struck a boy's skull and sent him flying to the ground among the others' feet. All around him Urrell smelt the fear of the cringeing mass, and he vividly recalled his own terrors of the abyss of the tusks.

He had been a boy then. Now he was grown, a healer, a player of music, strong with his own *poodooec*, so that the terror rising amid these cowering, shoving youths drew only disdain from him. And as for the guardians of the cavern, their faces masked behind animal skins, wielding their whirrers, he intended to observe them without drawing attention to himself, and to pit his own power against theirs. In the gloom he would not be noticed, whereas he would be able watch them, high above their prey on stones or stands.

When their herders deemed they had instilled terror enough into the troop of youths they began barking orders at them, with snarls and yells meaningless to Urrell who waited to see what the outcome of all this might be. It soon came. The animal-men hived off groups of youths, parting them from the packed mass with shoves and prods from their antlers, using these like staves of office. Each grouplet was driven off towards a side cave, those that Urrell had noticed on arrival, and disappeared within. He was one of the last to be rounded up, with the remaining four or five others, all practically out of their wits with fear, eyes staring, mouths dribbling, nether clouts none too clean.

They were shoved into a small chamber, unlit, and left there. Instinctively Urrell found the wall and edged round it in search of openings or any features, but the surface was unbroken. While he felt his way round, the others were whispering and moaning in a huddle somewhere in the middle, unused to total dark. There was nothing to which their eyes could become accustomed, not a glimmer to comfort their minds. They whimpered like small children. Meanwhile Urrell continued round the chamber wall, intent on finding clues as to why they were held there. His fingertips would tell him if anything was engraved on the walls, even a trace of painting, but they felt nothing. When he was something like halfway round, the floor grew wet underfoot. He went on feeling his way, ignoring the terror of his fellows, convinced the wet had to enter by some gap or hole which might explain why they were herded there. So, fingering his way he came to what seemed to be the source of the wet cave floor, a sort of alcove with water oozing from it. The recess was about an arm's length deep where, reaching in, his fingers traced water trickling down a slimy surface of spongy contours so flesh-like that he flinched back as from a body.

That seemed to be the signal for a chorus of shrieks from his companions. Something or someone was tormenting them. They were being whipped or prodded in the total dark and milling about to avoid the blows. Urrell kept back and waited to discover what would transpire.

He soon saw. One of the masked man-like beings entered with a light. Its feeble illumination revealed a tangle of terrified youths on the floor of the cave, cowering from a half-human half-animal shape, like a huge upright wild boar. It might have been a human or might have been a gryphon from campside stories of creatures that slid along the bottoms of lakes or lurked in the depths of forests for all the quaking youths knew. Urrell, in shadow out of range of the light, leant right back against the cave wall to watch. He felt detached.

With the tines of its whirrer the apparition prodded the youths to their feet. They, half upright, half crawling, were driven towards the recess from which Urrell had just stepped back into the shadows. As the jumbled bunch of fearful youths approached the recess the light disclosed a vague shape inside, glistening with damp. It was the thing Urrell had touched. He edged round behind the group and its tormentor to glimpse what it was – a female, heavy-bellied, over-breasted, so life-like that even Urrell was dumbstruck. In the poor light, a tremor ran over its skin. In front of the figure, squirming, terrified youths, some out of their wits, were being shoved and poked towards the thing. Each had to touch its breasts and belly, run his fingers down the slimy thighs and fall down before it. No words were uttered but the pelt-clad figure's instructions were clear enough.

This done, the youths were herded towards the other side of the chamber where the faint light revealed a gap wide enough for one at a time to go through. No one wanted to be first. Noises could be heard through the gap, coming from whatever lay beyond. They were more grunts and howls than human sounds. By dint of prodding and pushing by the figure, first one then the others were driven ahead into the cleft towards this, their next ordeal. Urrell hung well back. He felt in control, curious, pitting his wits against those of the cavemen. This sense of control flowed through him, like a new power, in some way connected with the chamber he was about to leave. It was then he heard – he was certain he heard – a long deep gurgling sigh from behind him, from the direction of the squelchy figure in its recess, which sent him hurrying to find the gap and grope his way down.

Faint but steady light in the still air of a large cavern lit up a scene to test the stoutest heart. Sprawled, crouching, trembling, his companions and the youths from other groups were assembled in one large mass. All must have undergone trials in side caves like the one he had witnessed. He hung back to watch what came next.

At some invisible signal, from several openings, bison-headed creatures leapt forward and charged the mass of defenceless youths. Yells echoed amid sobs and cries in the dimness. The beasts seemed half human. Urrell, squinting closely in the gloom, was certain he made out the fore legs of bison, complete with hooves, in several of the creatures that rushed forward on all fours, snorting and tossing their huge heads. Then no sooner had they arrived, knocking down quite a few of the youths, than they turned and disappeared back into their lairs.

Over all this the pelted bull-headed figure reigned, his seven-tined antler whirrer held aloft. He was waiting. Dozens of fear-crazed eyes were fixed on him. All they could see would have been what Urrell saw from his place in the darkness: an outsized creature, a man-beast in fur, with power of life and death over them.

The antler came down. On the signal, skin-clad figures sprang from the gloom. With switches they roused the youths from their prostration and drove them towards the back end of the cavern, beyond the range of the few lamps. Those behind, whipped by their tormentors, pushed and shoved those ahead who held back from stepping into total darkness. The seething mass slowly disappeared from Urrell's view. Not till he of the antler moved to follow did Urrell dare bestir himself, edging round the cave wall and keeping well out of range of the meagre light.

By feel, and by following the receding sound of moans and cries, careful not to stumble or dislodge anything that might betray his presence to whatever lurked in the side caves, Urrell worked his way forward. His groping fingers found loose flakes of stone and he was wondering whether to choose one as a weapon of defence when his hands fumbled on several staves leaning against the rock face. He felt along them, fingering incisions and carvings along their shafts. They were some kind of wands of office. On the heaviest, almost a cudgel, his exploring fingertips found the knob end carved with the head of a mammoth. His hand closed on it, this wand which had awaited his coming for so long in that forlorn passageway. Who might have placed it there? For him? That was not a question he would have asked himself a few moons ago. He would simply have accepted it. Now all his senses were alive to what this meant, sharpened by lack of food, drink, sleep, into a higher awareness of what might lie ahead. In his palm, the mammoth head settled.

Guided by sounds, Urrell moved on. He used the staff as a blind man uses his stick. And like a blind man's stick it acted as an extension of his arm, feeling its own way. It seemed to lead. He wondered at this, wondering if it was his imagining, or whether his heightened awareness was playing tricks on him. He had never thought like this before. Into his mind's eye rose the image of Agaratz, of Old Mother behind him, and beyond her his boyhood cave. He saw again the bear's outline, his trek in the summer warmth, home cave and the savannah. The bison hunt. Rakrak, Piura. They were many journeys away, in another time, beyond any harm from this cavern. While thus lulled – his detachment was suddenly shattered and he was back in the pit, the heaped tusks glinting under the guard of the huge skull perched on its boulder, and he was reliving his shivering boyhood terror as he had shinned up the pine bole to safety and to Agaratz.

His grip tightened on the mammoth carving; his fear receded as he held on, like a flush of fever; he felt well again, out of danger, and went on.

This passage seemed a long one, as far as he could judge in the near-total blackness, twisting and turning into the mountain. With care, led by the wand held before him, he advanced in the wake of the throng of youths, more aware of their smell than of the sounds they made, now fainter with distance while their body reek hung in the still air along with the smeech and reek of guttering lamps in the motionless atmosphere.

He caught up with them, turning a corner. They were crouching and being fed in a sort of dimly-lit hall. Figures in furs, masked, handed the youths morsels that Urrell could not make out. They were allowed to drink from what looked like skins full of liquid. Beyond them he vaguely discerned an overbearing dark shape. Keeping in the shadows, Urrell edged round, alert both to the scene before him and to the sense of an impending event that would explain why the youths had been driven here. He also wanted to make out what the shape might be.

To his surprise the youths were allowed to rest, to drowse. Accordingly, Urrell squatted too, with his back to the cave wall, feeling hunger for the first time at the sight of the food being handed out. He too dozed off.

When movements roused him he saw that the masked figures were urging the youths up to dance, each youth holding a short lance which must have been distributed while Urrell dozed. Their purpose he waited to see, through the dimness of smoky torches stuck in cracks in the cave walls. There was no pipe music for the dancers, just a drumming from somewhere out of sight, on hollow logs or the like. Urrell's eyes watered from the torch smoke as he watched the jigging mass go round and round the dark shape in the centre, urged on by their masters of ceremony. What the shape was he could still not make out, though it looked animal-like.

No rest was allowed the dancers. They were being goaded to ever greater speed as the drumming grew faster till Urrell realised that they must have been fed a stimulant of some sort with the food, like the fungus Agaratz had given him to chew in the mammoth cave. That would drive them till they fell, with little recollection afterwards of their feat of endurance.

How long the dance went on Urrell had no way of telling. In caves another, slower, time holds sway, or so those old men by the sea had told him when they recounted tales of bygone wonders and monsters. That, they said, is why the dead were laid in hollows in certain deep caverns, so that they could escape into the land of *mamu* deep in the centre of the earth, beyond time. He had listened round-eyed; now he thought he better understood.

CHAPTER 38

Youths were beginning to fall exhausted amid the feet of the others.

The rhythm became yet faster, as well as louder. Dancers stumbled under the urgency and prodding of the goads. The culmination was close.

Urrell strove to guess what it might be, peering with smarting eyes through the smoky air. He had almost stepped beyond the shadows to get a better look when, to a crescendo of drumming and a resounding yell from the masked figures, the mass of youths, as though caught in a spell, turned towards the shape and stabbed it repeatedly with their spears. The act released them and they stared around. Some spears stayed embedded in the shape. Some lay where they were dropped, as the mass of youths allowed themselves, almost sheepishly, to be led away down a tunnel, leaving Urrell with the whole vast chamber to himself, somewhat surprised at his own composure. He collected a guttering torch and approached the shape, sniffing the acrid smell of humans mixed with grease, the earthen floor churned and filthy from so many feet.

Close up, the shape was that of a bison, in clay, thrice life size, and covered along the back with a bison hide complete with head and horns. Urrell walked right round it, holding up his failing torch and his mammoth wand. Stab marks in the clay flanks were plain to see. He even pulled out a lance to see how deep it went and leapt back, startled, when liquid seeped from the wound. He screwed up his courage to look more closely. In the poor light he could not be sure whether it was blood or not that oozed.

The overhang. His boyhood fear of the unseen creature in the den.

On his neck the small hairs rose. Shivers seized him and he would have fled headlong down a combe had there been one, a boy again gripped by untellable fears. For the first time since entering the caverns he felt the huge strangeness of where he was, entirely alone, deep in the earth. The others had gone. Suddenly he longed for human company – theirs. He was about to hasten off in their wake when he heard, from an unimaginable distance, but in the opposite direction, the unmistakable trumpeting harrumph – he quivered – of a mammoth. He listened again. It had gone. Then it came again, the blare he knew from Agaratz's mimickries.

It was a summons.

Urrell's wand drew him on. He collected several torches from their niches, burning low but making a tolerable light, enough to show him that yet another gallery led off from the hall of the bison. It had been from deep inside that the mammoth sound had come. He entered, eager, and for the first time since the start of the trials and tests felt a presence steering him. His strength grew; he felt neither hunger nor thirst; no more was he that frightened boy.

It was a long gallery, with twists, turns, narrows – and total silence. Had he heard the sound? He had been in no doubt what it was, but had he really heard it? To venture so deep into an unknown gallery, with a poor light likely to burn out, was a folly, yet the head of his staff, warm in his palm, lent him confidence and seemed to tug him forward.

He tapped the side of the tunnel with its tip as he went, more for company from the tap than guidance. His light was still strong enough to see by. He knew anyway that, light or no light, he would go forward, that he could find his way back in pitch dark under the guidance of the wand, with a new-found confidence and sense of direction that the wand, or something else in the cavernous silence, seemed to give him.

The air was quite still, neither cold nor threatening, just the deep chill of a cave atmosphere. Though he scrutinised the cave wall as he went for any signs of engravings, dots, dashes, devices, within the patch of light his torch cast, he found nothing. He, Urrell, was treading where none had trodden before.

Lost in this thought he turned a bend and was stopped by a wall of pure cold. One step forward and the cold rose so dense it felt like an ice-sheet; one step back and he was in the cave air again, bearable in his light furs. He tried again. Again the ice–cold air barrier stopped him short, making him blink. In his hand the wand hung limp, an ordinary stick, powerless beyond the barrier. His last torch had sputtered out.

As this was happening his eyes were becoming aware of a faint luminosity beyond the cold, of a greenish-blue tint in the air, as if filtered through a wall of ice. He began to make out shapes, a bulky one with other smaller ones grouped round it.

Their outlines became clearer. In the centre the bulky shape took the form of a huge beast, encircled by humans or semi-humans, devotees swaddled in furs. Then it came to him why he, Urrell, had been guided hither to see this, for before him stood a full-grown cow mammoth. As he stared and squinted in the faint light, she raised her trunk and trumpeted a huge blaring note which reached him, despite her apparent nearness (he could even make out the creature's long eyelashes), from a great distance. He heard this remote signal – meant for him? — and watched as, having delivered it, she cumbersomely turned round and strode away out of sight followed by her escort of humanish beings. They raised their short, clumsy spears in a sort of salute, whether to him or to something else out of sight ahead, he would never know.

Then they were gone with their puzzling yet familiar gait. His impulse to follow them was cut dead by the barrier of pure cold. With them faded the faint light.

Urrell found himself back in total darkness, unsure of what he had seen, or if he had seen anything at all.

CHAPTER 39

He must have stayed there a good while, stunned. Hunger began to make itself felt. His body had awoken. It was time to find his way back, his light having burnt out, trusting to instinct, to his hunter's sense of direction. If ever he needed Agaratz's certainty, it was now. He held on to his mammoth-headed stick as to an amulet.

With outstretched hand along the cave wall, tapping ahead with his wand lest he stumble into a sink-hole or pit, one of those abysses that trap creatures blindly venturing underground, Urrell crept along. Hunger and thirst now plagued him. Water sometimes oozed down rock faces and his fingers found these traces so he was able to lick the wet stone to dampen lips and tongue. But of food there was none in this mineral world, not the least sound of insects or of tiny rodents in the eternal blackness. He was longing for light. Even sight of his companions' taskmasters wielding their command antlers would have been welcome: he might have rushed up to them in gratitude for their company.

Never straying from touching distance of the cave wall to his left he reached a point where a feeling of unease warned him that he must have reached the chamber where the youths had danced round the bison figure with their spears. No lights remained, nor even a whiff of their wicks hung in the air. The sharp odour of all those frightened bodies had vanished. It was as if nothing had happened. Yet he sensed the bison was there, in the never-ending dark, master of the chamber. Did it know he was edging round by touch back the way he had come, avoiding the masked and fur-swaddled masters of ceremonies bullying and driving his fellows until they lost their wits from fear and fatigue?

He had witnessed them being herded off. Should he try to guess the way and follow them? Hunger and thirst, weariness from how long he could not tell, were making him light-headed.

Better to retrace his way in.

Once he knew he was beyond the reach of the bison he let himself drop to on the floor, cuddling his wand, and fell into a sleep so deep it was akin to dreamless unconsciousness.

How long this lasted he could not have told. Ordinary sleep has markers, intervals when the mind works of its own, times when the sleeper rises almost to the surface of consciousness, like a fish approaching the surface, then replunges into the depths. Thus the sleeper marks some sort of rhythm and his body knows when to waken. Nothing like this occurred to Urrell. Sleepers like this may sleep till they die. It is akin to the sleep of hunters caught in the snows who drowse to death.

A hand on his shoulder shook him alert.

"Agaratz," he blurted, but he was alone. His back and limbs felt as stiff as the stone they lay on. With effort he sat up. The wand in his palm felt ready to go while an urgent need to urinate hinted how long he had lain, and its painful discharge how long he had drunk nothing.

As he moved again it felt less that the wand led him than that he was guided through the dark. Somewhere in a side cave the female shape oozed; elsewhere lay the caves where the masters of ceremonies must dwell, yet not the slightest sound, nor the least glimmer of light, told of their existence.

It was his sense of smell that warned him, when the air changed, that he was close to a mouth of the cavern. A little further on he reached the exit into overcast daylight and looked eagerly around for the shelters studded up the combe, but it was not the cavern he had entered with the throng of trembling youths, nor the open sward where the maidens had danced before the crowds. He must have come out of a side entrance. He would have to scout round the bluff, through the scrub and trees till he found the moot.

Hunger, muted so long while he had been cut off in the dark, woke as from a sleep of its own, hand in hand with its sister, thirst. The air felt chill, as if the season had advanced in his absence. He rubbed his face, with its growth of young beard, a true measure of the passing of days and nights. Withal, his feeling of a new, lean strength, of manhood, comforted him: he had entered the cavern a grown youth and had come out a grown man.

Right or left? He waited to know which way, as he had waited for a hint on that scarp brink as a boy. The wand would say. He held it tight, his keepsake of the cavern. In the gloaming he saw how old it was, the shaft made of a wood unknown to him, hardened almost to stone with age, its mammoth knob of yellowed ivory worn down with handling. Only now did he wonder who had propped those wands against that cave wall, and why, and how long ago; and why had it been this wand rather than another that had chosen his hand.

It led. Hunger drove him. He must find the camp. Brushing through the undergrowth in the chill lee of the bluff there rose the acrid smell of the mottled stems and the big leaves, and his fear of the hole beneath the scarp: a boy again, he was fleeing down dale to the women berry-picking in the sunlight below. But there was no combe, no sunlight, no berry-pickers.

He hastened on, almost scurrying. Cold air hung in the shadow of the cliff. There was nothing he recognised despite his weeks of roaming and hunting around the camp. He must have come out of a distant cave, he thought, far from the main cavern he had entered such a while ago. On and on be pressed, blundering and weaving his way through the thick growth along the base of the bluff, convinced, thanks to his sense of direction, that the camp and its shelters and clumps of people lay round the next outcrop.

But for his wand and the comforting warmth of its ivory head in his palm he would have felt lost, lost not like going astray in the wilderness but more as in those dreams where no landmarks or recognisable objects assist the dreamer to wrench his way back to wakefulness, like a drowner in a slough reaching out to grasp an overhanging branch. He had known dreams where he knew he was dreaming, but could not shake the dreaming off. He wondered if he was dreaming like that now.

That night he camped down in brush and ferns, armed only with his wand, unafraid of beasts as the undercliff was silent, empty of game. He had found raspberries and eaten them by the handful, ravenous. He felt again as he had as a lad, bedding in bracken brakes on his journey over the moorland, hungry on a diet of berries and birds' eggs.

Before dawn, chilled, he was on his way again. He half expected to meet a wounded bison, hunters crouching to slay it, a kindly crookback holding out a venison haunch…

CHAPTER 40

Urrell's puzzlement deepened: how could he not recognise the cliffs, outcrops, trees if he had foraged so far afield from camp – he could not be that far away from the entrance to the cavern, could he? It was trance-like, this ever-treading weary progress among fallen rocks, scrub, the outfalls of the bluffs overhead. A few wild apples, small red crabs, their acid juice oddly vivid, seemed to startle him into a greater awareness, making him truly awake.

Then, suddenly, there were the familiar clumps of trees lining the rim of that long descent he had made, it seemed long ago, with Agaratz when they had arrived to camp by their tree and the hidden hearth stones which Agaratz had known about, but how? He had never thought to ask.

Rakrak saw him first. Her yelps of greeting and dance of welcome brought faces to stare from shelters as he wove his way past. He must look a wraith to them. Even those who knew him seemed startled. Could he have been absent so long? Given up for lost?

Agaratz rose from his fireside. "Ho, Urrell, you eat now."

The food was hot and ready, as for an expected guest. Urrell scarcely gave it a thought. He was suddenly utterly famished, the hunger suspended all those days, gnawing at his insides like a living creature with a hunger of its own.

"Soon games, Urrell, wrestles, throw spears, girls dance." If those were the tests and ordeals that Agaratz had trained him for, and the youths who had cringed and snivelled in the caverns were to be his opponents, Urrell felt he had little to fear.

While he gorged, Agaratz gave the wand his complete attention. He turned it over, stroked the shaft, scrutinised each tiny carving, fingered the head, even smelt it. The yellow eyes darkened as he bent over it, more crookbacked than Urrell remembered. He held up the wand before him. Then said something to the air.

Urrell knew enough of Agaratz's shifting, subtle language to tell that these words to the air were not part of it, nor perhaps language at all. The sounds were addressed over and above the wand, which Agaratz held horizontally, at shoulder height.

While this was happening people had been creeping from shelters, alerted by the wanderer's return, emboldening one another forward to form an edgy half-moon of staring faces. Urrell's absence, while the other youths had come out of the cave, must have been noticed, he thought, with an agreeable little tingle of self-importance.

However, there was nothing for them to see, except Agaratz's shaggy shape, motionless, holding aloft a baton as if to ward off something invisible. The wait went on till the onlookers began to shuffle; a boy fidgeted; an infant nuzzled to suckle; the crescent of attention wavered. People drifted off.

But a gasped 'oh' from the lingerers brought drifters scurrying back. The wand, still held aloft, was emitting smoke from both ends, as if blown by something inside the shaft, threatening to make it burst into flame. With a little gesture of showmanship Agaratz released the stick in mid-air, where it stayed, to a greater round of 'ohs' tinged with a frisson of fear.

Urrell had paused in his eating, a meat bone in his hand, as agog as anyone. Rakrak crouching beside him, whimpered. What next? This trick of Agaratz's surpassed any other. Urrell wondered how he did it, or if the power to hang in the air lay in the wand itself, that wand which had led him out of the labyrinth, had warmed in his grip when he had been so alone deep in the black entrails of the mountain.

For his next trick Agaratz simply reached out to the wand, caught it and twirled it playfully at the crowd, sending them helter-skelter downhill. His grin as he laid the wand on the grass in the shelter was meant for Urrell alone, his apprentice.

"Agaratz, where is Piura?"

"Piura no more." He waved a hand into the faraway and Urrell knew his lioness, Old Mother's facesake, was gone. No cairn would mark where.

CHAPTER 41

Agaratz asked nothing of Urrell about his adventures in the cavern depths though his hardships had been severe, deserving of notice. Only the wand interested Agaratz.

As he thought about it, Urrell suspected that Agaratz had known all along what he, Urrell, was undergoing in those dark galleries, the scenes he had witnessed and the perils he had experienced. If so, why did the wand so intrigue him? In an obscure way Urrell felt that he had been sent to fetch this ceremonial object from where it had lain beyond Agaratz's reach, within the domain of the cave men and their horned leader. Would the wand be missed from its companions? He imagined hide-clad searchers pouring out of the cave mouth in his pursuit. Memories of the mammoth tusks in the pit rose before his mind's eye, and he relived his boyhood's terrified scurry up the pine-log from the guardians of the tusks as they had closed in on him. He glanced at the wand lying on the turf, half-expecting a sign from it, a squirm, a puff of smoke. But it lay where Agaratz had left it, its flint-hard shaft dull in the hearth's glow. It looked safe enough. Should he touch it?

As he wondered whether to do so, flute music stopped him in mid-move, notes from Agaratz in answer to his thoughts? At first these notes were ones Urrell knew, often played, but then the melody rose and wandered beyond anything he could have drawn from the ivory. Out of the corner of his eye he saw the wand bend, arching itself. A trick too many: it lay dead straight when he looked directly at it. Quickly he turned to Agaratz but the flute player was engrossed in his music-making, pausing only to say, "Dawn, begin games," before resuming his playing.

No trumpet call heralded the competitions, yet as the sun rose all was astir in the encampment. Urrell got ready, ate, and following the instructions of Agaratz rubbed his upper body with goose grease that his mentor produced from a pouch. He checked his lances. Then Agaratz kneaded his back and shoulders, twisted his head till his neck bones cracked and his skin tingled.

"Now you ready, Urrell."

They set off downhill.

An autumnal briskness filled the air. Watchers were banked many deep on the sloping ground to witness events. Children ran in and out, mothers held infants, men leant on staves or spears.

In the open area before the cave mouth youths waited to compete. Urrell joined them. Inside the cave mouth stood men in furs, faces painted with stripes, some masked, and in their midst the towering figure of the horn-wearing leader clad from head to foot in skins, his face masked. He held his trumpet in one hand and an antler-roarer in the other.

The first pair of young men faced up to wrestle. They pulled and tussled till one fell. Another pair entered the rink. Again they wrestled till one bested the other. It seemed simple enough and when Urrell was summoned he stuck his lances in the ground and stepped forward. Though his opponent was taller Urrell floored him with a feint taught him by Agaratz. A ripple of applause ran round the crowd. Two officiants led Urrell to one side with the other winners.

CHAPTER 42

Half the day went by like this. Then pairs of winners were pitted against each other. Again Urrell had little difficulty in upsetting his man. He glanced round the crowd to see if Agaratz was watching how his coaching was being successful, but there was no sign of him or of Rakrak.

His third bout proved harder. Stronger contestants were surviving the eliminations and this contender stood a handspan above Urrell. He had observed Urrell's technique and was ready to parry his feints. They clasped each other round the shoulders and swayed one way and the other, the big man trying to kick Urrell's legs from under him. Urrell stumbled onto one knee and it would have been over but for a surge of strength that came to him as from nowhere; he slid his grip to the man's waist and in an extraordinary effort lifted him off his feet and threw him on his back, winding the fellow.

The feat earned a murmur of applause from the throng as Urrell rejoined the winners' group. It was a subdued murmur. He sensed surprise among the onlookers at his unexpected throw and that it challenged something or someone. When he looked round for Agaratz to seek an explanation, the hunchback was again nowhere to be seen.

From the skin-clad officiants there came no corresponding congratulatory murmur. Behind his mask the horned man's eyes glittered.

A pause in proceedings followed, a sort of break for refreshments.

At their shelter Urrell found no-one, though the fire was banked and food laid out on leaves.

Hostility filled the air on his return. Urrell sensed that the onlookers awaited something to happen, that his outsider's successes had gone against expectations. His true test was to come.

Instead of the bullroarer's whir, and the blaring trumpet that had announced the earlier wrestling heats, there came a long echoing resonance from the mouth of the cave. Deep in its black throat huge hollow logs were being drummed. The resonance was enough to make Urrell wonder if blocks of stone might not be shaken loose from the cliff face on to the entrance. Old men during his boyhood by the winter sea had told of caverns sealed by falls, trapping people inside, whose cries could be heard by those with ears to hear pressed up against the rocks.

All of a sudden, with a clarity that surprised him, Urrell realised that the drumming was not intended for him, or his fellow competitors, but for the missing Agaratz. The apprentice would be tested in the absence of the master.

It was to be a spear-throwing contest.

He gripped his three lances and waited. At one end of the green a mark was being set up, a log with a human, lifelike shape and a white blaze in the middle.

Young men stood about, with lances. Most wore face paint, some had feathers in their hair, others were bedizened with splashes of colour and fur that Urrell assumed marked them out by clan or blood group. He recognised several from the band of tall dark men whose leader Agaratz had slain with that single spear-cast.

In the pushing and shoving for position Urrell received knocks and jabs in the ribs from ill-intentioned lance butts. On one he recognised the pattern of the javelin thrown at him and Agaratz aboard their raft on the River Nani. He had been recognised too.

The jostlers threw first, bullying aside competitors, eager to show off their greater skills. Lesser youths stood back, awed, in little clan groups. Urrell, belonging to no group, stood alone. He watched as the javelins flew at the mark, set at a good range. Several missed, some fell short to jeers from the crowd. Urrell began to realise that it would take him a powerful throw to reach the target, let alone hit it, but he felt confident enough to let other youths throw first. Few managed the range or hit true. Round them swaggered the swarthy louts, putting them off their aim. This, too, Urrell noted, with rising anger.

Then, as he stepped forward, two of the bullies jostled him and one muttered, in a broken version of Urrell's language, "Where's your lion?" The other let out a wolf's howl in mockery of Rakrak – a single swipe of Urrell's lance butt to the man's midriff crumpled him on its way to the leering face of his companion, cracking the fellow's jaw. Fired up, without faltering, Urrell drew the lance back and let it fly at the target. No need to aim or wait. A sort of exultation seized him. He hurled both other lances, one behind the other, almost before the first reached the mark, knowing with unthought certainty that both would follow the first to the target. All three lances stuck in the blaze side by side.

Silence from both the crowd and competitors greeted this feat of marksmanship, all eyes accompanied him to the log to retrieve the lances, the little strut in his stride the only hint that he, Urrell, allowed himself to signal that the apprentice had at last achieved his master's *poodooeic*.

To intensified drumming, two fur-clad men from the cavern stepped out and paced off a distance between contestants, Urrell at one end in a small group, a larger one at the other made up of what looked to Urrell like bigger, older men, swaggerers and shovers every one. It was to be a one-to-one contest, with javelins. A yelled signal and one of the tall, striped-faced men stepped forward and shouted a challenge or an insult. His face-streaks reminded Urrell of the clan which had wished to kill Rakrak, that day on the plains. Watching the man's bravado, he was pleased how little it affected him. A glance at the crowd for a glimpse of Agaratz and Rakrak was met by faces set with the cruel glee of watchers at a fight.

On a signal from the horned giant the duels began. Urrell held back to assess what was to happen, letting others from his side face the first flight of javelins. Two were hit, one seriously in the thigh. Their own throws did no damage. He of the bravado, encouraged by this poor showing, redoubled his strut up and down, raising his lances over his head and yelling defiance. Then, his parading before his group over, the man stepped forward and hurled a javelin straight at Urrell.

It was well aimed. Urrell saw the ripple of muscle in the hurler's shoulder; he saw the slight curve in the flight of the javelin; he noticed a tassel near its middle; he had time to dodge and catch the shaft as it flew past him. The crowd was hushed by the feat. Then, like Agaratz before him, Urrell gripped the shaft in both hands and snapped it with a strength that he knew was not his.

A gasped 'oh!' from the onlookers greeted this. Glancing round, Urrell again hoped to catch sight of Agaratz in the crowd. Instead, cruel faces now looked at him fearfully. What next? He looked towards the master of ceremonies for a hint: was he to skewer his opponent, as he knew he easily could with his new-found strength? Or what?

Then, for his ear only, Urrell distinctly heard the notes of his own mammoth-tusk flute. It was playing one of Agaratz's ineffable, unseizable melodies. He knew then and there what to do. Holding his three spears over his head he strode across the grass to the group of his opponents, who shrank away, unable to guess his intention.

Urrell went up to the one who had tried to kill him with his spear-throw and tapped him on the shoulder with his own spear tip, counting coup. After this, he walked along the line of others, supremely confident, and tapped each in turn on the shoulder before strolling back to his place across the sward to await events.

His bloodless gesture, he knew, was a direct challenge to the horned one, the blood-letter. Utter silence gripped the onlookers.

Again Agaratz's music played in his ear, this time the melody of the cavern where the mammoths had marched past, head to tail, while he had drawn their outline in tune to Agaratz's playing, the lead cow's eye watching him as she led her frieze past him and his crayon into the place whither no-one went and whence no-one came back, the land of *mamu*. That night he had been on the brink of knowing.

Now the air on the flute hinted as much, in his inner ear. No-one else heard it, neither the crowded banks nor the knots of youths. But did he of the horns, now back in his cavernous den as though to gather strength, hear it and know that it was aimed at him with the accuracy of Urrell's javelin?

Urrell would not have long to discover. Once more the trumpeting rang out and the huge fur-clad, horned figure stepped forth with his sequel of striped and painted followers, some masked, some near naked. The booming drums inside the cavern shook the very rocks of the cliff face. To Urrell's surprise these figures began a wild cavorting dance round the tall figure, shrieking and girning like men possessed. The crowd shrank back, so Urrell stood back a little himself with his group, more to follow suit than from concern at the strangeness of events.

But where was Agaratz? Playing his flute out of sight when his acolyte needed him most?

The performance, centred on the leader, rose in frenzy as the dancers leapt and skipped round the giant, driven by the drumbeat.

He was sucking their power from them. The air almost crackled.

Total stillness held the crowd, a tense expectation of something about to come. A distant rumble of thunder emphasised the crowd's stillness.

At a sign from the huge figure, the dancing stopped dead. The drumming fell silent. He stepped forward and in a deep voice boomed out a call that Urrell could not understand.

The crowd, however, did. Young girls and maidens were ushered and pushed into the grass area before the cavern's gape. They came shyly and formed groups. There was to be some kind of competition, female this time. Urrell looked keenly at each girl, hoping to see Guimera but she was not there.

As they lined up, the maidens formed pairs. At a signal they discarded their upper covering and stood bare-breasted, their girlish breasts stained and stippled with berry juices, their bare shoulders arrayed with designs of necklets and flowers, bird shapes and insect wings, painted or tattooed he could not tell.

The first pair faced each other. From somewhere inside the cavern a wailing chant of female voices issued to which the two girls began a dance. They jigged and twisted till the master of ceremonies raised his antler-roarer to decide the winner. She went to one side, near the cavern mouth, while the loser regained her place in the throng.

As with the youths' wrestling contest earlier Urrell saw that the heats would be eliminatory.

Winners in the first round competed against each other to louder chanting and stronger rhythms. The crowd entered into the spirit of the contest. Comments and catcalls increased as the heats went on until the last few girls remained, sweaty and streaked from their exertions.

The weather, till then warm and mild, was fast clouding over, the sky darkening. Black clouds billowed up from beyond the mountain where the cavern lay embedded with all its galleries and chambers, along which he, Urrell, had stumbled and wandered till he had encountered the ice barrier separating him from the she-mammoth and her troop of followers. They had half mocked, half beckoned him to follow, but how could he have gone beyond the ice-shield that shut him off from them, that prevented him from entering their time? Willingly would he have followed, mammoth-led. Were these clouds their vengeance, a jeering gesture at his powerlessness to penetrate their world?

But then he wondered whether it had been Agaratz who had barred his way through. Agaratz who found interstices in rock faces, gaps to wriggle through where none seemed to exist. He would have known if there was a way round the ice-shield, surely. Urrell's mind struggled with this. He felt, for the first time, forsaken, rejected as a grown cub must feel when its mother spurns its advances, forcing it to fend for itself.

With these thoughts in mind, he was startled by a flash of lightning from beyond the mountain, then a huge clap of thunder.

Even the horned man looked up uneasily. The girls cowered. As for the throng, their upturned faces formed a sea of noses, Urrell thought, a saw-edged pattern.

He scanned the sea of faces, hoping to spot Agaratz up to one of his tricks. Something or someone was teasing the mage, challenging him to a one-to-one contest.

As Urrell waited for what was to happen, he felt detached from events, an observer, a bystander. Not even the louring tempest that was building up, the flashes of lightning across the sky, concerned him. It was a performance to which he was a spectator.

The girls' competition ended and the winners were led into the cavern.

Then, to Urrell's surprise and joy, another bevy of older maidens came forth from the cavern, among them none other than Guimera, each girl draped in the flimsiest of garlands and strips of fur.

Had Guimera been secreted in the cavern all this while, hidden from him as he sought her in the encampment?

The judge this time was a female, huge, heavy-bellied, her big breasts sagging. Only when he looked carefully did Urrell make out that this apparition was entirely naked, like the spongy figure he had stumbled on in her grotto deep inside the cavern.

Of the young women, two were singled out, Guimera and another, both beauties, Guimera with her lion's mane hair to her waist, the other dark, a sibling perhaps of Urrell's foes, the swarthy spearmen. These the horned man drew forward, with the female deemer, nearer the crowd. Then, coinciding with yet another peal of thunder, he suddenly stripped each young woman of her whisps of apparel. There stood Guimera, his Guimera, nude. Her body she had adorned with stains and plant juices so that she appeared wreathed in sinuous designs. Her rival, just as ornamented, was streaked and stained in the manner of her clan, her dark hair thrown back.

Mutterings and growing sounds of threats from the men Urrell had bested, with others of their group milling behind, confirmed Urrell's surmise that Guimera's rival was indeed a sister of theirs. They meant their girl to win. And they wanted revenge.

Again thunder pealed overhead on the tail of the greatest, longest flash of lightning Urrell had ever seen. The ground shook. The air smelt. For a trice Urrell could not place the smell, then he did. It was like the brimstone stench from some of the geyser pools they had lingered by during their journey through the glacier.

Instead of frightening the crowd, the crashes and flashes among the rolling black clouds overhead seemed to excite them. They ignored the reddish tints in the sky. People pressed nearer the open area before the cavern where the contest was taking place, on one side of which Urrell and his little band of fellow spearmen had lingered to watch. They were outnumbered by the supporters of Guimera's rival. If it came to a clash, they would be overwhelmed, slain even. Yet Urrell surprised himself by feeling unconcerned, almost contemptuous of his adversaries. A nonchalant 'come what may' took over, a sense of of things being out of his hands. Now that he had Guimera before him, nothing and no-one could outface him.

It was at this point that once again he heard Agaratz's music of the cave where the mammoths had marched past, head to tail, while he had drawn their outline in tune to Agaratz's playing, the lead cow's little eye watching the lad in his daze as she led her frieze past his crayon into the unknown and the unknowable. Yet that night he had been on the brink of knowing.

Slivers of stone fell down the cliff near him, unheeded. The sky had lit up yet more, reddening the underside of the clouds rolling and swelling overhead. He sniffed the acrid air.

Meanwhile the mage and his assistants had paused to gaze with the crowd at the skies. Their unease showed. Urrell's mind-drift kept him calm, detached. The longer he stood there, waiting for whatever was to happen, the more he questioned matters that hitherto had been straightforward. And the more he thought, the less he understood.

These thoughts were soon cut short however as, with a burst of drumming that seemed to imperil yet further the arch of the cavern, shaken by the thunder, the horned man decided to proceed with the rituals and competitions. Some of his assistants ushered back onlookers and the disgruntled spearmen.

Now came the turn of the ponderous female judge, it seemed to Urrell, as she waddled forward to decide the winner in the beauty contest.

From the shouts and catcalls of the crowd it was plain that most supported their clanswoman as opposed to Guimera, the outsider. Both were tall and well made but to Urrell's eyes Guimera outshone her rival. Yet it was obvious which way the decision would go. Whirling his antler-roarer over his head the horned man stepped past the female judge to tip the dark-haired girl on the shoulder.

A clap of thunder, in the darkling clouds, seemed, to Urrell at least, to signal dissent at the decision. With a yell the dark girl's supporters rushed into the arena intent on clinching the win by avenging themselves on Urrell and his small group.

They tried to seize Guimera, knocking aside the mage's men, even jostling the mage himself. He, enraged to have his authority disregarded, drove them back, whirling his antler-roarer at them. Urrell waited to intervene, ready to rescue Guimera.

Driven back they might be but the spearmen still had revenge in mind. They hurled javelins and stones, yelled insults and issued what sounded like challenges to single combat across the grass at Urrell and his little band.

Urrell now watched as from nowhere Agaratz appeared.

The yells fell silent. The crowd stared intently at the apparition. Agaratz, shrunken in Urrell's eyes, circled the arena with his familiar rolling gait, going up to the spearmen and forcing them back with a simple twirl of a baton: the one Urrell had retrieved. It had puffed smoke, lain stone-like on the grass, arched to flute music.

Guimera, the other girl, their female judge, the mage and his men stood struck still. Over their heads the sky had reddened so much that it seemed to reflect a cauldron of fire beyond the cliffs and caverns. Rumblings sent tremors through the ground underfoot. Loose stones fell from the cavern roof.

Agaratz turned his attention to the horned man as he limped

towards the two beauty competitors. Both men's eyes locked.

Then, in the silence between two claps of thunder, Agaratz began what Urrell immediately recognised from their years together, from that very first encounter between a famished boy and a singular creature bearing food. Agaratz was about to mimick a creature into reality.

For an instant he hoped it would be a mammoth.

Instead Agaratz moved about with jerky movements, spinning on his goat foot, flapping his arms with invisible speed: to all those watching eyes he became the bee, symbol of womanhood, maker of honey, best of flies, fertility itself. He seemed to rise off the grass.

A swarm appeared and hovered over him.

In total silence the crowd, now gripped not so much by fear as by awe, stared transfixed by the scene.

The swarm buzzed round the hunchback, controlled by his twirling hands and Urrell's wand. He held the insects aloft, as he stood eye to eye with the glittering glare of the masked man, twice his height, escorted by his henchmen in their motley garbs and guises.

Breath pent, the crowd awaited. Overhead a flash of lightning tore through the clouds, followed by a roll and clap of thunder louder than anyone had heard so far, rocking the ground underfoot and bringing down more rock from the face of the cavern.

Agaratz rose with the bees, lifted by their whirling density till his good foot and his goat foot seemed to clear the ground.

He seemed slighter to Urrell, shrunken, drained of substance.

The crowd, up the bank, could not all see the gap under his feet. Voices and cries of those who could shouted their astonishment to those higher up.

But this was more than one of Agaratz's sleights.

Urrell kept his eyes on the mage and his gang to see what their

239

reaction might be to this fight to the death, of one against many, of force pitted against force. No shaman could live down being outfaced like this.

Both beauty contestants had remained standing still in their places. Would the mage's men close in on them, or try to seize Agaratz?

Again lightning flashed, holding long enough for the swirling bees to be visible as a dark mass hovering over the two maidens. Agaratz had vanished. The swarm, in one swoop, alighted on Guimera, clothing her from her russet hair to her thighs in a teeming mass, as though drawn to the sinuous designs of flowers and twining plants that adorned her nakedness.

A roar this time rose from the assembly. She had won. The bees had chosen their queen.

People surged forward to her. Women to touch her. The horned one and his men backed off into the cavern as the crowd poured down and the world seemed to quake. Urrell was borne along, nearer his beloved.

The trembling of the ground increased and there were shouts and screams as the top of the cavern, loosened by the quaking, crashed down. Within minutes the throng had dispersed, the bees leaving Guimera a naked princess in her regal body paintings for Urrell to embrace and carry off.

They came to the camp, where Rakrak lay crouching alone. He noticed how grizzled she was round the snout. Of Agaratz there was nothing to be seen. Had he perished in the collapse of the cavern?

That night they slept together, wed.

In the morning, the skies now clear as after a storm, Agaratz was still nowhere to be seen. Urrell sought high and low, enquiring of the last few of the crowd gathering their belongings ready to disperse to their hunting grounds in time for the onset of winter.

He looked for the baton, for the ivory flute, for his very identity. All had vanished. He descended to the silent cavern entrance, half blocked by falls of stone, even climbing over the rubble to look inside. Nothing of the inhabitants, their master, their lamps remained. He had a distinct sense that they had never been, or at another time long ago, so damp and uninhabited did the gloomy place feel. He shouted. His voice rang away into the blackness and he was struck by the lack of an echo. That blackness sucked in the sound and gave nothing back.

Then they both heard the distant flute-playing. In Guimera's eyes Urrell saw the look, that remote look that was Agaratz's.

The flute bade them depart. It was time to bury the hearthstones and turn towards home cave. They would just have time to reach the grasslands and cross them amid the heaving migrating herds of bison, horse and deer to reach the bluffs he knew so well, he, Urrell, clan leader, before winter set in.

When spring returned, he would take his woman upstream by raft along the Nani, to the island in mid-river where Agaratz, curled up and shrivelled in his pit with his forebears, would be awaiting their arrival and the libation of egg-yolk accompanied by the keening of Guimera in their antique tongue, evokatrix of memories of the age of the mammoths.

Finis